PRAISE FOR LIZ TOLSMA

"Liz Tolsma delivers engaging ch .... Deft
plot twists and vivid, turn-of-the .... etting
will keep readers turning pages. 7 .... read.
Lovers of history, mystery, and ror .... "
                    —Lisa Carter, a .... _..u uound of *Falling Leaves*

"Whenever I pick up a Liz Tolsma novel, I brace myself to get lost in her wonderfully evocative settings and story lines. Clear your calendar, settle in, and prepare to be captivated!"
                    —Elizabeth Camden, RITA and Christy Award–winning author

"Liz Tolsma's novel is a delicious combination of mystery and romance, with a rich historical setting and fascinating details. The twists kept me turning the pages well into the night, a series of exciting surprises revealing themselves at every turn. It's the kind of story that will linger in my mind for a good long while."
                    —Dana Mentink, *Publisher's Weekly* bestselling author

the SILVER SHADOW

LIZ TOLSMA

BARBOUR
PUBLISHING

Cover Photograph © Sandra Cunningham / Trevillion Images

Published by Barbour Publishing, Inc., 1810 Barbour Drive, Uhrichsville, Ohio 44683, www.barbourbooks.com

Our mission is to inspire the world with the life-changing message of the Bible.

Member of the
Evangelical Christian
Publishers Association

Printed in the United States of America.

*To Jon. You're already part of the Tolsma family.
Welcome to this crazy writing family! I pray that
God will bless your endeavors and that you
will continue to use your many talents.*

Chapter 1

What is this?" Balding Joe Ward, his light-colored hair curling over his ears, smacked his copy of the *Denver Post* against his desk. A whiff of newsprint filled the city editor's office.

A headache started at the base of Polly Blythe's neck and stretched up and over until her temples throbbed. The click-clack of typewriters behind her as her fellow reporters wrote their newspaper stories didn't help at all. "My article?"

"Yes, your article." The middle-aged Mr. Ward came to his feet and stared down at Polly.

She hunched over. "Is there something wrong?"

"Wrong? You're asking what's wrong? Everything." He drew out the last word.

"What do you mean by everything?"

"It's facts. Nothing but the facts."

"Well, I mean, Mrs. Pettigrew sent me the information about her daughter, so I wrote my article about her engagement from that."

Mr. Ward slapped his wide forehead. "Mrs. Pettigrew is as dull as they come. Your article matches the woman well. But there are rumors about the haste of the wedding. You should have included that. We want sensational. Attention-grabbing. Articles that will leave the entire city buzzing." He gestured wide, almost knocking over his coffee cup. "We want people to have to buy the *Post* to find out all there is to find out. Mr. Tammen and Mr. Bonfils would not be pleased with this. Not at all."

Under the weight of Mr. Ward's glare, Polly sagged. "Did you want me to lie about Miss Pettigrew?"

"There's a difference between lying and embellishing. Learning to walk that line is what makes or breaks a reporter. That's why I don't hire anyone who hasn't completed school or who hasn't worked for a publication before."

If only Pa had let her further her education. But her family needed money. She'd had to get a job. Her brother Lyle got to finish college because Pa said education was wasted on women but not on men. She'd worked hard to move from cleaning the newspaper offices to writing for the *Post*.

All Mr. Ward could see was that cleaning girl.

"Please, sir, I'm so sorry. It will never happen again. I promise. From now on, you'll have the most sensational stories ever. You won't be disappointed in me. I'll do my job, and I'll do it well. Just don't sack me."

Mr. Ward stroked his prominent, clean-shaven chin. "By rights, I should let you go. Or at least reduce you to a cleaning position again." He raked his gaze from her head to her feet and back. "Still, you're a nice addition to the staff."

She cringed. Had he hired her because he thought she was pretty? A piece to spruce up the office?

"I'll give you another chance. One more. Take this as your warning. Another mistake like that, and you'll find yourself on the street. Do you understand? Now, get out of here. It's well after eight on a Friday night, and I just want to go home."

He'd made his point crystal clear. She gave a single nod, turned on her heel, and returned to her little corner of the office.

She stared at the sheet in the roller of her typewriter, the paper table proudly pronouncing it to be a Remington.

A sigh escaped her lips. Another Denver society piece. How many stories could she write about wealthy young women's engagements to the most eligible bachelors in the city? How many stories about weddings and comings out? How could she possibly make them exciting and titillating enough for Mr. Ward?

Mr. Ward lumbered past, leering at her as he went by. She shivered.

Well, the article wouldn't write itself. Until it was completed and turned in, she couldn't go home. She typed a sentence. Gracious, that was awful. Even she agreed it was as dull as dirty dishwater.

She ripped the paper from the typewriter, crumpled it, and tossed it in the metal trash can. Who cared about those society girls? There was nothing fun or fascinating about them at all. The only reason to write these pieces was because the prominent people they featured wanted to read about themselves.

If only Polly could get this done. She could go home for the day. Already, she'd missed supper at her boardinghouse.

A commotion rippled through the newsroom, a buzz that moved from the front and found its way to Polly. Something about a mugging. Two women. Much more interesting than society stories.

Polly turned in her chair and leaned toward the desk beside her, occupied by Harry Gray, who had just returned from a dinner break. He glanced at her, his fingers flying over his typewriter keys.

She kept her voice low. "What's going on? Some kind of big story?"

Harry turned his skinny lips into a frown, his dark mustache also dipping, and shook his head. "A woman cracked over the head. Nothing new. She was crazy to be out by herself at this hour. A woman in Denver in this day and age should always have an escort. Colorado gives you the right to vote, and now you think you can waltz the streets alone at any hour. I'll bang out a little piece about it before I leave."

Maybe so. Denver was a dangerous place. But it wasn't always possible or practical to have an escort. Sometimes women needed to go places in the evenings. Polly always held her breath until she arrived safely at her destination.

She let his comment slide. "Where did this happen?"

"On Pearl Street near Sixteenth Avenue."

"How far is it from here to Pearl Street?" Polly rolled her chair closer to his desk.

Harry waved her away. "Maybe ten or fifteen minutes by streetcar. The mugging will probably be a page-ten story. Perhaps you'd like a shot at it. See if you could get that one right. It should be easy enough for you to make it exciting." He cackled, the small scar above his eye crinkling.

She sucked in a breath. "Really?" Oh, a chance to get a true story.

One with some meat. Sure, maybe it wouldn't appear on the front page or have a big headline in red, but it was a start. A start toward getting recognized for her work, despite being a woman.

This was her chance to prove herself after her failure with Miss Pettigrew. Perhaps she could get Mr. Ward to view her as more than simply a newsroom showpiece. "But can you assign articles?" Harry was, after all, just a reporter like herself.

"With Ward gone, yeah. It's yours. Three paragraphs. No more. Got it? But make it sing."

At Harry's words, Polly grimaced. "I won't let the paper down."

"You'd better not. I'll tell the typesetters and press operators to leave space on page ten for it. Now get out of my face. I need to finish my work."

"Yes, of course." Polly slid back to her rolltop desk. She would do a bang-up job on the piece. They would see. Mr. Ward wouldn't be disappointed.

Harry mumbled something else that Polly didn't catch. No matter. She had her first real story to report.

She would show Mr. Ward and Harry. And everyone else who had ever doubted her. This was big. She stood and bounced on her tiptoes. Now, to get going. Without a moment's thought, she settled her rather unflattering fedora on her head, the paper stuck in the band proclaiming her a member of the press, swiped her notebook and pencil from her desk, and swept from the building into the darkening Denver evening.

In spite of the August heat, she shivered. That woman had been on the street alone. Polly had to make the trek herself. Alone. A few blocks to catch the streetcar. A few more after she got off.

What if the perpetrator hadn't been caught yet?

Another mugging. Two of them, to be exact. Edwin Price sat back in his office chair in the middle of the Denver Police Department and sighed. There was nothing unusual about that. Muggings were an almost daily occurrence. Some people apparently still believed Denver to be the Wild West. And nothing the cops did changed the numbers.

He'd joined the force to make up for that night he had done

nothing. To absolve himself. To make a difference this time.

Some difference he was making.

"What have you got there?" Edwin's partner, Ralph O'Fallon, nodded to the file in Edwin's hand.

"Two more muggings. Women out alone. Happened within a two-minute walk of each other."

"That's a little bit different." O'Fallon positioned himself on the corner of Edwin's desk. The only clutter-free corner of it. "Anything else to it?"

Edwin adjusted his wire-rimmed glasses and glanced over his scribbled reports. He'd taken them in such haste, he had a difficult time reading them. "They were both struck over the head. And"—he scanned the page—"this is strange. Neither of them was robbed or violated."

"That's very different." O'Fallon snatched the notebook from Edwin. "What do you make of it?"

"Not much. A pretty typical day in Denver. I just hope both women are going to be okay." Edwin gestured for the paper, and Ralph returned it. "I'll go interview Mrs. Lillian Bell first. What is this world coming to when someone attacks a widow? Hopefully I'll get the chance to speak to the other one at some point."

"Looks like a late night."

Edwin excavated his coffee cup from where it was buried under an avalanche of papers and took a swig of the almost-cold brew. Yes, it was going to be a long night.

As he settled into his chair to review his notes before questioning the victim, he caught a uniformed officer leading a slender, doe-eyed woman through the station. Her dark blue skirt swished across the floor as she followed him. Was this one of the victims? If so, she didn't bear any signs of being mugged. No cuts, no bruises. In fact, her skin was flawless.

As she approached, she straightened the fedora on her head, the paper tucked in the band labeling her as a member of the press. Fabulous. Just what he needed.

When the officer stopped at Edwin's desk, he scraped his chair back and stood. "What can I help you with?"

From the reticule that matched the color of her skirt, the woman withdrew a pad of paper and a pencil, then pulled herself straight and flashed him a soft smile. "I'm Polly Blythe from the *Denver Post*. I understand there was a mugging tonight on Pearl Street. What more can you tell me about the case?"

Edwin glared at the officer. "That will be all."

"Yes, sir." The man scurried away.

"Miss Blythe, you said?"

"That's correct. From the *Denver Post*."

The news just got better and better. The *Post* was a sensational publication with flamboyant owners who weren't afraid to exaggerate a bit to lure in readers. They even printed their headlines in red ink. "I caught that part. You're a reporter there?"

Those eyes hardened, and she pointed to her hat. "You don't believe women can be good newspaper reporters?"

"I never said anything about good or not. I want to make sure I have your credentials correct before I speak on the record."

"Oh." A little of the starch left her spine.

"I don't know much about either of the cases at this point."

"Either of the cases?"

"Yes, there were two victims."

"Two?" She scratched something onto the paper.

"That's correct. Both in close proximity to each other. One, as you said, on Pearl Street. The other on Sixteenth Avenue, a few blocks from Pearl. The investigation is in its very earliest stages. All I can tell you is that neither of the victims was robbed or, um, violated. If you would like to leave me your information, I can give you a statement when I have more details. I have yet to question the victims. Until then. . ." He gestured toward the door.

"Detective. . . I'm sorry, I don't believe you gave me your name."

Mother would have his head if she knew of his lack of manners. "My apologies. Detective Price. Edwin Price."

"Detective Price." The strain in her voice was hard to miss. She wasn't about to be easily dismissed. "Do you believe these two cases to be related?"

"No. Multiple muggings on a single night in Denver isn't uncommon."

"But would you characterize multiple muggings within a short distance of each other on the same night as out of the ordinary?"

"Not really. Could be nothing more than a coincidence."

"Could that be why these incidents continue to occur? Because the police department doesn't take them seriously?"

Edwin fisted his hands then forced himself to relax them. Was she trying to goad him? That wouldn't be out of character for a *Post* reporter. "Of course we take them seriously."

He, of all people, knew how hard they worked to bring these criminals to justice. Sometimes, no matter how hard they tried, they couldn't locate the perpetrator. Like they had never caught the man from that awful night so long ago. "I have a stack of cases that will take me until the next century to solve."

"But you haven't interviewed the victims from tonight's incidents yet. You said so yourself."

By the way she crowed, you'd think she'd just been crowned queen of England. "I was on my way to one of the victim's homes. In fact, you have detained me."

"Let's be off then."

He stared at this spitfire of a woman. "You cannot come with me on an investigation."

"Her home just so happens to be my next stop as well."

He quirked an eyebrow. "You don't even know her address. Or her name."

"Which makes it so providential for me to have come to you. And since you're going there, it's perfect timing, really, as you wouldn't want me wandering the streets alone at night, would you?"

Edwin gulped. No, he wouldn't. He had forbidden his sister, Amelia, from leaving the house at night unattended. Not that women from their social class usually did, but she was almost as much of a handful as Miss Blythe. "Fine. You can come with me. But you can't be in the room while I'm interviewing the victim. Is that clear?"

She gestured to shake his hand, and when he did so, he discovered it was quite small and soft. Not an unpleasant experience at all.

Once he had slipped on his suit coat, he led Miss Blythe from the station into the warm late-summer evening and set a brisk pace. After a block or so, she pulled on his arm. "Did you hear that?"

"What?" He furrowed his brow. It may be getting late in the day, but Denver still hummed. People milled about the streets, music played from the saloons, children cried. The streetcar bell clanging only added to the cacophony that was the city.

"I heard a sound in the alley. Listen."

There did come a quiet mewling. The woman had good hearing. "Stay put. It's probably nothing more than a kitten."

He crept down the passage, around refuse, a rat racing in front of him at one point.

What he found about halfway in, though, was no cat.

It was a woman. One he recognized.

Blood poured from a gash in her head.

Chapter 2

Polly knelt beside the beaten woman and pressed her handkerchief to the back of her head in a vain attempt to staunch the bleeding.

"Let's get her to my house. I don't live far from here." Mr. Price's voice wobbled.

Not far from here? They were in Capitol Hill, one of the nicest areas of Denver.

Mr. Price grasped the handkerchief and, still pressing it to the woman's head, picked her up and cradled her like a baby. Polly found the woman's reticule and grabbed it.

He raced from the alley onto the streetlamp lit road. "Rachel, Rachel, can you hear me?"

He knew her name? This man was an enigma. His strides were long and rapid, and Polly had to run to keep up with him.

"Rachel, you're going to be okay." Mr. Price's voice cracked. "Please, please, you have to come out of this. How could someone do this to you? How?"

Polly struck up the nerve to touch his arm. "Do you think she'll be all right?"

"If anything happens to her. . ."

Breathless from trying to keep up with him, Polly couldn't answer. Was there a romantic relationship between the two?

Mr. Price turned up the walk of an elegant brick Georgian home with a curved entrance and three third-story dormers. Polly scurried ahead of him and came to a screeching halt at the door.

"Open it." He barked the command as if she were one of his police underlings, but she obeyed.

They stepped into the grand hall.

"Nancy! Nancy!" Mr. Price's cries echoed in the large, marble-floored space. His face was as white as the mountain snows, and blood stained his shirt and coated his hands. Rachel's breathing was shallow.

A woman in a black gown with a white apron, a frilled white cap on her head emerged from the back of the house. "Edwin, what happened?"

"It's Rachel. She's been attacked, beaten over the head. Telephone for the doctor. I'll take her to the blue room." As Nancy retreated to make the call, Mr. Price headed for the stairs.

Polly followed him, at first at a safe distance. When he didn't scold her, she closed the gap. Two women met them at the top of the curved staircase, both in elegant gowns, one older than the other. Perhaps his mother and sister?

The younger one gasped. "Is that. . .?"

"Get a fire lit in the blue room." He was the model of efficiency. "Bring towels and sheets, plenty of them. Boil water. Do whatever you have to do to keep her alive until Dr. Klein arrives."

Without much visible effort, Mr. Price carried the victim to a large room painted in sky blue, white clouds on the ceiling. As he lowered her to the four-poster bed, the woman moaned, and her eyes fluttered open. She flicked her glance between Mr. Price and Polly.

Mr. Price stepped forward and took Rachel by the hand. "You're at my house. We found you in an alley."

"My head."

"Yes, you've received a rather nasty gash. Do you remember what happened?"

She scrunched her eyes shut for a moment before reopening them. "Just a noise behind me. Lots of pain. That's all."

"You've been unconscious. But the doctor will be here soon, and he'll take care of you."

The two women returned with the requested items and bustled about the room.

In a very short amount of time, the doctor arrived and shooed Polly and the others into the hall.

Polly shifted from one foot to the other. "She's in a bad way, isn't she?"

The three of them stared at Polly as if she'd grown angel wings. Mr. Price blinked several times. "You're still here?"

"I thought I could be of use."

He sighed. "Mother, Amelia, this is. . . I'm sorry, I've forgotten your name."

Heat rose in Polly's face. Then again, she'd always been invisible. "Miss Polly Blythe with the *Denver Post.*"

"Miss Blythe, this is my mother, Mrs. Price, and my sister, Amelia."

She smiled in their direction. "I happened to be at the police station and was on my way with Mr. Price to interview a mugging victim when we found Rachel in the alley."

Amelia, her dark red hair a contrast to her alabaster face, smiled. "Thank you for all of your help, Miss Blythe. We do appreciate it." Then she turned to her brother. "Are Rachel's wounds serious?"

"I'm afraid so." His words were measured and heavy.

Silence hung over the group. Perhaps they were praying for this woman they knew.

Polly fingered Rachel's reticule that she'd been holding the entire time. She handed it to Mr. Price. "Don't you think it odd that she was mugged but the perpetrator didn't steal her purse?"

He furrowed his eyebrows and took it from her. "It's heavy." He passed it to his mother. "I can't rifle through it. That's not gentlemanly."

"Don't I have the most thoughtful son?" Mrs. Price directed the comment and her stare at Polly. Then she opened the reticule and withdrew a coin purse, which she opened. It was filled with cash.

Whoever had assaulted Rachel hadn't done it to steal from her. "She wasn't robbed," Polly said. "Don't you find that unusual?"

"That is unusual, Edwin, you have to admit." Mrs. Price shook her head. "What is this world coming to?"

He adjusted his glasses. "It was the same with the other two muggings tonight."

His mother and sister exclaimed over the news.

Polly trembled a little. "This person, whoever he is, is committing these crimes for the fun of it. That makes him particularly dangerous."

"Thank you, Miss Blythe. I'm capable of doing my job. And I have no proof that these three muggings are related. The streets of Denver are naturally dangerous."

"Edwin, be polite." Mrs. Price gave her son a narrow-eyed stare.

Polly fumbled. "I didn't mean—"

"But you did. I'm invested in these cases, more than you know. I want to apprehend this attacker as much as anyone, including the victims. Please, don't tell me what kind of perpetrator or perpetrators we're dealing with here. I'm very well aware."

So she had struck some kind of nerve with him. "Then I suggest we interview the victim we were on the way to see."

"We?" He raised one ginger eyebrow.

"Yes, we."

"I believe our bargain is that you aren't to be in the room when I interview the victim."

"I know. But I'll be waiting right outside the door. Because once you're finished, I must interview her." She gave him her best what-are-you-going-to-do-about-that smile.

"Go on, Edwin." His mother nodded. "There's nothing you can do for Rachel right now. If there's someone who can give you information on who did this, then you need to get those details."

"But I need to interview Rachel too."

"If she's able, we'll ask her a few questions. Chances are, she's not going to be in any shape to talk for a while."

He huffed but nodded, and he and Polly left the house and caught the streetcar to ride to the first victim's home. There was no way Polly was going to make a mistake on this story. She had to prove to Mr. Ward that she could be as good a reporter as anyone else.

And she had to prove to Pa that education wasn't wasted on a woman.

They arrived at Mrs. Lillian Bell's residence, where the rather shriveled boardinghouse keeper, Mrs. Frankel, led them to the widow's room. "She's resting, and praise the Lord, the doctor says she'll mend in time."

While Mr. Price spoke to Mrs. Bell, Polly paced in the hall in a vain attempt to burn off some nervous energy. Mrs. Frankel, despite her dour appearance, was kind and offered her tea, but she couldn't drink it. Mrs. Frankel then asked her to sit in the parlor, but Polly wasn't able to settle.

Though Mr. Ward's dressing down had hurt, she had to heed his advice to keep her job.

Or did she?

Plenty of other reporters embellished their stories until there was little resemblance to the truth. But she would make sure people knew the truth. Nothing but the truth. This one was sensational enough. No need putting ribbons and bells on it.

Mr. Price would play a role in the story. What an interesting angle. He knew Rachel. With the tender way he treated her, they had to be sweethearts.

Polly wouldn't doubt it. Mr. Price, with his ginger hair, his green eyes large behind his glasses, his neat mustache, and his intelligent manner, was a good-looking man. And Rachel, raven-haired and fair-skinned, was beautiful, even when she was bleeding from the head.

After a few more courses up and down the hall, Polly leaned against the plastered wall and sighed. Why was she even thinking such thoughts? Mr. Price was none of her business. She'd only just met him, and they hadn't gotten off to the best of starts.

No. She gave herself a shake. She had a job to do. A point to prove. And prove it she would.

What did he mean that the cases may not be related? Couldn't he see what was right in front of his eyes? None of the women were robbed. None were violated. All were struck over the head. That couldn't be coincidence.

By the time Mr. Price exited the room, Polly must have paced the hall a hundred times or more. At last he stepped out, tucking a notebook into his jacket pocket, and came to her. "Thank you for your patience, Miss Blythe. Mrs. Bell is quite tired, so please don't badger her. Be respectful of the ordeal she has been through."

"Of course. Contrary to your opinion, journalists do have hearts."

Mr. Price rewarded that line with a guffaw. "I'll keep that in mind.

When you're finished, I'll walk you back to your place."

"Oh, I can't go home yet. I must return to the newspaper office and write the article. As it is, I won't be able to do a full report on the incidents for tomorrow's edition, but I do want to be able to get some news of this out so the public can be on the lookout for the criminal." No cause to inform him that Harry had restricted her to three paragraphs.

"Very well then. I'll escort you to the office."

"There's no need, really."

"I insist."

"But surely you want to get back to Rachel."

"No more arguments. While you speak to Mrs. Bell, I'll telephone home and see how Rachel is doing. By then, you should be finished." He strode down the hall and around the corner.

With a huff, Polly entered Mrs. Bell's room.

After about twelve drafts of her little three-paragraph, page-ten story, Polly at last had an article to be proud of. She had jammed her piece full of over-the-top details. Hard to do when her entire article wasn't more than a dozen sentences. No matter. She would show Mr. Ward that she could do her job properly. More than properly. She could do it very well.

He was gone for the night, so she hurried it to the printing room herself. What a surprise awaited him in the morning when he opened to page ten and found her piece there. Her well-written piece, if she did say so herself.

As she entered the noisy room, the whir of the presses and the swish of the paper through them drowned out every other sound. She waved to David, an olive-skinned, dark-haired man, and he sauntered to her.

"What you got there, Miss Blythe? Another engagement?" David wasn't just one of the paper's best press operators. He was a sympathetic listener.

"No." She couldn't hide the excitement in her voice. "This is an article, a real article that Harry Gray assigned to me. Even though Mr.

Ward wasn't happy with the piece on Miss Pettigrew, Harry told me this assignment was mine. Isn't that divine? Anyway, here it is. He said he would tell you to hold three paragraphs on page ten for it."

The smile that creased David's face dimmed. "Page ten, you say?"

"That's right."

"Miss Blythe, I don't know how to tell you this, but Gray didn't tell me to hold any places on any pages tonight. None at all. In fact, he came down here and gave me an article for page ten himself."

"What?" She leaned forward and clenched her jaw.

"Just like I said."

"That's impossible." She swallowed hard. "He told me. He promised me."

"There's nothing I can do about it, 'specially not tonight. We're already running the morning edition. Maybe you got mixed up, and it's supposed to be in the afternoon paper?"

"No, I'm sure he said he would hold it for the morning." Or had he? Maybe she had misunderstood him.

Or maybe he was playing games with her.

"Thank you, David. I guess I'll be heading home then."

"You be careful out there now. I heard about some goings-on tonight."

"How did you hear?"

"From Harry's article. A woman needs to watch her step. I'd take you home myself, but I can't leave right now."

Harry assigned her the article and then took it back? He probably thought he could have a little fun at her expense. She clenched her jaw and her fists but forced her voice to remain steady and even. "Don't you worry. It's late enough that even the more unsavory of the city's residents are in bed." Including the rat who sat at the desk beside her. Late enough that Mrs. Mannheim, who ran the boardinghouse where Polly lived, was sure to scold her for being out at such an hour and causing her so much worry.

Mr. Price had walked her here after she had completed her interview with Mrs. Bell, but then Polly had sent him on his way, assuring him that one of the men who worked at the paper would see her home.

If he ever found out she was unescorted—which he wouldn't—he would scold her.

Gracious, but Polly had had enough of scoldings for one day. Then again, no one said this life would be easy. If she wanted to make it to the top, she had to take her lumps. But she wouldn't stand for Harry's treatment of her.

With feet that might as well have been cast iron, she dragged from the office building and down the street toward the boardinghouse she called home. The evening had darkened into deep night, and a certain stillness had settled over the city. No moon illuminated the Rockies tonight.

In the distance, a cat howled his nightly cry, answered by the barking of a dog, almost as if they taunted each other. From one of the open widows above Polly came the wail of a hungry infant.

She wasn't more than two blocks from home when a rustling sounded behind her. Then a soft, even rhythm, one that matched her footfalls.

She stopped.

So did the sounds.

She walked again.

The sounds came along.

Was someone following her? Could it be the same person who had injured three women already tonight?

A picture of a beautiful young woman bleeding from a wide laceration on her head flashed through Polly's mind.

Would she be the next victim?

She increased her pace.

Whoever came behind her increased his.

She sped up.

So did he.

She hoisted her skirts and broke into a full sprint, pumping her legs as fast as she could.

The footsteps behind her pounded the street. Closer, ever closer they came.

A stitch of pain raced through her side. She couldn't keep this pace up much longer. He was going to catch her. And then what? Was she going to end up like Rachel or Mrs. Bell? Or worse?

God, protect me. Keep him away from me. Don't allow any harm to come to me.

She couldn't outpace the man. If only her legs were longer. But she wasn't used to running.

She rounded a corner. Why wasn't anyone out tonight? Was it truly that late? Did a city really sleep at some point?

If she screamed, would anyone hear her? Come to her rescue? Perhaps it would be enough to scare off her would-be assailant. She opened her mouth and drew in as deep a breath as possible.

Then she released her loudest, wake-the-dead shriek. "Help me! Help me!"

Her lungs protested, demanded air. But if she stopped, who knew what fate would befall her? She kept up her pace, as fast as she could, shouting and yelling for at least half a lifetime.

At another intersection, she turned again.

And ran smack into someone.

Someone who wrapped her in his arms. With all her might, she kicked and fought him and continued to scream.

To no avail.

Chapter 3

Whoa there, what has your dander up?" Edwin gazed at the woman in his arms, her brown hair tumbling from its pins, her deep-set eyes wide and wild. He held her fast lest she kick him or take a swing at him.

Wait a minute. She bore some familiarity. Not only in her looks, but in her attitude. "Miss Blythe?"

She stilled, though she breathed hard. "Oh, Mr. Price, am I ever glad to see you. Someone is—is after me." She peered over her shoulder.

The street behind her was silent. "I don't see anyone."

"I was on my way home from the office. I heard footsteps behind me. They moved when I moved and stopped when I stopped. When I sped up, so did they. You have to believe me. A man really and truly was chasing me."

"Of course I do." There were plenty of men with less than honorable intentions out at this time of night. "Though you promised me someone would walk you home."

Still in his grasp, she sagged. "Thank you for believing me." She trembled. "And I did promise to have an escort, but no one was available. As it is, Mrs. Mannheim is going to be terribly put out because I'm so late in returning to the boardinghouse."

He released her. It would do her reputation no good to be discovered in a man's arms at this time of night. "I did try to warn you of what might happen if you were alone."

She gave a shaky half laugh and smoothed her hair. "Perhaps after all it was nothing more than my overactive imagination. Pa always said

I spent more time with my head in the clouds than anywhere else."

"Even so, you can't be too careful. Please, allow me to see you the rest of the way home."

She bit her lip, as if weighing her options. "Thank you. I'd be obliged."

He offered her his elbow, and once she had pointed out the house, they set off.

"How is your investigation coming?" She kept her gaze straight ahead.

"As you know from speaking with Mrs. Bell, there isn't much to go on. She didn't see anything. In the morning, I'll chat with the shop-keepers in the vicinity, find out if they noticed anyone unusual or sus-picious hanging around, though I doubt that will yield any valuable information."

"How is your friend?"

"The last time I telephoned home, my friend had slipped into unconsciousness. For now, she needs her rest."

"For someone whose friend was attacked tonight, you don't seem in much of a hurry to apprehend a suspect." Her words rose in pitch.

"Why are you so bent on having someone in custody within five minutes of the crime?"

"To protect the population, of course. Anarchy cannot be allowed to reign on our streets and throughout our country. Law and order. As a police detective, you should understand that."

"Of course I do. But I'm also a realist. Much as we want to, we don't always catch the criminals. Much as we want to, we don't solve every crime." The acid that thought churned up burned a hole in his stomach.

As soon as they approached Miss Blythe's boardinghouse, a woman he assumed to be her landlady stepped onto the front porch. "Miss Blythe, what is the meaning of this? I have been frantic for news of you. And now I find you in the company of an unknown man."

Before Miss Blythe could open her mouth, Edwin answered. "She was working late at the paper, and I escorted her home. Detective Edwin Price with the Denver Police Department, ma'am."

"Oh well." The flustered woman bustled back into the house.

A chuckle burst from Miss Blythe. "Thank you for defending my honor. She means well but is overprotective of the young women under her care."

"There's nothing wrong with that."

"Thank you for seeing me home. I do appreciate it, however unnecessary it was."

"Unnecessary? When you had someone chasing you?"

In the pale moonlight, he caught sight of pink rising in her cheeks. "Perhaps not unnecessary, then."

"Think nothing of it."

They bid each other good night. Though Edwin had said he would allow Rachel the chance to rest tonight, he hurried home to check on her condition. The update he'd received when he telephoned home hadn't been reassuring. He had to know how she was doing. He had prayed the entire way that she would wake up and be fine.

As he entered the house, noise came from the parlor. Weeping. Wailing. As he entered the room, his blood chilled. There were Mr. and Mrs. Quincy, Rachel's parents. Mrs. Quincy held an embroidered handkerchief to her eyes as she sobbed, and her sober husband held her in his arms. Amelia sat in the armchair opposite them, tears streaming down her cheeks. Rachel's brother Bernard stood behind her and rubbed her shoulders, even as his own heaved.

God in heaven, no!

Edwin crossed the room to Amelia. "What has happened?" He bit the inside of his cheek, steeling himself against the pain that surely must be coming.

Bernard withdrew a handkerchief from his pants pocket and blew his nose. "You haven't heard?" His voice cracked.

A wave of coldness, like a winter gust from the mountains, swept over Edwin. "What don't I know?"

Amelia stood and flung herself into his arms. "Oh, Edwin, it's awful, just awful." She sobbed into his chest, soaking his bloodstained shirt with her tears.

"What has happened? Tell me."

She stepped back, her green eyes shimmering. "Edwin, Rachel is dead."

The word hit Edwin like a punch in the stomach. "Dead?" It couldn't be. At one point in his life, he had loved her. Enough to ask for her hand in marriage, though they soon realized they were better suited as friends. But a dear friend she had been.

And now she was gone. Forever. Because some madman decided to have a little fun tonight.

Miss Blythe was right about one thing. They needed to arrest whoever had done this.

Now.

Saturday, August 25, 1900

He sat at his kitchen table as the early-morning sun floated through the dirty window. He flipped through the newspaper until he reached page ten. There it was in the *Denver Post*.

Three attacks last night should have been enough to garner a front-page story, but he had to be content. No rushing this. Hopefully it didn't get lost with all the advertisements for Payn's Sure-Raising Flour and Coca-Cola. In time, with enough activity on his part, it would attract more attention. It would get its big, bold, red headline.

Because the world needed to know what he was doing.

Some might call them crimes. He wouldn't. He was a teacher. An instructor. Teaching women their place, their role in the world. It was a new century, and women were acting like they were taking over the country.

Let them try. Let them try as hard as they wanted, but he wasn't going to stand by and let that happen. No way, no how. This ridiculousness had started with the passage of suffrage in Colorado seven years ago. The lawmakers who signed that into law should be strung up by their toes. They had created this problem.

A woman's place was in the home, raising children, caring for her husband, keeping house. She had no business out working a job, thinking she didn't need a man.

And then these women who were gallivanting the streets at night. Nothing but hussies. Loose, immoral women, the lot of them. If they were in any way respectable ladies, they would be at home, fixing dinner for their families. No, instead they were out doing who knows what with who knows who.

He was only trying to protect them. Keep them safe from predators who might take advantage of them. There was nothing worse than a spoiled dove. A woman with no honor was no woman at all. They needed to learn this lesson. They had to learn how to stay home and put their husbands and their families first.

Not like Beatrice. That backstabbing, conniving good-for-nothing. He should have known the day he met her. Should have known the day he first laid eyes on her. No one came in such a pretty package and had anything good in store for the likes of him.

But he deserved better. All men did. No matter how pretty the face, no man deserved to be humiliated, disgraced, cuckolded the way he was. She got herself a little job as a typist. Just to earn some extra money to buy the nice things she liked.

At least that's what she said.

That's not what she did. Oh, she did have a job. But more than the extra cash it afforded her, it gave her the chance to flaunt herself in front of all those men at the bank where she worked. Flirting with them, throwing herself at them when she should have been at home, cooking his dinner, keeping his house, giving him children.

The one child born to them was clearly not his. As plain as the nose on his face. How did she ever think she could pass off that kid as belonging to him? He didn't look like either of them.

Though he had suspected all along, when that baby came, that's when it was obvious. He could no longer deny the fact that his wife had not been faithful to him.

She had cheated on him and produced a child that wasn't his. When they went to church, people stared down their noses at him. His coworkers laughed behind his back. His friends walked away.

Because he was no kind of man.

He would show them. He would show all of them. He wasn't a man to let a woman get the best of him. Those women would realize where their proper place was in the world. If it took him the rest of his life, he would teach them what a true woman acted like.

The women tonight were prime examples of those who should be home. The pretty one with the dark hair. No one like that should be strutting about after dark. The same for the one who had gotten away. Two young women out by themselves. All of them, especially the older one, should have been with their families, enjoying a quiet evening of cards and reading.

Soon enough, every female in Denver would get the message. They would be too scared to leave the house after dark. They would learn. He would be their teacher.

Chapter 4

Edwin placed a light knock on the red door of the two-story house with a large bay window and stepped back to wait for an answer. The late summer morning had turned golden, spotlighting the mountains that drank in their just-risen rays. A slight breeze ruffled his hair, and he adjusted his glasses.

Hopefully Mrs. Jessup would be of more help than Mrs. Bell had been. The older woman remembered nothing of her attack.

After a minute or two, a man with bags under his dark eyes answered. "Yes?"

"Edwin Price with the Denver Police Department." He flashed his silver badge, a star in the middle of it. "I'm looking for Elva Jessup. I'd like to speak to her about last night's incident."

"I'm her husband, Alvin." He motioned for Edwin to enter. "She's resting, but I'll get her. As you can imagine, she didn't get much sleep last night."

"I'm sorry to disturb her, but I do need to talk to her as soon as possible. The more time passes, the less likely it will be that we will catch the person who did this."

"And believe me, we want him caught." Alvin disappeared up the stairs and returned a few minutes later leading his pale wife.

He settled her on the dark green davenport in the sunny alcove, fluffing pillows behind her back and draping a black and yellow afghan over her lap.

"I'm sorry to disturb you, Mrs. Jessup, but I need to ask you some questions about the mugging last night."

A shudder passed through the heavyset woman with a hint of lines around her eyes. "It was just awful." She rubbed the back of her head.

"How are you feeling this morning?"

"I have quite a lump on my noggin and rather a bad headache, but the doctor says I'm lucky. I believe I heard that a woman was attacked last night and died."

The sour taste of bile rose in Edwin's mouth. He fought it back. Rachel. Gone. For no purpose whatsoever. He swallowed against the burning in his throat.

Getting out of bed after almost no sleep last night had been more than difficult. Pulling the covers over his head and pretending the world outside didn't exist, that evil such as he had witnessed last night didn't exist, tempted him. But for Rachel's sake, he had to open his eyes and face the day.

For her sake, he would catch this man. The one who hunted women for sport. "Can you tell me what you remember?"

"Not too much. I was walking home from the service at Temple Emanuel. Alvin had gone home earlier, and I stayed to chat with a few of my friends. It's only a few blocks between here and the temple, so we didn't think anything of it."

Edwin wrote furiously in his notepad while Mrs. Jessup spoke.

"I wasn't far from home at all. Maybe a block, if that. I'll admit that I wasn't paying the best attention. The night was so beautiful and warm. From behind me came this rustling sound, and that's the last I remember. Next thing I knew, I woke up in my bedroom with the worst headache of my life."

"Did the assailant take anything from you?"

She shook her head, wincing as she did so.

"Were you"—such a delicate question to ask in front of the woman's husband—"hurt in any other way?"

"No." Mrs. Jessup's word rushed out in a breath of air.

None of the three had been violated. None had been robbed. All had been hit over the head. Edwin ground his teeth. "Are you sure you didn't see someone? Perhaps when you left the synagogue? Anyone who was acting uncomfortable or unusual? This is very important." More than she knew.

She scrunched her dark eyebrows together and rubbed her forehead. The mantel clock ticked away the minutes while she thought. Then she shook her head. "I'm sorry, Detective, but I can't remember a thing. Nothing out of the ordinary other than the sound behind me right before I blacked out."

This wasn't helping his investigation. Yet experience had taught him that pressuring Mrs. Jessup wouldn't help her bring any clues to mind. He resisted huffing out a breath. "I understand. Thank you for trying. If you should think of anything, even the smallest detail, please let me know immediately." He withdrew his business card from his jacket pocket and handed it to her. "You never know what might be important."

Alvin assisted his wife to her feet. "We'll keep that in mind. If there's nothing else, I'd really like my wife to rest."

"Of course. Thank you again for your time."

Edwin left the house and all but stomped down the street. A dead end. Poor choice of words. Words that brought Rachel to mind. She hadn't deserved to die. For her, for Bernard, for the entire Quincy family, he had to bring this perpetrator to justice.

He didn't pay much attention to where he was going until he found himself in front of the police station. He hiked up the stairs, into the building, and thumped into his chair at his desk.

His partner descended on him like a vulture on a deer carcass. "What did you find out? Do you have a suspect?"

Edwin flashed O'Fallon a look that hopefully conveyed his great annoyance at the questions. "Nothing. Absolutely nothing. Neither Mrs. Jessup nor Mrs. Bell remembers a thing from the muggings. You can interview people from the nearby businesses, but without witnesses, we have no leads. No leads mean no suspects. No suspects mean no arrests or convictions. No justice." He rubbed his throbbing temples.

"Don't worry, Price. Something'll come up. It always does."

"This is different. Far different. This time it's personal. I've known Rachel Quincy and her family my entire life."

"Oh." O'Fallon's mouth hung open. Then, as if he realized it, he shut it with a click of his teeth. "I didn't realize you knew Miss Quincy. I'm so sorry."

"Thank you."

"If nothing else, whoever did this will get what he deserves when he stands in front of God's judgment seat. That has to bring you a measure of comfort."

It didn't. Not really. The man—for what woman would do such a thing?—was a menace to society. He had already killed once. He could well kill again.

Edwin gazed at the water-stained ceiling. "God, you have to help me here. Send me a break. Help me solve Rachel's murder." He wouldn't be able to rest easy until he did so.

O'Fallon slapped Edwin on the back. "You keep up those prayers."

He would, no doubt about it. They were all he had to go on.

Polly sat at her desk, the afternoon copy of the *Post* sitting in front of her. Inside was her article. Her first. Harry had assured her that she had misunderstood, that he would write the one for the morning edition, and hers would be in the afternoon's.

She couldn't read it yet, even though she had memorized every word of the three paragraphs.

Because what if it wasn't as good as she had thought it to be last night?

What if Mr. Ward had taken Harry to task for allowing her to write that article and hadn't printed it after all? She glanced at Harry, skin so fair it would make any woman jealous. He flashed her a cheeky grin that sent a shiver skittering down her spine, then stood and headed toward Mr. Ward's office.

Even on a Saturday afternoon, the newsroom buzzed. While voices hummed and typewriters clacked around her, Polly straightened the sharpened pencils in the cup on her desk. She lifted a stack of papers and tapped them to make them even. She wiped away imaginary crumbs.

At last, with nothing else to put in its place or to clean, she unfolded the paper, her hands shaking. Starting with the front page, she scanned the edition. Perhaps Mr. Ward had thought the article so good and important that he had moved it to a different page.

Page one, page two, page three. No article. Heart thumping, she thumbed through the paper. As she turned to page ten, she drew in a deep breath. This should be it.

She flicked her gaze up and down the page. Both sides. Advertisements for Shiloh's Consumption Cure, Bremmer Tailors, and Ewing Reducing Garments. A piece on a bank theft. A story about a boy who had saved a cat from a tree.

But no article by Polly Blythe.

As fast as possible, she flipped through the rest of the paper. Mr. Ward hadn't printed it. It wasn't here anywhere. Like a furnace, heat built low in her stomach and spread to her face. Grasping the paper in her hand, she marched to his office and flung open the door. He sat in his chair, puffing on a cigar, and Harry Gray sat across from him doing the same. The two of them in cahoots. Their laughter came to an abrupt halt as she strode into the room.

"Mr. Ward. Where is my—"

"The one Harry said you could write? It was not what we were looking for, Miss Blythe."

"Not what you were looking for? I sensationalized it as much as I could. The story itself was fascinating enough. And I incorporated information that I had verified directly from the sources. Including the Denver police. You printed Harry's. Why not mine?"

Mr. Ward leaned back in his chair, a smirk crossing his face. He puffed on his cigar a few more times. "You stated that all three victims survived. But that was wrong. The truth is even better than what you wrote."

"Wrong?" She steadied herself against his desk.

Harry cleared his throat. "One of the women passed away."

"Who?"

He had the gall to smirk. "A Miss Quincy."

No. Not the young woman they had found. Mr. Price's friend. He was so concerned for her, so tender with her. He would be devastated, and so would her family. "When I wrote this piece, all three women were alive."

"Not by the time I went to print the article."

"It would have been accurate if my piece had gone in the morning's edition." She glared at her fine-boned coworker and forced herself to control her breathing.

"Your article wasn't ready in time. We can't hold the presses for a page-ten story. You should have updated your facts before submitting for the afternoon edition."

"But—"

"You should have followed up."

"So there's no mention of the crimes at all?"

"Another few muggings. That's hardly news these days. It's hard to keep them as page-turning as we want."

"But a woman died."

"If you want to be a success in this business, you have to learn how to take your lumps." He rose from his chair. "Frankly, you're almost out of chances. Back to the society pages for you."

Harry guffawed. "Just where you belong."

"No, please." He couldn't do this to her, especially over an inaccuracy that wasn't her fault. This was her chance. Perhaps her only one.

"And if you can't write the way we want you to, you'll get the hatchet." Mr. Ward sat back down.

Harry leaned back in his chair and puffed harder on his cigar.

If Ma hadn't taught Polly better, she would have stomped on his foot.

"That will be all, Miss Blythe."

With the greatest of restraint, she closed the office door without slamming it. Try as she might, she couldn't stop the sting of tears at the back of her throat. Two days. Two dressing downs.

Maybe Pa was right. Maybe only men were worthy of education and jobs.

No. She shook her head hard, as if that might shake those thoughts right out of it. She would prove to Harry and Mr. Ward and everyone else that she was as good as any man. They might sabotage her, but she would show them. For now, she'd write those inane society page articles and make them as exciting as possible.

But these three muggings—and now the murder—were connected. Somehow, in her bones, she knew it. Not that she had proof. But she would get it.

She would go to Mr. Price. After the help he gave her when she believed she was being followed, they had a connection. At least an acquaintance. And because his friend died, he would be motivated to solve this case.

Together they could work to prove that these cases were related, and together they could apprehend the suspect.

She grabbed her pressman's hat from the edge of her desk, slapped it onto her head, and set off in the direction of the police station.

At least it wasn't dark. No chance of a repeat of last night's events. Those poor women who weren't as fortunate as she had been to escape, especially Rachel. They must have been terrified. Only by God's grace had Polly not come to harm.

Once she arrived, a uniformed officer wearing a long blue coat with a single row of brass buttons led her to Mr. Price's desk, much as he had done last evening. Was that less than twenty-four hours ago?

He peered through his glasses at her, a pockmarked, blond-haired man standing beside him.

Mr. Price came to his feet. "Miss Blythe. To what do I owe this pleasure?"

"First of all, I have come to express my sympathies to you on the passing of Miss Quincy. My condolences to you and your family."

A shadow passed across his long, thin face, and he swallowed hard. "We were longtime family friends, and thank you. Was there something else?"

All of a sudden, her heart went fluttery. She clasped her hands and cleared her throat. "I was badly shaken last night because I was almost mugged, and I would like to work with you to solve these cases."

He studied her for a long moment. So long, she squirmed under his scrutiny. At last he whipped off his glasses and nodded. "I'm thankful I was in the right place at the right time to help you. Purely providential. As for your offer of help, there's something more to it, isn't there?"

How had he seen clean through her like that?

Would he allow her to work with him? To get this story that would make or break her career?

Chapter 5

Edwin would have to have a heart made of stone to say that Miss Blythe's big deep-set eyes and her still-quavering voice didn't strike a chord with him. There she stood, in front of his desk, her hands clasped, her mouth downturned. She had been through an ordeal. She could have been the night's fourth victim.

Despite all that, she had taken the time to come and express her condolences to him. Yet, though he knew her little, there was more than sympathy on her mind when she paid him this visit. If he were a wagering man, he would place a bet on it.

She twisted the ribbon on her reticule until it wrapped around her delicate wrist. "You lost someone you cared about last night. I was almost accosted. We both have our reasons to want to solve this case. These cases."

"In your expert opinion, then, you believe these cases to be related." He cringed at the harshness of his words. "Forgive me. I shouldn't have said that to you." He could make grief and lack of sleep his excuses, but he wouldn't. If Mother were here, she would give him that look again.

"You don't think so?"

"They do bear a striking resemblance to each other, I can't deny that. But why are some attacks, like the one on Rachel, so violent, and others, like on Mrs. Bell, less injurious?"

"I, uh, don't know."

"And so, until we have concrete proof that this is the same person committing these crimes, eyewitness statements from people that corroborate the same person struck each of these women, we can't make that leap. Right now we treat this as if we are looking for three suspects." One, of course, he wanted to catch more than anyone.

There could very well be a connection between them all. Personally, he may believe that. Professionally, he couldn't rely on it. They had no idea whom they were dealing with. If it was the same man, he was bold and he was violent.

Miss Blythe seated herself across from him, smoothing her dark green skirt and fiddling with the reticle ribbon again. "Can we speak one-on-one?" She gazed at O'Fallon.

What was he to say to that? She intrigued him. Soft and vulnerable one minute, hard and determined the next. But someone interesting. Not the society women Mother foisted on him. A person who would bring a spark of light to his life. Or drive him crazy. It was too early to tell.

Then again, he shouldn't be considering such things. Rachel, the woman he had once planned to marry, had died last night. Just last night. How could he be so unfaithful to her memory?

Still, he turned to O'Fallon. "Just give us a minute."

His partner wandered away, and Edwin returned his attention to the woman in front of him. "Go ahead."

She leaned forward. "I'm going to be honest and straightforward with you. Yes, there is another reason I came here, other than extending my sympathies, which I am sincere about."

"I don't doubt that." And he didn't.

"I, well, I've been having trouble at my job. Mr. Ward, the editor, will only allow me to report on society stories. I want more than that. I'm trying to show him that a woman is capable of writing a real piece of journalism. But he just won't see it."

"So if you are able to connect these cases and write a sensational article about them, he might take more notice of you. Perhaps you would be allowed to write more crime stories in the future."

Her countenance brightened. "Exactly. You are very discerning."

At the compliment, he swallowed hard. This was no practiced nicety. She was forthright. A breath of fresh air. "However much I may wish to help you, Miss Blythe, I already have a partner. And given how dangerous this man is, I would hate to have you mixed up in any activity that could put your life in jeopardy. Just think of Rachel."

"Could you at least keep me informed of your progress on the case? Let me know before any other reporters are able to get the scoop?" She kept her voice low, so low Edwin had to lean forward to hear her, their noses almost touching.

How could this tingle be racing through him? He jerked back. "You want me to give you an advantage?"

She too leaned away. "Yes, I suppose that's what I'm asking."

"Wouldn't that be unfair to the other reporters?"

"I can do this job. I know I can. But there are so many roadblocks, so many obstacles to my proving myself, I need just a little help. Anything you can do to give me a hand will be very much appreciated." She stood and straightened her pressman's hat. "I hope to hear from you soon."

With a swish of her skirts, she turned and flounced across the room and through the door.

So abrupt was her leaving, Edwin didn't even have a chance to say anything else to her. Fascinating creature. He would do what he could to help her. Besides, if he could get the media's attention with the case, it might help him solve Rachel's murder.

That had to be his focus. His priority. Nothing else took precedence at the moment.

O'Fallon returned to his side. "What was that all about? She left here in quite the huff."

"Not really. She didn't want anything in particular." No need for O'Fallon to know. He was such a joker, he would never let Edwin live down the fact that he was helping a woman journalist. He would make kissing sounds every time he passed Edwin's desk. Not what he needed. Not right now.

Rachel deserved justice. Edwin would be the one to give that to her. He owed her that much.

Hamilton Armstrong, the chief of detectives, approached and handed Edwin a file. Edwin raised his eyebrows. "What's this?"

Armstrong tipped his head toward the file in Edwin's hand. "Take a look at it. I think you'll find some information in there that's very interesting."

With O'Fallon peering over his shoulder, Edwin opened the folder. The coroner's report on Rachel's death. Physicians' reports on the other women. All suffered blunt-force trauma to the head. A single stroke.

Edwin sucked in a breath. The supposed weapon in each of the cases was the same—a metal pipe, according to the coroner and the attending physicians.

He broke out in a sweat. They had a monster on the loose.

More than ever, they needed to catch him. Next time, more than one woman might die.

Monday, September 24, 1900

The Denver air held a distinct chill. Summer had fled, and autumn had filled the void. Polly sat at the little desk in the cramped room she rented and scribbled in her journal. Not words, not even drawings. Just lines and circles and squares.

For a month, all had been quiet. No more of the unusual muggings. No more deaths. Praise the Lord for that. But no more exciting stories. Now that wedding season was over and the social season had yet to begin, there was little for Polly to do at the paper.

She hadn't heard a word from Mr. Price. The few times she had stopped into the station, he hadn't been around. Once he'd been at Rachel's funeral. Another time the officer who spoke to her told her he was working a case. The officer, however, refused to tell her what case it was.

She sighed and peered at the gathering gloom, a storm rolling over the Rockies, only the gas lamps along the streets providing any light. In the distance, lightning flashed, too far away for the noise of the thunder to reach her.

A knock sounded at her door. "Polly, are you in?"

Sophie. Polly couldn't help but smile. Sophie was the best friend she had among the women in the boardinghouse. Probably her best friend in the world. "Come on in."

With her usual enthusiasm, Sophie bounded into the room, her blond curls wisping around her heart-shaped face. She wore her dark blue wool coat and a matching hat with a wide brim. "What are you doing? More work? Mr. Ward keeps you too busy."

"Not work tonight. Just thinking, I suppose."

"That's not very much fun." She held up a fan of tickets. "I know you said you didn't want to see this show with us, but Mary can't make it now, so we have an extra. Won't you please join us? Please?"

"I'm not in the mood. Besides, it's Monday. We all have to work tomorrow."

"Posh. You'll have loads of fun. You know you will. For the past few weeks, you've been spending too much time cooped up in here."

"Really, I wouldn't be a good companion. Next time. I promise. You have fun."

Sophie sighed but came farther into the room and hugged Polly from behind. "I love you."

"And I love you."

After another quick squeeze, Sophie almost skipped from the room and shut the door.

Another flash of lightning lit the black sky.

When Polly and her brother Lyle had been younger, they had watched through the glass windowpanes in their small cottage as the sky had brightened with lightning streaks. Each time thunder tickled Polly's toes, she would shriek.

Always the big brother, Lyle would wrap her close to himself. "Look, Pols, look at how beautiful it is. Wild and untamed. Powerful. Always hitting the mark. That's how you're going to be. You're going to grow into a great woman."

Funny how her brother, the only one her father would allow to attend college, was also the only one who encouraged her in her dreams. She picked up Lyle's latest letter. He was working hard in a law firm. Pa was so proud of him. Would he ever be proud of her?

Lyle, at least, told her to keep trying, no matter what. Told her not to let Mr. Ward get to her. If nothing else, she could always come and work for him.

But that's not what she wanted. She wanted to make it on her own. At the end of the day, she would succeed without help from anyone else.

Including, it seemed, the elusive Mr. Price.

From outside came a screech. A cat trying to match the howling of the wind? Polly listened a moment more. No, definitely not. She rose and brushed aside the curtains to peer onto the street below.

Though the darkness hid much, she could just make out a silvery, shadowy figure racing down the street. A man, judging by the way he sprinted. She didn't take her attention from him until he turned the corner.

Had he been running to get home ahead of the rain?

As she turned to get back to her doodling, she caught sight of something from the corner of her eye. A figure on the ground. Hunched. No, crumpled.

Her heart thudded, stopped, restarted. Within seconds, she had her gray knit shawl wrapped around shoulders and was racing down the stairs.

"You just missed Sophie. I don't know if you can catch her." Mrs. Mannheim stood at the bottom of the stairs, her skinny arms crossed over her scrawny body.

Before Mrs. Mannheim had finished speaking, Polly was out of the house, slamming the door behind her.

She scurried down the walk, out the gate, and down the street. In no time, she almost stumbled over the woman curled in a ball, lying on the side of the road.

Polly knelt beside the whimpering woman.

The blue coat. The blue hat. No. No! Not Sophie. Not Sophie. Blood gushed from a wide-open gash on the back of her head, staining her fair hair.

Polly stroked her back. "Hush, hush. You're okay. I'm here now. I'll get you help, and you'll be fine. You'll see."

At this point, the darkness didn't matter. Sophie's only answer was more whimpering.

"Do you know what happened? Who did this to you?"

Sophie drew in a shuddering breath. "Mama. Mama. Mama."

"Listen to me, Sophie. You have to listen and be calm. Who did this?"

"I want Mama."

"She isn't here, sweetie, but I am. I'm going to help you. You'll be fine. You'll see. In no time, you'll be off to the theater again. Stay here. I have to get help to get you inside." As Polly turned toward the gray Queen Anne with red trim, the first big drops of rain splattered her face.

A roll of thunder shook the ground under her feet. She needed to get Sophie inside. Fast. A soaking would do her no good.

Polly slammed inside. "Mrs. Mannheim! Mrs. Mannheim!"

She emerged from the kitchen, drying her hands on a towel. "What is it, child? You sound as if the devil is after you."

"Sophie. Outside. Attacked. Need you to help."

A few of the other residents scurried from various places. Mrs. Mannheim, Polly, and another woman carried Sophie inside and, with the greatest of care, laid her on her side on the davenport. Within seconds, blood stained the couch's fabric, a spot of brilliant red spreading like crimson ice cream.

Polly turned to two of her housemates hovering behind the couch. "Hurry. Both of you go together for the doctor."

They stood, wide-eyed and open-mouthed.

"Hurry. Do you want her to die?" Polly almost choked on the last word. But the urgent tone of her voice snapped them into action, and they were soon out the door. "Mrs. Mannheim, a towel. Quickly, please. To stop the bleeding." Why was everyone moving at a tortoise's pace?

Sophie moaned, her eyes flickering open then shutting again.

"Please, sweetie, don't die. Don't leave us." Another burst of lightning, another tremble of thunder, another gust of wind.

"Mama?"

"No, I'm not your mama, but the doctor will be here soon, and she'll make you better. Between her and God, nothing is going to happen to you. Just hang on until she gets here."

Mrs. Mannheim returned with the towel, and Polly pressed it to Sophie's head. Though in Polly's mind half a lifetime passed before the doctor arrived, it was probably no more than fifteen minutes. The young female physician, tall and strong-featured, an apron already over her dark skirt, commanded attention.

"We telephoned the police before we left the office. They should be here shortly. In the meantime, I would like to examine the patient in private. If you could all remove yourselves, I'll let you know if I need anything."

As she left to obey the doctor's orders, Polly spotted Sophie's reticule still dangling from her wrist. "May I?" She directed her question to the doctor.

"Of course."

Once in the kitchen, Polly opened it. Sophie's money was still inside. So was her little silver compact and the tickets to the play. Nothing had been stolen. Not a thing.

The women paced the kitchen, the only sound breaking the silence that of Mrs. Mannheim stirring the stove's fire and putting the kettle on to boil. That and rain pinging at the windows and pounding on the roof.

Polly must have paced a mile or more, a thousand prayers rising to heaven, before the doctor, her apron now bloody and her dark hair disheveled, entered the kitchen. "How is she, doctor? Is she going to recover?"

She shook her head, a few more pins dislodging themselves. "She has sustained a serious head injury. Right now she's confused and doesn't remember the attack."

"Will her memory return?" Mrs. Mannheim poured the doctor a cup of tea, which she accepted with a wan smile.

"I can't say. The brain is an amazing organ with a great capacity to heal itself. Sometimes, though, it doesn't, and we can't explain why or do much about it. I wish I could give you a more definitive answer, but I can't."

She sipped her tea. "Just watch her carefully the next few days. She shouldn't be left alone. You'll have to take shifts nursing her. She may remain unconscious for a while, but try to get some liquids into her. I'll be back tomorrow to check on her, but don't hesitate to call for me again if her condition changes for the worse in the meantime."

Polly saw the doctor to the door. Before she opened it, she turned to the woman. "Was Sophie, you know, violated?" Thunder, a little more distant, rumbled low and long.

"No, praise the Lord. Her only injury is the one to the back of her head."

"You never answered my question. Will Sophie recover?"

"Because I don't have the answer. I've done what I can. The rest is in God's hands."

If only the police would hurry and arrive. Because there was no doubt in Polly's mind.

Their culprit had struck again.

Chapter 6

Another late night for Edwin. The station around him had quieted. Not so many voices. Not so many telephones. Not so many people moving about.

As he stared at the stack of folders teetering on the edge of his desk, he sighed. How was he supposed to make any progress on Rachel's case when he had so much else to do? And the workload only increased. Muggings continued, but none that fit the pattern of the three a month ago.

Exactly a month ago.

He scrubbed his face, his stubble rough beneath his fingers. He needed a shave. Supper. A good night's sleep.

None of that was in his future.

He opened several of the folders in front of him and scanned each of them, searching for clues. Any kind of clue. The smallest detail he had overlooked the hundreds of other times he had studied these cases.

Especially Rachel's.

Nothing.

Absolutely nothing.

What would motivate a man to bash women over the head without robbing or violating them? Why waste a life for nothing? None of it made sense. A piece was missing. Why couldn't he figure it out?

The telephone on O'Fallon's desk rang. Since Edwin was the only one even close to his partner's workstation, he rolled his chair over and answered. "Detective Price."

"This is Dr. Lawson." The voice was feminine and took him aback for a moment.

"How can I help you?"

"I've been summoned to treat a young woman at a boardinghouse on Emmerson Street near Sixteenth Avenue who was struck over the head. I don't know how serious her injuries are, but I wanted to inform you."

Edwin went cold all over. Not another one. This hadn't been a one-night crime spree by a drunken despot. This was calculated. "Do you have the address?"

As she provided it to him, he scribbled it down, stopping in the middle. "Are you sure?"

A muffled voice sounded in the background before the doctor came back on the line. "Yes, that's correct."

Polly. She lived at that address. "Who is it?"

Another muted conversation, then the doctor again. "A young lady by the name of—"

"Hello? Hello? Are you still there?"

The operator came on the line. "I'm sorry, sir. The call got cut off. Would you like me to try that number again?"

"Yes, yes."

She did, several times. There was no answer. Likely, the doctor and whoever was with her were already out the door. All he was doing was wasting time. He'd discover the victim's name soon enough.

With tightness in his chest, he sprang to his feet and grabbed his jacket from the back of his chair. Perhaps the woman's injury wasn't severe. Perhaps she had seen the man. Perhaps she could give him a description. This might just be the break he'd been waiting four long weeks for.

"Price."

Not Armstrong. Not now. "I'm on my way out to a call. Another one of those mysterious muggings, at least by the sound of it."

"I'm not worried about that. What I want you to concentrate on is the robbery over at First National Bank."

"Sir, I've been working this mugging case for over a month. Now we have another possible incident."

"That's peanuts. Happens all the time in this city. Everyone should take more care when they're out at night. But this heist is a big deal. A lot of money stolen. And in broad daylight. This is the case we need to solve."

"I'll get on it as soon as I get back from interviewing the latest mugging victim." Whoever that might be.

"You'll work on it now." Armstrong narrowed his eyes and stroked his mustache.

"I told them I would be right there. What if the woman loses consciousness? Or worse?" He bit back bile. "We could miss the chance to crack this case and make the streets safe for everyone, day or night." He turned on his heel.

"Get back here, Price. If you walk out that door—"

That's just what he did, the slamming of it drowning out the rest of Armstrong's threats. He wouldn't give up on the case. He wouldn't let Rachel down. Not like he had his family.

Pouring rain greeted him when he stepped from the station. As was his practice, he eschewed a hat and popped open his umbrella. He dashed from underneath the small cover the portico provided. A streak of lightning illuminated the gloomy night, and thunder crashed around him.

Perhaps he should hop aboard the streetcar, but it wasn't that far. Still, the wind blew the rain straight under his umbrella, soaking him.

By the time he arrived at the house, he was shivering from the cold. No sooner had he turned up the walk than the door opened. Miss Blythe stood in the entrance, beckoning him inside.

Thank goodness she wasn't hurt.

She took his wet coat and umbrella. "I'm so glad it's you who came. Sophie isn't good, not at all. The doctor has been and gone."

"Yes, I apologize for the delay. Another case popped up that I had to push to the back burner. What happened?"

"Sophie, one of the boarders here, was on her way to the theater. She hadn't even gone from in front of the house when she was attacked. I heard her scream and ran outside."

Edwin sucked in a breath. "Did you see anything? Can you identify the perpetrator?"

"I didn't see anything but a silver shadow running away."

His hopes were crushed before they'd had a chance to fully bloom.

"I'm so sorry. Under any other circumstances, I would have run after him, but I was so concerned for Sophie, I couldn't even think straight." Tears gathered in the corners of Miss Blythe's eyes.

"You did what you could." Not that the words would make her feel any better. They never did anything to lift his guilt. "Your friend needed you more in that moment. How is she?"

"Come in and see for yourself."

A young woman lay on the davenport, her head wrapped in a white bandage. An older woman knelt on a Turkish rug beside her, spooning broth into the younger woman's mouth.

Polly came alongside him. "The doctor isn't sure if Sophie's confusion or memory loss will ever resolve itself. She may have suffered permanent damage. Only time will tell."

He huffed out a breath and shook his head. Such a shame. "Was anything of hers stolen? Or was she. . .?"

"No. Just like the others, this act was committed for no obvious reason."

Again, a senseless attack. Why hurt an innocent young woman for no reason at all? "Can we sit? I'd like to ask you a few questions."

"Of course." She relayed her story to Edwin as he made notes on his pad. Nothing of substance. Nothing that was immediately helpful. But he took down her information. You never knew. Perhaps one day very soon something would click and he would have the answers. Answers for Rachel. Answers for all the women of Denver.

"I wish I could help you more."

"Not at all. You did what you had to in the situation. At least you'll get the scoop on the story."

She shook her head. "This is one case where I wish I didn't know the story as well as I do. Now it's my turn to ask you something. Would you be willing to go on the record and say that these events are related? The ones from a month ago and tonight's incident?"

"I can't make such a statement on the record. The chief would have my head on a platter. All communication with the newspaper comes from him and him alone. You know how well your bosses like the police department." He flashed a wry smile.

"Like oil likes water. So I have to speak to him?"

"I suppose you have to. He won't be available until the morning. He won't appreciate being disturbed at home unless it's urgent. Which he doesn't consider this to be."

"Then I'll have to write my story without his input."

"He's more focused on other cases, like the bank robbery at First National. Not on these mysterious muggings."

"Not even your friend's death?"

"No. He should be, but he isn't. He wants the high-profile cases that will get him noticed. He's been eyeing the police chief's job for a while."

"He doesn't care about the city's women?"

With the way his constricting throat was closing off Edwin's breathing, all he could do was shake his head. The chief's attitude about the muggings laid all the responsibility on his shoulders. He would have to solve this case on his own.

And he would.

"Someone has to do something about it." She set her features.

"Watch your step. You might get the wrong people angry."

"But don't you agree that a fire needs to be lit underneath the police department so that these cases will get solved?"

She was right. As much as he hated to admit it, she was right.

Feeling self-satisfied, he poured himself a cup of coffee and sat at the small kitchen table. He'd done it again. Taught another woman a lesson she wouldn't soon forget. Warmth spread throughout him, and not from the hot liquid streaming down his throat.

There was one less woman in Denver who would be running around at night when she should be home.

It wasn't as if he enjoyed this. But the pastors in the churches didn't preach against this kind of immoral behavior. The schools didn't prepare young women to be good wives and homemakers. Fathers didn't keep a tight rein on their daughters.

That left the job up to him. If not for him, the women of this city would never learn. They would never become the kind of women they should be. Women who knew their place and kept to it.

Surely now someone would recognize what he was doing. It was no coincidence that he had picked tonight, exactly one month since his last lesson. Those dolts at the police station weren't bright, but even they couldn't deny the connection.

Tonight his heart had beat a little faster. Instead of slinking into the shadows, he'd had to run in front of the woman. Though he wore darker clothes and a low-slung hat, perhaps she had glimpsed him. He hadn't gotten as good of an angle as he'd wanted.

Then again, she had gone down hard.

No matter. With the incompetence of the Denver Police Department, there was no way they would catch him. Ever. He had nothing to worry about.

A knock sounded at the door. His hands shook, and he dribbled a bit of coffee from his cup. Who could it be? Perhaps he had been too confident. Perhaps the police knew more than they were letting on.

Next time, if there was a next time, he would have to be more careful. He was getting sloppy. Sloppy could get you into a heap of trouble.

Maybe if he sat still and quiet, whoever was at the door would go away. But the knock came again. And again. More persistent and demanding each time.

Whoever it was wasn't leaving.

He rose to his feet and crossed the distance to his home's entrance. He opened the door the smallest of cracks. "Yes?"

"Ralph O'Fallon with the Denver police." The broad, muscular man flashed a silver badge. "Right in this very neighborhood, not far from here, a woman was attacked tonight on her way to see a play. Did you see or hear anything around six o'clock this evening? Whatever you can tell me would be most helpful."

He bit the inside of his cheek, the metallic taste of blood filling his mouth. A cop dressed in civilian clothes. He was getting careless. Of course the police and others would look for him in the neighborhood where he'd struck. He'd been so intent on making sure the authorities and media could connect the dots, he hadn't thought it would bring suspicion on those who lived in the neighborhood.

"Nothing. As far as I know, all's been quiet. I've been here all evening and haven't heard a thing. Sorry I can't help you, Officer." He went to close the door, but the policeman stuck his foot on the threshold to prevent it.

"If you do remember something, however insignificant you believe it is, please get in touch with us immediately." The man handed him a card, which he pocketed.

"If there is nothing else."

"That's all. Have a good evening."

He closed the door, his heart slamming against his chest hard enough to break his ribs. From now on, he might have to venture a bit away from home. Still in the same general area, enough for the police to figure out that what was happening to these women was connected but far enough that they wouldn't question anyone in this neighborhood.

For though his goal was to send a message to the women of Denver to be good daughters, wives, and mothers, he couldn't get that message out if he sat in prison. That wouldn't do at all. And he couldn't bear it if his wife heard of it. She would gloat and have the last laugh.

He could never let that happen.

From deep in a chest at the end of his unmade bed, he pulled out a map of the city of Denver. He'd lived here long enough that he should know every street by heart, but if he wanted to avoid detection, he would have to be more strategic.

So far, he had carried out all his attacks in the Capitol Hill area, in a cluster in the same neighborhood. Before tonight he hadn't even thought the police cared about the attacks. They were more concerned about rounding up barkeeps and inmates to vote in the election next year than in keeping the streets safe.

In a way, that was good for him. Helped him avoid detection. Especially with the rampage of other crimes happening. On the other hand, they were too busy to take notice of the message he was sending to Denver's female population.

He studied the map some more. If he stayed on the same trajectory but moved a number of blocks away, a little bit north perhaps, he could throw the search in a different direction but still give the detectives working the case, like that idiot at the door, enough clues to connect what was happening to these women.

He squinted harder at the lines that marked the city's streets. With his finger, he followed them up the map. A smile crossed his face. Yes, that would be the perfect location. And he knew just the date and time for it to happen.

Chapter 7

Tuesday, September 25, 1900

Polly stumbled from her room, down the stairs, and into the dining room where Mrs. Mannheim was setting out flapjacks and bacon for breakfast. Most of the seven girls who lived in the boardinghouse had already made their way to the table, and a general din ran through the room. The morning light gleamed on the silver tea service.

Though she rubbed the grit from her eyes, Polly couldn't stifle a yawn. Not that she'd slept much. Every time she had dozed, she jerked herself awake, afraid to take her attention from Sophie. What if she took a turn for the worse while Polly slept? For her friend's sake, she'd had to stay alert.

Even the sweet aroma of bacon and coffee didn't quite do it.

Hardly able to keep her eyes open, she yanked her chair from the mahogany table and plopped down. The scattered conversations came to an abrupt end.

Laura, the young, delicate teacher sitting beside her, eyed Polly. "How is Sophie?"

Polly made an attempt to loosen her shoulders. "The same." She directed her gaze around the table. "The few times she's awakened, she's been confused. She begs for her mother and wants her dolly."

"Oh my." Mrs. Mannheim lifted her apron to her eyes and fled to the kitchen.

Laura bit her lower lip. "I'm so sorry to hear that. I wish we'd have waited for her before going to the play. She told us she'd catch up. If she had been with us, none of this would have happened."

"And I wish I had gone with her." Pa would say this was why

young women needed to stay home, either under the protection of their father or their husband. Perhaps he was right. Maybe, just maybe, he had a point.

Laura looked troubled. "By the end of the day, I'm sure this will be all the talk around school. Why, now I'm afraid to walk home after a late night at work or after evening church services."

The other girls murmured their assent, then returned their attention to their meals.

"The trouble is that the police don't do anything about it." Everyone but Mr. Price, that was. "They consider these incidents as just part of the crime problem in the city. When I can see that they're related because of the nature of the attacks and the fact that nothing is stolen from the victims, why can't they?"

Laura shrugged. "I'm sure you have a thought on that."

"Of course I do."

"I would expect nothing less." A dimple appeared in Laura's cheek.

"They're concentrating on getting the right people elected next fall so they can keep their jobs. Just sweep the city's woes under the rug so no one notices. Make it look like they're doing what they're supposed to, and then they won't get fired for their incompetence because they have the mayor and the councilmen right where they want them."

Laura stared at Polly, her green eyes wide. "Wow, I didn't realize all that was going on."

"Well, it is. Yesterday was one month to the day since the first of the attacks."

"Isn't that when Mr. Ward decided not to print your story in the paper?"

"Exactly. Though I did get last night's attack stuck on page twelve." Mr. Price had been gracious enough to take her story with him and drop it at the paper so it would make this morning's edition.

"That's better than nothing."

"Have you ever read the paper all the way through to page twelve?"

A blush rose in Laura's freckled cheeks. "Well, no."

"And neither does anyone else." Polly poured herself a cup of tea and spooned in some sugar.

"So what are you going to do about it?"

"I don't know. Mr. Ward is trying everything he can to push me to the side. He doesn't want a woman reporter on his paper. Only Mr. Defils's insistence that they need a woman's point of view keeps me on. Thank goodness Mr. Ward has to listen to the paper's owner."

"What about a letter to the editor instead of an article?"

Polly tapped her spoon against the china cup. What an idea. Mr. Ward pretty much printed whatever the editorial board put in front of him. If she could convince them to include it in the paper, perhaps even on the front page of the editorial section, the story would at least get noticed. "I think, Miss Laura Stark, that you are one brilliant young woman."

Polly jumped up, squeezed Laura around the neck, and hurried out. Mrs. Mannheim called after her, but she didn't pay the woman any heed.

Before long she was settled behind her desk at the newspaper, a fresh, crisp white sheet rolled into the barrel of her typewriter.

Harry leaned over. "What are you working on?"

Good thing she hadn't typed a single word yet. "Nothing much." Not anything he needed to stick his nose into, especially not with the way he was chummy with Mr. Ward.

"I heard about your friend. What was she doing gallivanting about the city alone at night?"

"She wasn't gallivanting. She was on her way to a play. And she didn't want to be out alone. Just before the attack, she asked me to join her. I declined." Polly swallowed the lump in her throat. It wouldn't do for Harry to see her emotional. He'd claim she couldn't do the job. "How I wish I hadn't."

"I don't care how many of you are on the streets at night. No respectable woman is ever without an escort. That's how they get in trouble."

She chomped her tongue so hard it was amazing she didn't bite off the tip. Once she swallowed, she turned a lightbulb-bright smile on Harry. "Thank you for sharing your views with me. Now, if you don't mind, I believe we both have work to do."

"Just watch your step, Miss Blythe." With that, Harry slid back to his desk.

She shuddered. It was men like him who forced her to write this editorial. She didn't have to spend much time thinking about what she was going to say. She had reworked and rehearsed it until she had the piece pretty much memorized.

Dear Editor,

As a concerned citizen of this fine city we inhabit, the time has come for me to speak up. I've stayed silent far too long. The streets of Denver are no longer safe for women to walk. A terrorist is holding the women of the city hostage.

On the evening of August 24 of this year, three innocent women were attacked in the most heinous manner. All three of them, walking home from activities such as work or religious services, were struck over the head, each of them suffering deep gashes. One young woman, but twenty-two years old, lost her life to this madman.

Rachel Quincy was doing nothing more than returning home after purchasing some headache powders for her mother. For this, she gave her life. Nothing was taken from her person. Not her cash, not her watch, not her earrings.

The attacks continued on September 24, exactly one month from the date of the first. This time Miss Sophie Hanover was struck over the head and left lying bleeding in the middle of the street. We can thank the good Lord that Miss Hanover's life was spared. Again, she suffered this crime through no fault of her own. Once more, nothing was stolen from her person.

What kind of individual would commit such offenses? What kind of man would perpetrate such deeds against defenseless women? Isn't it instead a man's job to protect a woman's welfare?

Only the basest and crassest of human beings would stoop so low as to purposely injure and kill a woman who did nothing to provoke such an attack. Only the cruelest and most heartless among us would do such a thing.

What is being done to solve this string of crimes? Absolutely nothing. That's right, fellow citizens, not a finger has been lifted toward bringing this murderous individual to justice. Our esteemed police chief and the chief of detectives have been sitting on their hands. They cannot see that these crimes are related to one another.

Has one man faced a judge in this case? No. Has one suspect been questioned in this case? No. Has one man been apprehended in this case? No. I ask, why not?

Because the police chief and those working for him are more worried about retaining their jobs. They are doing what they must do to curry favor with those in power, hoping to keep them in power so they will retain their positions.

This should not be so. The welfare of women should not be sold for an election. People of Denver, you should be outraged. The time for apathy is over. The time for action has come. We must demand the police do their due diligence and catch this thug. How many more lives must be lost before the police chief stops twiddling his thumbs and begins doing his job?

With a flourish, she signed her name.

The afternoon edition of the *Denver Post* trembled in Edwin's hands as he read the editorial section. His eyes were probably bugging out of his head. *What is being done to solve this string of crimes? Absolutely nothing.*

Nothing? Nothing! Whoever concocted this drivel had no idea what they were talking about. Had no idea how he slaved day and night tracking down the least little lead in Rachel's death. Mother had expressed her concern for him last Sunday at dinner. The dark bags under his eyes must have given away the fact that he hadn't slept much in over a month.

Swallowing hard, he forced himself to read on. *The police chief and those working for him are more worried about retaining their jobs.* What kind of nonsense was that? Hang his job if it meant he brought Rachel's killer to justice.

Before he finished, before he glanced at the name of the letter's author, it struck him. Miss Polly Blythe. There was no one else who could have written the editorial. She had knowledge of these events. She was the one who found Miss Hanover in front of her building. She knew what was happening—and not happening—inside the police department. In fact, he had mentioned to her the other night about his frustration with the chief.

Yet the conclusions she jumped to were ludicrous. If she wanted to inflame the city in general and him in particular, she had accomplished her goal.

He glanced at the name at the bottom of the editorial. He was right. Polly Blythe.

Edwin turned to O'Fallon. "I'm going out. Finish that report on the attack on Miss Hanover. Go back through the other files. See if you can find any similarities to Miss Hanover's case. When I return, I'll be interested to hear what you have to say."

Ralph saluted him. "Aye, aye, sir."

"I won't be gone long." He shrugged into his coat before stepping into the cool fall day, the wind ruffling his hair.

The walk wasn't far, just six blocks or so. Though the breeze was bracing, it was better than that broiling office. Every now and again, the streetcar clanged by. Businessmen crowded the road. He passed the May Company building, shoppers flocking to the department store. Soon he went by Parini Brothers Umbrellas, the *Post's* neighbor.

He strode up to the brick building with glass store fronts on the main level. The painted slogan on the windows proclaimed *Every Day in the Year*. He marched through the door. The secretary in her neat white blouse with a blue ribbon tied at her throat peered at him, her typing coming to a halt. "Yes, sir?"

"I need to speak to Polly Blythe. Immediately." He clenched his fists so hard, his fingernails were sure to leave half-moon imprints in his palms.

"Let me see if she's available." The secretary scurried off and returned a few short minutes later with Miss Blythe in tow.

"Mr. Price. What a surprise to see you here. To what do I owe this pleasure?"

Her voice was a little too syrupy sweet. She knew exactly why he was here. Perhaps she had even been expecting him. "May we step someplace where we can speak a little more privately?"

The bottom of her maroon skirt dusted the tops of her brown shoes. She led him to an empty office with a large window overlooking the newsroom. Tendrils of russet hair escaped her Gibson girl updo and brushed her fair cheek. "Now, do you care to tell me why you're here?"

He inhaled a few deep breaths before he began, just so he didn't lose his temper. "I believe you know why. I read your article in the paper this morning."

She had the grace to blush. No, he shouldn't be noticing how attractive that made her. Not that she wasn't very becoming already. Drat. He was allowing her to muddle his thoughts.

"I was hoping someone would notice. If it means that the police chief will take me, you—us—seriously, I would be happy. It was the only way I was going to get an article about the muggings onto any prominent page of the paper. The only way I was going to garner attention for the story. And your coming here is proof that it worked."

"Publishing such inflammatory rhetoric, though, isn't going to make you any friends at the department."

"If it lights a fire underneath them, it was worth it."

"And in the process, it gets your editor to notice you."

"I suppose. Now, on to more important business." She sat in the leather chair in front of the large desk and motioned for him to sit in the matching chair beside her. "Do you believe that the cases are related?"

Edwin settled into the seat. "It can't be coincidence that all four of these women were attacked and nothing was taken from them. But what would motivate someone to just walk up to an unsuspecting woman and whack her over the head?"

"I don't have an answer for that. Do you?"

"It might be that he was wronged by a woman in some way. Perhaps mistreated by his mother."

"Why take it out on innocents?"

"We can't plumb the depths of man's depravity."

Miss Blythe shivered and rubbed her arms. "So where we do go from here?"

"That's a very good question." The heat in his chest had subsided.

Yes, Miss Blythe had scorched the police, without merit in part. But she did have a point. Perhaps this would enlighten the public as to what was taking place in their city and would force Armstrong to take these crimes seriously. "We continue our investigation. I'm going to return to the station and speak to my boss. You may have done me and my case a great favor, Miss Blythe."

"Why, Mr. Price, I believe you just complimented me."

He stood and studied his feet as he shuffled them. "Then come to Sunday dinner at my family's home."

Oh goodness, what had he just said? Why had he blurted that out? Now she would think he was interested in her. His focus had to remain on Rachel's case. He owed Rachel that. To become distracted would be to sully her name.

"That sounds lovely."

What had he gotten himself into?

Chapter 8

Though his kitchen was cold, no fire in the stove, he couldn't stop the grin that spread across his face any more than he could stop the hands on the clock from moving forward. He read the editorial in the *Post* a second and a third time. "*The streets of Denver are no longer safe for women to walk. A terrorist is holding the women of the city hostage.*"

He paced in a circle around the room and back again. Exactly what he wanted. Women off the streets at night. Women at hearth and home, watching over their families. Women faithful to their husbands.

His tactics were working.

He had to have patience and stick to his plan. In time, it would all come to fruition.

He laid the paper on the small table in front of him. The table where he and his wife used to sit and have dinner. They ate. They talked. They laughed. Life was good.

What had gone wrong? Why had Beatrice left? Why did she conceive a child with another man?

Because love wasn't enough. She wanted great wealth. Prestige. Social standing. All things he couldn't give her. At least not fast enough.

So she walked away on the arm of a man who could.

After all he'd done for her, she didn't even look back.

The editorial spoke about a woman's need to be protected. What about a man's? The need to protect his heart once he gave it to his wife. These modern women didn't give a second thought to that. Instead, they gadded about the city day and night. Always on the lookout for something—or someone—better.

He picked up the map from beside the paper. On it he had marked where he had struck. The time was drawing near for another lesson. And that editorial would get the police working on the case.

Soon they would fit the puzzle pieces together and figure out what he was trying to tell the world.

He did have to change where he struck. Police presence in the area he'd been working would be increased. Women would be more cautious, perhaps not going out without an escort.

He circled the next place. Twenty-three blocks from the last attack. A more affluent area. Fitting. Beatrice's punishment, in a way, for being too hoity-toity.

He gazed to the side, to the picture calendar hanging above the stove. He circled the date, big and bold and black. Just a few more days.

Like a bolt of electricity, energy zipped through his body. Yes, yes, everything was working just the right way. His entire plan was coming together. People were recognizing that he wasn't trying to rob women or assault their womanhood, but that he was trying to show them their proper place in the world.

It wouldn't be long. Not long at all. Another attack, this one's location much more deliberate. Deliberately chosen to send a very specific message. To Beatrice. To all the others like her.

Sunday, September 30, 1900

Everything around Polly whirled and swirled. The bright electric lights. The gleaming silverware. The maid serving dinner.

Even the sumptuous food set in front of her, including duck and scalloped potatoes and a large, elaborate cake that sat as a centerpiece in the middle of the long, polished dining room table.

Her best church gown, dark green with puffy sleeves and lace at the collar, was no match for her elegant surroundings.

Edwin nudged her. "You're rather quiet."

"I, I . . ."

"Edwin tells me you are quite the intrepid young reporter, Miss Blythe." Mrs. Price buttered her dinner roll and gazed at her.

Polly refrained from squirming under her scrutiny. "Yes, I suppose you could say I am. My goal is to someday be an editor. First, though, I suppose I have to get a story on the front page."

Mrs. Price chuckled, warm and smooth. Not at all stuffy. Though Polly had met her the night of the first attacks, she hadn't gotten to know what she was really like. Some of the tension eased from Polly's shoulders. Enough that she picked up her fork and knife and got to work on the duck breast on her plate.

"Good for you, I say." Edwin turned his attention to Polly. "I like a woman with a bit of spunk."

"Oh now, you stop it before you find yourself embarrassing poor Miss Blythe." Mrs. Price turned and smiled at Polly, the warmth reaching her eyes, which were the same color as Edwin's.

Amelia, who was seated across from Polly, shook her head. "You'll have to forgive my brother. You know how men can be sometimes. That's why I volunteer, tutoring at church a couple of nights a week. I simply have to get out of the house." Mirth filled her rich laugh, and a dimple shone in one cheek of her oval face.

This time Polly couldn't help but laugh along. Despite their obvious high position in life, the Price family was down-to-earth. They treated each other with genuine affection.

In Polly's home, it was all about Lyle. Pa didn't even see her. Didn't notice when she came or went. And certainly didn't believe she should have a job. "How interesting it must be to train young minds."

"I so enjoy it." Amelia sipped from the cut crystal glass. "By working with disadvantaged youths, I'm able to help lift them from poverty and make their dreams come true. I tell them they can become anything they imagine, even president of the United States."

"Is that why you got involved in law enforcement, Mr. Price?" Polly wiped her fingers on the napkin in her lap. "So you could help others?"

Without warning, his face froze. He coughed and gulped his water, then wiped the corner of his mouth with his napkin. "No. Because of my father." His voice was soft, barely audible, and he focused his gaze on the plate in front of him.

From the corner of her eye, Polly caught a glance that passed between Mrs. Price and Amelia. One that communicated more than words could ever say, but one that was indecipherable to anyone outside the family relationship.

Polly forked her scalloped potatoes. "Why because of your father?"

A muscle jumped in Edwin's clenched jaw as he cut his meat. For a long moment, silence covered the room.

Mrs. Price clutched her napkin, moisture glistening in her eyes. "My husband was murdered."

"Murdered? How very awful for your family. I'm so sorry."

Mrs. Price dabbed her eyes. "We miss him every day. Even though it's been well over a decade since that terrible night, the ache is still there. We don't like to talk about it. But we rejoice because he is rejoicing in heaven." After a while, she collected herself and motioned for the maid to gather the dinner dishes.

Polly ached with the question she didn't dare ask. What exactly had happened to Edwin's father—Mrs. Price had referred to it as a terrible night—that had spurred him to join the force?

Before she had much chance to ponder the matter, the maid came in and sliced the chocolate cake that had been the table's centerpiece. She placed a plate in front of each person.

"They say turnabout is fair play." Edwin had regained his composure. "What about you, Polly? Why did you decide to become a newspaper reporter?"

She didn't miss his use of her Christian name. Apparently, after dining in his home, they were well enough acquainted that they could be more informal with each other. But his question hit her in the gut. How did she go about answering? Certainly she couldn't say that it was to prove to her father that women could do anything men could do. "I, uh, always enjoyed, um, reading about current events. I wasn't interested in marriage, so I thought I might as well find a job that I would like. It seemed like a natural fit."

Amelia widened her eyes. "It must be so exciting, getting to meet all sorts of famous people and writing about what's going on in the city, the history that's being made all around you. I mean, the election is coming up. Do you think President McKinley will win a second term?"

Mrs. Price cleared her throat. "No politics at the table. You know the rule."

"This isn't politics, Mother." Amelia tipped her head and curled her lips into a little-girl pout. "This is about news. And speaking of news, what about the rash of muggings? My brother has been telling me about your theory regarding them. I must say, I have to agree with you."

"That's another unpleasant topic for Sunday dinner." Edwin forked a piece of chocolate cake into his mouth. "I've warned you about not walking home by yourself after tutoring."

"Said like a true big brother." Polly giggled, then bit into the cake herself. Oh my, what a slice of dessert heaven.

"I give you the same warning." Edwin narrowed his eyes. "No woman should be on the streets alone after dark. If you're going to be late, Polly, please make sure you have an escort. And Amelia, I'll make sure you either have someone to walk you home or I'll send the carriage for you."

"Do you have any brothers, Polly?" Amelia dug into her cake with a great deal of relish.

"An older one, yes. So I understand how they can be."

"Overbearing, you mean."

"Hey, I am in the room." Edwin glared first at his sister then at Polly.

"And overprotective." Polly couldn't resist continuing the banter.

"That's it. Women like you can't be trusted. You can be sure I'll be watching both of you like a hawk." Edwin gave a single nod of his head, as if to say the matter was closed for discussion.

But his words were more of a promise than a threat. And Polly found herself unable to be upset or offended by them.

Friday, October 5, 1900

What a crazy, hectic, insane day it had been. Case after case after case, almost without ceasing. Edwin had managed to grab a very quick bite at lunch but nothing since then, even though it was well after seven o'clock.

He was long past hungry. And had no time to dwell on it. Amelia's tutoring class would be over soon. Mother and a few of her friends had taken the carriage to attend the theater, so it was up to him to get from the station to the church and walk Amelia home. At least it had been almost two weeks since the attacker had last struck. Nevertheless, that didn't mean she should be out alone after dark.

Armstrong wandered over and leaned against Edwin's overflowing desk. "How's everything going, Price?"

"Just fine. About to finish up here for the night."

Edwin's tall, well-seasoned boss eyed the stacks of papers and piles of files covering every inch of the desk's surface. "You sure about that? Seems to me like you have an awful lot left to accomplish before you can call it a day."

"I'm not doing that, sir. I mean, I would like to, but I need to see my sister home from church. Since this string of muggings, these vicious attacks on women, I don't want her out by herself. Everyone else in my family is otherwise engaged, so it's up to me. I'll return as soon as she is safely settled."

"Isn't that sweet?" Armstrong tipped his head and puckered his lips. "Looking out for your baby sister while the other women of Denver must fend for themselves."

Armstrong's condescending tone scraped at Edwin's nerves. He rose and lifted his coat from the rack. "If you'll excuse me, I'll be going. I should be back within the hour."

Armstrong stepped into Edwin's path. "You think you're better than everyone else, don't you?"

Where on earth was this coming from? Not that Edwin had time to answer that question now. "Please, sir, I must be on my way. Already, I'm late. I wouldn't doubt that Amelia is the last one left at church. I don't want her walking home without me."

"If the rest of us can't leave to even have supper, neither can you."

"Like everyone else on duty, I haven't eaten. And I don't plan to. I simply want to see my sister home. To make sure she's safe."

"But your bevy of servants will have a piping hot meal waiting for you that you won't be able to resist."

Edwin couldn't come up with any good retort. "Excuse me, I'm leaving now." He attempted, without success, to duck around Armstrong, who fisted his hands.

"Sit down, Price, and finish your paperwork. That is an order." A bear's growl would be less intimidating.

Edwin crushed his coat between his hands. He ground his teeth together.

"I said sit down. Work, like the rest of us."

Attempting to control his breathing, Edwin thumped into his chair. As soon as Armstrong turned away, he'd hightail it out the door. He reached for his pen, praying that the Lord would keep Amelia at church and safe until he could make his escape.

The weight of Armstrong's stare pressed on Edwin's shoulders.

Before he had a single line on the form in front of him filled out, a uniformed officer approached his desk, breathless. "Detective Price?"

"What is it, Brown?"

"Just had a call come in. Another mugging, like the others. Hit over the head, nothing taken."

"How serious?"

"I don't have that information yet. But sir?"

"What is it?" Edwin was already shrugging into his coat.

"The victim's name is Amelia Price."

Chapter 9

With his chest tight and his blood whooshing in his ears, Edwin dashed up the steps of his home and flew through the front door, slamming it behind him.

Mother met him in the hall as a harried Nancy carried an armful of bloodied towels down the stairs. "I'm glad you got here so quickly." Tears thickened her voice.

"I came as soon as I heard. How is she? Is it true, that she was struck in much the same way Rachel was?"

"Unfortunately." Mother covered her mouth.

Edwin clung to the banister for support. This couldn't be happening again. How was it possible that two people he loved would meet the same fate? "Is she. . .?" He couldn't voice the question. Not about his sister.

"The doctor is still in with her. That's all I know."

"Was she conscious when they brought her here?"

Mother shrugged. "Nancy rang the theater, and they informed us. By the time we arrived, Dr. Klein was already with her. I feel so helpless. All I've been doing is standing here and praying and praying for God to spare my baby's life."

Edwin blew out a breath. "I can't talk to God right now. This is all my fault. If I hadn't gotten tied up at work, I would have been able to meet her to see her home." His weak legs refused to hold him any longer. He slumped to the marble step. "I should have been there. I should have defied Armstrong."

Mother came to him and touched his shoulder. "This isn't anyone's fault but the assailant's. He's the one who committed the crime. You've always taken so much responsibility on your shoulders."

"Because I should have done more the night of the robbery all those years ago. I should have done more to protect Rachel a few weeks ago. And now look at my poor sister. She's suffered the same fate because of my negligence."

"We don't know what's going to happen to her. Right now we trust that her life is in the Lord's hands and whatever happens to her is within His will." Mother's voice cracked.

Edwin's lip trembled, and his throat burned. "It's my job as a detective and a brother to take care of her and protect her. Especially since she doesn't have a father to do it for her. I did neither. She was relying on me, and I let her down."

"I could say the same thing, Edwin." Mother fiddled with the strand of pearls around her neck. "If only I hadn't gone to the theater. If only I had hired a carriage so she would have had a way home. We can ask those questions all we want. Nothing will change her circumstances. God will protect her."

"I have to see her." He rose.

Mother gripped his arm, firm and sure. "Let Dr. Klein do his work. Another body in the room isn't going to do any good."

He pent up the shouts that built in his chest. Demands to know about Amelia. Demands to see her. Demands that wouldn't get him anywhere and wouldn't accomplish anything.

One, two, three deep breaths. By the time he had himself back under control, Nancy was on her way through the hall after ridding herself of the towels.

She stopped in front of them.

"How is she?" The question burst from Edwin.

"Bleeding heavily. Unconscious."

Edwin squished his eyes shut, then opened them. "What is the doctor saying?"

"Not much. Just that the next few hours are critical. I really must get back to her."

"Yes. Go, go." Edwin shooed her away.

That didn't sound good. Not good at all. Mother climbed the stairs toward Amelia's room. Before she was even halfway up, a prayer was on her lips, one almost inaudible to Edwin.

Though he attempted to speak to the Almighty, the words wouldn't come. Nothing more than, "Lord, please. Lord, please. Lord, please."

He paced the black-and-white tiled foyer, a scattering of potted plants filling the space. Back and forth and back and forth. What was taking Dr. Klein so long? When would they have answers? Amelia's condition must be serious.

The doorbell rang the Westminster Chimes. With Nancy otherwise occupied, Edwin broke off his pacing and turned to open the door himself. As he did, a gust of chilled air followed.

He'd be a monkey's uncle if it wasn't Polly sweeping in. She scurried inside, unbuttoning her coat as if she'd been invited to stay. "Oh Edwin, I was at the paper when the word came. I'm so very sorry to hear about your sister. What a terrible thing to happen."

He led her to the parlor and motioned for her to sit. When she did so, he settled himself in the armchair beside her. "This is what I was warning both of you about on Sunday. But what happened is my fault. I got caught up at work and lost track of the time. Then my boss detained me. I should have been there for her."

"Don't take any of the blame on yourself. Circumstances were beyond your control."

Easy words to say. Hard words to believe.

"How's she doing?"

He rose and resumed pacing. "They don't know. Nancy and Dr. Klein are with her. Nancy said Amelia is unconscious and losing a great deal of blood."

Polly came to him and touched his shoulder, her hand gentle on him, just enough for him to stop. "What good is pacing accomplishing?"

He inhaled and huffed out the breath. "It's helping me to pass the time."

"Sit, and we'll talk. A much better way to wait."

He obeyed but couldn't stop his leg from jiggling. "What do you want to talk about?"

"Thank you again for the invitation to Sunday dinner. I so enjoyed myself. You have a wonderful family."

"I do." He squeaked out the words between his tight vocal cords. "I couldn't ask for better. That's why, if we lose Amelia, it would be devastating. To all of us."

"I understand." But her voice was flat.

"You didn't say much about your family."

"My pa was always adamant that a woman's place is in the home. I. . . Well, it doesn't matter. He'll see soon all I'm capable of."

What must it be like to grow up with a parent who didn't respect your choices in life? "What about your mother?"

"She passed away several years ago. This isn't helping. I meant that we should talk about light, happy subjects."

"I'm not sure my heart would be in it." Such a weight bore down on him.

"Did you and Amelia get along well growing up?"

"For the most part. She could be a pesky little sister. Always wanting to play cops and robbers with me and my friends, insisting on being the heroine who needed rescuing. Except that by the time my friends and I had our shootouts, she usually had rescued herself." A small chuckle passed his lips despite himself.

"I can well imagine that she would. I would have done the same."

"Did you play with your brother? Bother him something awful?"

"He didn't play much. Oh, don't get me wrong. He was always good to me and kind, but he had his mind on his studies. Pa rode him hard to get good grades. I'm sure he would have rather been outside with me."

"How awful that he missed out on so much of his childhood. But there has to be a time or two you remember."

"Once, when we were a little older and Ma and Pa left us alone for an afternoon, Lyle ditched his books, and we ran to the river. Though he promised not to get me wet, he splashed me so hard, I was soaked." She relaxed against the back of the chair, and her eyes glassed over, like she was whisked to the past. "I suppose I deserved it. I did splash him first."

Shoes squeaked on the floor behind them, followed by Mother's distinctive sweet flowery toilet water scent. Edwin turned. Dr. Klein stood beside Mother, who twisted her handkerchief in her hands.

The doctor gave a single nod. "I have news."

Polly's breath caught as she stared at the gray-haired man in a dark suit, a stethoscope around his neck. Edwin grasped Polly by the hand and squeezed so hard, she bit back a little squeak.

"Yes." His voice warbled.

His mother, dressed in a gorgeous peach gown with gold accents and lacy three-quarter-length sleeves, stood stock still beside the physician.

Edwin squeezed Polly's hand even harder. She would have a difficult time stretching out her fingers when he finally let go.

The doctor adjusted the stethoscope around his neck. "Amelia sustained a serious injury to her head. She's been in and out of consciousness. When she is alert, she is able to tell me things like the date and who is president. All of that is encouraging. I've stitched and bandaged her up and will watch her carefully for infection."

"Will she make a full recovery?" Edwin asked.

The doctor sighed, and Edwin stiffened. "There are so many possible complications, but I'm cautiously optimistic."

The pressure on Polly's hand eased, and Edwin's mother gave the slightest of smiles. Once Edwin shook the doctor's hand and showed him out, he returned to Mrs. Price and Polly. "I would very much like to see her."

Polly settled deeper into the mauve velvet armchair, ready for a long wait. The family wouldn't allow her to see Amelia for a while. Maybe not until tomorrow. Maybe not until she recovered.

If she recovered. *Dear God, may it be so.*

Before Edwin made it to the parlor's entrance, he turned to her. "Aren't you coming?"

She glanced around the room. Was he speaking to her? There was no one else there. Mrs. Price had already gone back upstairs. "You want me to come with you?"

"Please."

She jumped up and climbed the steps with him to a sumptuous bedroom. Amelia lay still and quiet in the bed, her auburn hair spread across the pillow. A white bandage swathed her head. Hopefully the doctor didn't have to cut too much of her hair for the stitches.

With soft footfalls across the thick Persian carpet on the floor, Mrs. Price and Nancy exited.

Polly stood in the doorway while Edwin went to Amelia.

He stroked her upper arm, and her eyes flitted open. "Edwin." Her voice was weak.

"Let me get you some water," Polly said. She moved into the room and poured from a pitcher on a table beside the bed. She handed it to Edwin, who assisted his sister in taking a sip.

"Thank you." Amelia attempted a weak smile.

Edwin pulled up a chair and sat beside her. "I'm so glad you're awake. Alive. Not that I want to badger you by playing detective, but do you remember what happened?"

Amelia closed her eyes, scrunched them, then opened them again. "It's a little foggy. You didn't come for me."

"I'm so sorry. Sorrier than you'll ever know."

"I decided not to wait for you. I was tired and wanted to get home. I hadn't gone far when all of a sudden, with no warning whatsoever, a man whacked me on the head from behind. Oh, the pain."

Was she speaking about when the attack happened or now? Most likely, both.

"As I fell to the ground, I caught a glimpse of him."

Polly grasped the end of the bed. "What did he look like?" She breathed out the question before Edwin had a chance. Then she bit her tongue. Any minute, he would ask her to leave. Up to this point, he hadn't allowed her to be in the room when he questioned a witness.

Amelia motioned her brother closer. "Edwin, can you help me adjust my pillows?"

When he did as Amelia bid, she moaned.

"Sorry, Sis. Didn't mean to hurt you."

"Just a little dizzy. It's passing."

But apparently Edwin couldn't hold in the question any more than Polly had been able to. "So what did he look like?"

"I didn't get a good glimpse. Small. Pale. A dark mustache. That's it."

Edwin glanced at Polly. "It's more than we had to go on before."

We. He had referred to them as *we*. Like he wanted to partner with her. She wouldn't allow this chance to slip through her fingers. "You're right. Is there anything else you remember, Amelia?"

She worked the edge of the blanket then peered at Polly. "I'd shake my head, but it would hurt too much."

Edwin leaned over Amelia and tucked the blanket around her slim shoulders. "You should rest. We'll leave you be for now." He kissed her forehead and moved toward the hall, Polly following him.

With a touch to his elbow, she stopped him. "I'm going to hurry to the paper and get this article written up. With your family being so prominent and the latest victim the sister of a police detective, it's sure to garner a great deal of attention. Amelia seems to be doing well."

"It is a great relief to hear her talking, to see her wanting to sit up."

"Though I'm sorry this happened to her, I'm sure it's going to be the break in the case. This is the first time someone has been able to describe the attacker."

"I don't know if it's enough, but it's a start. Perhaps enough to convince Armstrong this is worth going after."

Before Polly could turn to leave, Edwin's mother came up the stairs.

She dabbed at her moist eyes with a lace-edged handkerchief and hurried to Edwin. "Did you see what that maniac did to her? You have to catch him. He must be brought to justice."

"Don't worry, Mother." Edwin's deep voice echoed through the canyon-like hall. "One thing is for sure. We will find who committed such a despicable act, and we will prosecute him to the fullest extent of the law. I've decided to offer a $200 reward for anyone with information that can lead to an arrest and conviction in the case."

Polly bounced on her toes. "Is that on the record, Edwin?"

"It certainly is. I don't care what Armstrong thinks about me talking to the press. You make sure that the editor at your paper puts this story and the reward offer right on the front page. He can telephone me if he has a problem with that."

His family carried that much power? "I'm not sure he's going to do that if I write the article."

"But you're the one who's been with her. You're the one who's seen my sister with your own two eyes. Who better to write the article? I'll do what I have to, including throwing around the Price name, in order to get you that story."

Polly could barely breathe. Apparently the Price family was rather influential. "Thank you." It was too bad that Amelia's misfortune had led to the biggest opportunity of Polly's life.

But that didn't mean she wouldn't take full advantage of it. Pa would surely be proud of her now.

Chapter 10

Monday, October 8, 1900

The table wobbled as he leaned against it. He couldn't believe what he was seeing. The story about his mission last night had made the front page of the *Denver Post*. Written by Polly Blythe. There stood the headline in bold red letters.

The Silver Shadow Strikes Again

The Silver Shadow. Though he hated that she'd written the article, the moniker was nice. Rather fit him. A shadow could slither in and out, usually without detection.

Yes, his plan was working to perfection. Each little piece was falling into position. Soon the women of the city would know their place and would stay in it.

No more hurt and heartache for their men. No more shame or scorn for any of them.

He read further in the article. Amelia Price. That was the name of the young lady—though he barely dared to use that term to describe her—who was walking home after helping at her local church. Well, wasn't that dandy? She may have claimed to have been doing charity work, but isn't that what they all said? Behind closed doors, their words held little truth. They were up to no good.

You couldn't trust a woman unless she was in your sight at all times.

Amelia Price was the twenty-one-year-old daughter of the late prominent Denver businessman Jacob Price.

And the sister of Detective Edwin Price.

He sucked in an unsteady breath. Oh no, what had he done? His windpipe closed, and darkness threatened. He clutched the edge of the polished table in a vain attempt to steady himself.

No, no, it would be fine. He forced himself to stand straighter. In fact, it was better than fine. It was ideal. He poked at the words printed on the page.

He needed to savor this. He poured himself a cup of coffee, flavored it with a good helping of sugar and milk, and settled into his chair near the stove. After he'd enjoyed several sips, he picked up the paper and continued his perusal of the article.

He hadn't gone far before he put it down again and rubbed his aching temples.

A $200 reward.

For his capture.

There was a bounty on his head.

That was the last thing he needed. He couldn't have the police and the city's citizens hunting him down like he was a rabid dog. That would never do.

His head throbbed as if the hammers and picks that miners used were inside his brain. Things were going horribly wrong.

This wasn't the way it was supposed to play out. This wasn't the way it was supposed to happen. People were supposed to be happy about what he was doing. Men would applaud him. Women would thank him for reminding them of their proper roles.

Not this. Definitely not this.

He stared at the map by his left hand and scratched his aching forehead. He could strike elsewhere in the city. A place where people and the police wouldn't suspect.

But even that was too dangerous.

Men and women all over the city read the *Post*. There was even a description of him in it. Pale. Small. Dark mustache. He would have to shave it.

It put a target on his back.

One he wanted to remove.

There was only one option.

But it would be difficult.

Edwin's eyes had long since blurred from long hours spent poring over the case files for each of the Silver Shadow's muggings. That's what Polly had dubbed Amelia's attacker in this morning's paper. A fitting nickname.

Around him, the station came to life. Men filtered into the building. Chatter filled the air. Typewriters clacked.

Prodded by an officer, a painted woman, her neckline scandalously low, passed Edwin's desk, all the while declaring her innocence of "these ridiculous solicitation charges."

Edwin forced his attention back to the files. Files that now included his own sister's. He had to be missing something. There was a clue to the man's identity hidden in here. He just had to find it.

When he had checked with Mother this morning before leaving the house, she informed him that Amelia had had a good night's rest and was still sleeping. Though it would have been nice to see her before he left, sleep was the best medicine for her.

The fragrant bitterness of brewed coffee infiltrated the air around him a moment before a cup appeared in front of his face.

"Hope this will help keep you awake." O'Fallon stood at his side, two steaming mugs in his hands.

"Thanks." Edwin lifted his glasses and rubbed the bridge of his nose.

"Have you been here all night?" O'Fallon set one mug on Edwin's desk and then sat at his own desk beside Edwin's.

"No, but I was so worried about my sister, I didn't get much sleep. I've been here for a while already."

"I heard about that. So sorry. I also heard about your family's reward. $200." O'Fallon whistled. "That's a lot. Someone is sure to come forward now and turn in whoever did this."

"That's the hope."

"Anything so far?"

"Not a peep from anyone. No telephone calls. No one stopping in."

"It's still early. They haven't had a chance to get their coffee and read the paper yet. Maybe they have to get the kids off to school. Soon they'll be pounding down the door. I bet we'll have the suspect in custody by lunch."

"From your lips to God's ears." One thing Edwin liked the most about his partner was his eternal optimism. He was young though. Even younger than Edwin when he'd joined the force. Give O'Fallon time. He'd become as jaded as the rest of them soon enough.

"Hand me those files and let me see what I can glean. You need a break from them." O'Fallon reached for them, and Edwin passed them over.

A fresh set of eyes couldn't hurt.

"Why don't you go home, be with your family, and sleep for about a week?"

To borrow a phrase from Amelia, that sounded delicious. "I might just take you up on that offer."

"Good. I'll keep working this. Would it be all right with you if I stopped by later and interviewed Amelia? I've had dinner with your family enough that she's comfortable with me. There might be things she's willing to share with me that she wouldn't be as open with you about. I'll telephone before I come."

Edwin shrugged. "I doubt it, but it's worth a try." He gathered a few papers from his desk. "If anyone comes in or rings with information, call my house as soon as possible. I'll leave word with the maid to wake me. And just tell Armstrong I'm out on a case. That's not a lie. I plan to spend some time with my sister to see if she's remembered anything since last night."

"Sure, Mr. Moneybags. See you later."

The nickname grated on Edwin's nerves. While no one here except Armstrong treated him any differently because of his family's status, the label stung. He was his own person, making his own way in the world.

Just as he came to his feet, Armstrong exited his office and called to him. "Price, don't run out on me. I need to see you. Right now."

Edwin followed the skinny, balding man to his office.

"Have a seat."

Fatigue pressed on Edwin's shoulders. His bed was calling to him ever louder.

Eyes set deep in his narrow face, Armstrong stared at Edwin and cracked his knuckles a couple of times. Was he trying to unnerve Edwin?

Stillness settled over the room. In his vest pocket, Edwin's watch ticked away the minutes.

At last Armstrong cleared his throat. "It has come to my attention through various sources around the station that you have been spending a great deal of time with a Miss Polly Blythe of the *Denver Post*. In fact, reports have reached me that she had Sunday dinner at your home and met your family."

Ralph O'Fallon was a good young man, but he did have a mouth the size of Pinnacle Peak. "I'm not sure why this would be something we would need to address. Especially when my sister is confined to bed with a serious blow to her head and an uncertain future."

"As I said, Miss Blythe is employed by the newspaper."

"I'm well aware of that fact."

"She tended one of the victims after they were attacked, and she was with you at your house last night after the attack on your sister. Do I have my facts correct?"

"Yes, sir, you do." What was Armstrong's point?

"I'm not happy about your association with the young lady."

"I can assure you, sir, that there is nothing dishonorable happening between us." How could he even think such a thing?

Armstrong waved him off. "I wasn't suggesting anything of the sort. There is the matter of you consorting with the media."

"Consorting?"

"You are giving Miss Blythe preferential treatment, inside access to the police department, because she is a beautiful young woman. One you might possibly become involved with, if you aren't already."

"Sir, I assure you, Miss Blythe and I are not involved in any way other than professionally."

"Then why the dinner at your home? Surely you introduced her to your mother."

Edwin huffed. Armstrong made a good point. Why had he invited Polly to dinner? Why did his palms go sweaty and his mouth dry whenever she appeared? There was no doubt she was beautiful. A small, soft mouth. Sweet eyes. A clear countenance. Very lovely, indeed.

And also bullheaded.

He had blurted out the invitation. But he had enjoyed her company. A great deal.

Armstrong scratched behind one of his large ears. "I'm warning you, Price. Any dalliance with this young woman could impair your judgment and might well jeopardize the case. That's not what you want, is it?"

Edwin shifted in his chair. "No, sir." But it was important for these cases to be on the front page. Polly had made that happen. She had spunk and tenacity in spades. Something this case desperately needed.

A dalliance? No. An alliance? Certainly.

Before Armstrong dismissed Edwin, a red-faced man strode into the room. Though the newcomer wasn't a physically imposing presence, Edwin still jumped to his feet. This was Police Chief Farley. A man not to be trifled with. Not if you valued your job.

"Armstrong."

Armstrong shrunk into himself. Well, there was at least one person in the world the captain feared.

Farley rattled the newspaper in his hand. "What is this all about? A string of muggings that weren't brought to my attention? Apparently not given much attention at all?"

Farley must not read the editorial section. Or travel in social circles with anyone who did.

"Sir, I can explain."

Farley tapped his foot. Edwin itched to join in.

"We've been working on solving these crimes for weeks, months now, sir. Very hard. And making progress, I must say. Last night's incident was the break we've been waiting for. We're just about ready to bring in a suspect for questioning. Isn't that right?"

"Chief." Edwin nodded in the man's direction. "We—"

"That certainly had better be the case. A $200 reward from the Price family. That would be you, I believe." Farley's pointed stare stabbed straight through Edwin.

He swallowed the lump in his throat. "Yes, sir."

"I'm sorry about your sister. But this makes the case higher profile than ever. I need these crimes solved and this miscreant put behind bars faster than an out-of-control locomotive. Understood?"

Both Edwin and Armstrong nodded. Farley turned on his heel and marched out, slamming the door behind him.

Armstrong stood. "You heard him, Price. Let's get going."

They exited to the station, which had fallen quiet. Chief Farley's visit hadn't gone unnoticed.

Armstrong puffed out his chest. "Listen up, men. This string of crimes against women in our fair city has gone on long enough. It's time to bring this menace to justice. We have a description of the suspect from Detective Price's sister. I'm going to send a sketch artist to the house right away. Once we have that, I want you on the streets, bringing in every man who fits the description. Is that clear?"

With several nods, the usual din of the station returned.

What was Armstrong talking about? "Sir, if I could have a moment of your time?"

"Just a moment. I have a case to solve."

Strange that as of five minutes ago, he hadn't given the cases a second thought. All of a sudden, because of Farley's blustering, he was determined to solve them. "Are you sure it's wise to round up every man in the city who looks like the man Amelia saw? She didn't catch more than a glimpse."

"You leave it to me." He pointed to his chest. "I'll bring in the man myself."

"But—"

"Leave it to me. You're dismissed."

Chapter 11

"Sissy, Sissy, you came to see me." As she sat in bed with her oatmeal on a tray, Sophie clapped her hands.

Polly drew up a chair beside Sophie's bed. Sophie's legs were covered by a red, blue, and green quilt. "Of course I did. I wouldn't forget to visit you." Sophie's right mind had yet to return. It was pointless to argue with her. No matter how often Polly explained the situation to her friend, she never grasped it.

"What are we going to do today? Will you play dominoes with me?" Sophie fiddled with the sleeve of her pink dressing gown.

"First of all, you have to finish your breakfast. Then we'll see. I do have to scurry to work very soon."

"Then I'll eat fast."

"No. We don't want you to get a stomachache. There will be time later."

As Sophie cleaned her bowl, they chatted about the weather and what friends Sophie had at school and how she liked to play with her dolly when she didn't have chores. A heavy ache settled in Polly's chest. Her bright, witty friend was gone. Would she ever come back?

Just as Sophie finished the last scoop of oatmeal, Laura burst into the room, waving an envelope and the paper.

The paper. Her article. Would it be there? It had to be. Just had to be.

"Look, look." Laura bounced on her toes. "A letter for Polly."

Polly jumped up and swiped the envelope from Laura's hands. Before she had a chance to look at who sent it, Laura grabbed it back and placed it on the table. "Oh no. I'm going to read this morning's headline to you first. Ahem. 'The Silver Shadow Strikes Again. $200 Reward for His Arrest and Prosecution.' How do you like that?"

A squeal escaped Polly's lips. "That's my article. Please, let me see it. I have to know if there's a byline. Please, please."

"Well, it says here this story was written by Polly Blythe. You wouldn't happen to know her, would you?"

"Quit teasing me." Polly refused to believe it until she saw her name and her article in black-and-white-and-red print.

"Fine." Though she huffed out the word, a dimple appeared in Laura's cheek. She handed the newspaper to Polly.

And there it was. Her headline. Just as she had written it. And her name. With reverence, she traced the letters.

Laura squeezed her shoulders. "You did it. Look at that. My friend and boardinghouse mate, a real, true journalist. A bona fide reporter."

"Let me see. Let me see." Sophie wriggled in bed.

"Whoa, there." Laura caught the tray just as Sophie was about to tip it over. "Let's not make a mess. I'll let you see it in a little bit. Let her savor her triumph."

A deep frown marred Sophie's face, but she stilled.

Polly clutched the paper to her chest. "I have to go buy every copy in the city." She rushed from the house without even a coat, all but sprinted to the corner newspaper stand, and used the last of her coins to buy several copies of the morning edition. She couldn't help informing the newspaper boy that was her article on the front page.

Soon she was home, but before she left for the office, there was one more task she had to complete. With the greatest of care, she cut out the article and folded it so the big red headline would be visible and prominent.

Then she penned a letter.

Dear Pa,

I know you don't approve of my working for a newspaper in a big city. You feel I should be married with a home of my own. Perhaps one day God will bless me with a husband. But I think writing will always be in my blood.

I've worked hard these past several months, and God has rewarded my perseverance. I have enclosed my very first front-page story, which includes my byline. My greatest hope in life is that you will be proud of me. I hope this makes up for the times I disappointed you. For the times I displeased you. Though I may not be following the plan you laid out for my life, I am following the plan God laid out for me.

Love,
Polly

Perhaps now she would be worthy of his love. A worthy daughter. A worthy woman. Even though he had denied her the education she had so longed for, by sheer force of will she had accomplished this. Of course God had helped her, no doubt, but she'd put in the time and effort.

Didn't that deserve a reward? Just a kind word and a smile?

After Ma died, Pa never smiled at her again.

She shook off those morose thoughts. If she was to continue writing front-page articles, she would have to be more focused than ever on her career.

Before she left, she popped into Sophie's room. "I have to go to work now. I'll see you later."

"Sissy, why don't you stay and play dolls? Only grown-up boys have jobs." An open letter sat on the bed beside Sophie. In her excitement over her article, Polly had forgotten about the letter she had received.

"And sometimes, so do grown-up women." Though pressed for time, Polly entered, picked up the note, and scanned it.

Her stomach dropped like a stagecoach over a ravine.

The note had been pieced together with letters cut from the newspaper. Including red ones, like the ones in her headline.

MISS BLYTHE.
BE CAREFUL. LEARN YOUR LESSON. OR YOU WILL BE NEXT.
THE SILVER SHADOW

Polly drew in a breath but didn't release it.

"What's wrong?"

Polly shook her head, gathered the note and her skirts, and raced from the room. When she reached the bottom of the stairs, she bumped into Mrs. Mannheim, the air whooshing from her lungs.

"Goodness, girl, what has you all flustered? Your hat is askew, and your cheeks are red."

"I have to go."

But would he be out there waiting for her?

Thursday, October 11, 1900

Edwin steepled his fingers and rubbed his nose, knocking his glasses onto his forehead. Every part of his body ached. He had no leads. Nothing to go on. He and O'Fallon had canvassed the area where Amelia's attack had taken place. As usual, no one saw or heard anything. And none of the men who answered their doors bore any resemblance to the Silver Shadow.

Polly had picked a good moniker for this menace. He slunk about the city, no one ever getting a good glimpse of what he truly looked like. Much in the way a shadow disappeared when clouds covered the sun, so this shadow disappeared after his dirty deeds were done.

Edwin leaned back in his chair and rubbed his sore neck. Why couldn't he crack this case?

"I don't care if he's busy. I need to see him. Now. It's urgent."

Edwin glanced up. Polly pushed her way by the uniformed officer at the door and barreled toward him, her blue-feathered hat tipping at a dangerous angle.

"Edwin." She clutched a piece of paper to her heaving chest.

"Did you run all the way here?"

She nodded. "Look." As she handed him the note, her hands shook.

"Sit down. Let me get you a glass of water."

"Just read it."

His eyes took in the words, but his brain didn't want to process them.

Learn your lesson. Or you will be next.

Whoever sent it had seen what Polly had written in the paper.

"On what should be the happiest day of my life, this happens." She motioned to the letter he still held in his hands. "Who?" Her voice quavered.

He gave her credit for not fainting to the floor like many women he knew would have. "We'll find out who. Don't worry."

"Don't worry? He's threatening my life."

He rubbed his taut shoulder. "I know. But we'll catch him. I promise you that." Would it prove to be an empty promise, like the one he'd made to his father as he lay dying on the floor?

"What should I do?"

"Be very cautious. Don't go out after dark alone. In fact, don't go out after dark at all."

"That's impossible. Sometimes I have to work late. With winter coming on, the days are getting shorter."

All true.

"Can't I, maybe, have an escort?"

He raised an eyebrow.

"A guard. You know, someone to watch out for me."

She did beat all. "Much as I would love to put one of the officers on such a detail, I'm afraid that isn't feasible. We don't have enough staff to guard every woman in the city."

She thumped into a nearby chair. "But not every woman's life is being threatened."

He leaned forward and stared into her coffee-colored eyes. "I know you're scared. And I know that you are very much tied to this case and invested in it. I will do everything I can to catch this menace. In the meantime, I need you to be extra careful. When I can, I'll walk you home. If I can't, find someone who can or call for a carriage. Even if it's only a few blocks. His pattern doesn't suggest that he would break into a place to get to you, so as long as you watch yourself on the streets, you'll be fine. I'll do my job. You do yours. Okay?"

She nodded. "Thank you, Edwin." She smoothed her skirt, her hands not shaking quite as much. "I appreciate your calming me down.

Do you think it's safe to walk the streets during the day? Oh, I didn't even think about that on the way here, I was so anxious to get to you."

"Stay with the crowds. No back alleys. You should be fine." He prayed she would be.

She rose and passed him a small smile. "Thank you again for, well, everything." Her cheeks pinked like a sunset.

As she sashayed from the room, he stared at her until she exited.

Back to the case. Back to sifting through the files. And to trying to figure out how this note to Polly played into everything.

Just about the time he was ready to bang his head on the desk, Mr. and Mrs. Quincy, Rachel's parents, approached him. He forced himself to focus and stood, reaching out to shake Mr. Quincy's hand. "Good to see you, sir. I've been thinking about you so much these past few weeks. How are you doing?"

Mrs. Quincy, dressed in black, dabbed her eyes with a dark-edged handkerchief. "It's so difficult to lose a child. Until it happens to you, you never fully understand it. I know God is good, but I can't fathom why He chose to take our daughter from us like that. All she was doing was getting me headache powders."

The silence between the three of them continued for several seconds, the din around them fading into the background.

Mr. Quincy pulled out a chair and motioned for his wife to sit. Edwin should have done that. Where were his manners?

"We are also so sorry about what happened to Amelia." Mrs. Quincy's voice was weak. "How is she doing?"

"About as well as can be expected. She gets severe headaches and is weak, but she is making progress. I think we're all beginning to be able to breathe again."

"That's good to hear."

If only they'd had the same kind of news about Rachel. Edwin fingered his watch chain. "I assume this isn't a social call."

"You've always been good to our family." Mr. Quincy straightened his spine. "Even when you and Rachel decided you were better friends than spouses, we appreciated the gentleness with which you handled the situation. Since we hadn't heard from you in a while, we were wondering if there was anything new in the case. Especially since what happened to Amelia."

Edwin took a few moments to compose himself. If he had a hard enough time dealing with the fact that he hadn't solved Rachel's murder and Amelia's attack, imagine the pain of Rachel's parents and all they were going through.

"I'll do better. I promise. We just haven't had any breaks." Up until now. He didn't know enough about Polly's letter to know if that would help them solve these crimes or not. "We thought we had one when Amelia could identify a few of the Shadow's characteristics, but so far that hasn't panned out. There is so little to go on. This Shadow is elusive and as tough to catch as your own shadow."

"Listen, son." Mr. Quincy grasped the back of his wife's chair. "We don't want to pressure you. We truly don't. But we need answers. Nora doesn't sleep much at all, afraid that whoever did this to Rachel could do the same to any of us."

Edwin's gut clenched. Sleep was a difficult commodity to come by these days. "I understand, but rest assured, Mrs. Quincy, that it is not likely the shadow will attack you in your home. These are random assaults on the street. Muggings, really, but without robbery as a motive. I hope that will give you a measure of comfort and help you get some rest."

She nodded, still dabbing at her eyes from time to time.

"We are Christian people. We don't hold grudges." At this point, something changed in Mr. Quincy's eyes. A new sort of darkness settled into their brown depths. "But we do want this criminal brought to justice. Our Rachel doesn't get to live her life. Why should he be free to live his?"

Edwin scrubbed his cheeks. What more could he say? "I know, I know. Trust me. Our family wants this as much as yours. Perhaps the reward will help. People who may have been too scared to come forward might be motivated to do so by the money."

"Has it brought any leads so far?"

Edwin was forced to shake his head.

"We will contribute another $200."

"That's very generous. I'm sure it will help."

"Is it only you who has been working this case?"

"My partner and me. Though now the police chief is quite upset about this and the notoriety it's gaining. The inability to solve this case and the ongoing crimes are making the department look bad. Captain Armstrong has joined the crusade. He assures me that he will be apprehending a suspect or suspects in the near future."

"Now, that is good news." Mr. Quincy leaned over the desk and slapped Edwin's shoulder. "Why didn't you start with that?"

"Please, don't get your hopes up. There's no guarantee that we will make any arrests." In fact, the likelihood that they would was slim. Very slim. From the sounds of it, Armstrong planned on rounding up every male Denverite who matched the Shadow's description. Maybe even a few females, if he knew Armstrong.

"We'll keep praying for the perpetrator to get his just deserts. And you keep working hard. Press for more men on the case. Tell your boss that this takes precedence over everything else. Nothing, and I mean nothing, is more important to me than seeing my daughter's murderer convicted."

"I feel the same."

Just as the Quincys were rising to leave, O'Fallon rushed over. "This was just delivered. Addressed to you."

The plain envelope bore no return address. The handwriting was block writing. Edwin slit it open and a note fell out. Written with letters cut from magazines and newspapers, it sent him to shaking from head to toe.

When will you learn? How many more times must I strike before you get the message?

Chapter 12

As Polly stepped into the full-to-overflowing police station, the dank odor of unwashed bodies and alcohol-laden breath almost overwhelmed her. She steeled her stomach against the onslaught.

Everywhere she gazed, there were men. All with mustaches. All small and pale. Just the description Amelia had given of the Silver Shadow. How many small, pale men with facial hair were there in this city? Captain Armstrong must have brought in every one of them. And if the Shadow was smart, he would have shaved that mustache by now.

She had to be imagining things. With the worry over the letter the Shadow sent her, she hadn't slept well last night.

She rubbed her eyes.

The men were still here.

A few fidgeted with their hats. Several of them paced in the little room there was to maneuver. Most of them stood and chatted with the others around them.

Like a tightrope walker, she picked her way through the over-crowded office. Once she approached Edwin's desk, she inhaled enough to prevent herself from fainting. "Good morning. I came to check on the letter I brought the other day, and instead I find a three-ring circus. I thought the *Post* was the only business in town with such promotional stunts."

He rubbed his unshaven cheek, the dark half-moons under his eyes magnified by his glasses. So uncharacteristic for him to be disheveled. "As you can see, we have suspects in Amelia's case."

"Suspects?" She gestured wide, taking in the entire room. "All of these men are suspects?"

He swigged something from the mug on his desk. "Chief Farley is hot under the collar. Captain Armstrong, who is gunning for Farley's job, got a little overzealous in solving the crime. Might have something to do with the reward. The Quincys doubled the amount."

"This—this is ridiculous." The words sputtered from her mouth before she could check them. "How are you ever going to question all of them?"

"And how am I supposed to identify one of them?"

At the quiet voice at Polly's elbow, she spun to find Amelia standing there, her eyes wide in her thin face.

Edwin was at his sister's side in a flash. "Are you sure you're well enough to be here? I know you're still having awful headaches."

"I'm fine. Or I was until I saw this, this. . . Words fail me."

Edwin motioned back a few men who milled around his desk, pulled out two chairs, and gestured for both ladies to sit. "You can wait to try to identify your assailant. You don't have to do it today."

"But wouldn't it be more helpful if I did so as soon as possible? Before the assailant can attack someone else?"

Polly settled herself and fingered the lace at her wrists. "Before he can make good on the threat he sent me."

Edwin's Adam's apple bobbed several times. "Of course that's ideal."

"Will you stay with me?" Amelia glanced between Edwin and Polly. "Both of you?"

Why would someone like Amelia, who probably had all kinds of society friends, ask Polly to stay? Yet it would give her an in on the story. Perhaps that's why Amelia asked. "I'd be honored to. I'll support you any way you need me to."

"Thank you." Amelia squeezed Polly's hand, the gesture warm and filled with the promise of friendship.

"And I'll be by your side too." Edwin nodded at Polly over Amelia's head.

His suggestion warmed her just as much.

"All you have to do is let me know when you're ready," he said.

"And when it gets to be too much for you, just tell me, and we'll stop. We can finish another day."

"That's fine." Amelia tucked a stray strand of red hair back into its pins. "I'm ready."

"I'll arrange for you to look at the first suspects."

Edwin left, and Amelia turned toward Polly. "I appreciate you being here."

"You are quite a brave, strong woman. I can't imagine being in your place."

"You? I so admire your pluck. I could never be a career woman like you, working with nothing but men. But that's why I'm here. To show I can be strong and courageous. How is your friend Sophie?"

Polly held the tears at bay. "She's much the same, still stuck in the past. It's like someone turned her mind back to when she was a small child."

Amelia tsked. "What a shame."

"To make matters worse, we received a letter from her family a couple of days ago. They don't have the money to come bring her home. It's all they can do to pay for her doctor's bills. For now, Mrs. Mannheim is allowing her to stay at the boardinghouse for free. How long that will last, I can't tell you."

"That's so sad. My heart breaks for her. And makes me all the more grateful that I'm sound in both mind and body."

"God was watching over you. No doubt about that."

"Perhaps there is something we can do for your friend. Let me talk to Edwin about it."

"I don't know what would help, but thank you."

A short while later, after Polly and Amelia had enjoyed a nice chat, Edwin returned and showed them to a small room where a dozen or so men stood against a white plaster wall. Only a table with uneven legs separated the men from Amelia and Polly. It was here that Polly set her reticule.

Good gravy. There was very little difference in appearance between the suspects.

Polly stole a glance at Amelia. She was about as colorless as the men in front of her, and she bit her lip until a droplet of blood appeared.

Polly squeezed her hand. "Do any of them look familiar to you?"

"I. . ." She swept her gaze up and down the line and back again, then studied each man for a longer time. At last she sighed. "I don't think so."

"Are you sure?" Edwin's voice came from right behind them, soft but urgent.

"Pretty sure. They all look so much alike."

How would Amelia ever be able to tell which one was the Shadow?

Edwin nodded, and the uniformed policeman ushered the men from the room. A short while later, he returned with another group of men. They repeated this process several times. Each time the outcome was the same. Amelia didn't recognize any of them.

At last she turned to her brother. "That's about all I can take. My head is pounding. They're blurring together. I don't know. I didn't get a good enough look at the man who attacked me. Really and truly." A single tear trickled down her cheek.

Polly hugged her and led her to a chair in the room. "Don't worry about it. Your brother is a wonderful detective, and he'll sort out this mess and find the man who smacked you." And the man who sent her the letter.

Edwin sighed. "I don't know. There are so many of them. I'm not sure we can hold them long enough to interrogate all of them. Honestly, Armstrong is out of his mind, suddenly so desperate to solve this case that he'll bring in the entire city for questioning."

Amelia wiped the moisture from her eyes and gazed at Edwin. "I have every faith in you. You'll do it. You'll arrest the man who injured me and make sure he doesn't hurt anyone else."

But given the way his shoulders sagged and the lack of light in his eyes, Edwin wasn't as confident as his sister. It was insanity to round up men and bring them in for questioning and lineups just because of the way they appeared. Why, they might as well bring in Harry Gray while they were at it. He would fit right in with this crowd.

"Thank you, Polly." Amelia gazed up at her. "You've been a good friend. I appreciate it." She turned her attention to her brother. "Edwin, I'm ready to go home. Would you mind walking me to the carriage?"

"I can do it." Polly gathered her reticule from the table. "I have to go to the newspaper office. Mr. Ward wanted to see me."

"I'll walk both of you ladies out." Edwin gathered a stack of papers and held the door open for them as they exited.

A chill breeze greeted them, a portend of the long winter to come. Behind them flowed the South Platte River.

He helped Amelia into the carriage and sent it off before turning to Polly. "I want to reiterate my sister's thoughts. You've been a good friend to her, and we are indebted to you. I know this is more than a story to you now."

Polly tossed his words around in her head. He was right. This had become more than a story. It had evolved into a quest.

A quest to bring justice to Denver's women. Once she did, her editor would have to take notice. Her father would have to take notice.

"I'm happy to do whatever I can to help you and Amelia. To help the entire city." The wind picked up, and she held on to her hat lest it fly off her head.

"You made this difficult day easier for her. Having another woman in the room helped a great deal, I'm sure."

"Have you ever thought of Harry Gray as a suspect? He matches the description we have. If you're rounding up everyone else, why not him?"

"Your rival at the paper?"

"I don't know if I would call him my rival, but yes. He knows my movements and where I live. As a reporter on this story, he has access to inside information."

"And that's all you have to go on?"

"He hates women. That's more than you have on most of these men, I'm assuming."

"It's ludicrous."

"Why is it any crazier than what's happening here right now?"

Edwin shook his head. "That's the point. All of this is crazy. None of these men should be here without just cause. Without evidence against them. Bringing in Harry Gray would be just as insane." He rubbed his temples. "Anyway, thank you again for being there for Amelia. I do need to get back inside."

"And I need to get going. If I want to get a story into this evening's paper, I have to get to work."

He gave her hands a squeeze. "I'll see you later. And thank you again." He turned and strode into the police station.

The walk to the office did nothing to cool the heat in her face, despite the chilly late-fall temperatures. They would be in for their first snow soon.

With a glare from Harry, she settled herself at her desk and pulled a sheet of paper from her desk drawer.

Harry. Small. Pale. He'd had a mustache, but he'd shaved it.

No. Edwin was right. Harry might be a lot of things, but a woman beater wasn't one of them. Why, he couldn't even kill a spider. She'd asked him to do so once, and he'd refused.

She shook away the thought and returned to her article. But before she had a chance to roll the paper through the barrel, Mr. Ward emerged from his office and stood in front of her. "I need to speak with you, Miss Blythe. Right now." He scowled.

He had mentioned wanting to see her, and judging by his mood, this couldn't be good. What on earth had she done wrong now? She'd made her stories as sensational as she possibly could. How titillating could you make the society pages?

"Have a seat." Mr. Ward's normal frown deepened, pulling down his sagging eyes.

She did as he bid.

"You've done a good job with the Silver Shadow story."

Was it possible for her face to heat even more? "Thank you, sir." But if he had called her in to compliment her, why the scowl?

"I'm taking you off the assignment and giving it to Gray."

She must have heard him wrong. "Did you say you're letting Harry Gray take over the story?"

"He's our most experienced reporter. Such a big news item should be his. And this is something best handled by a man."

"Excuse me?"

"This story is beyond a woman's sensitivities."

Her chest tightened, and she fought to keep her voice steady and even. "I have to disagree with you. This is exactly the kind of story that calls for a woman's sensitivities. The events are happening to women. The story should be told from a female perspective. Ladies are the ones reading what is going on. They need to know how to protect themselves. How will a man understand what women are feeling, how they think and react to such news?"

Mr. Ward stared at Polly, narrow-eyed. Her pulse thrummed in her neck. What had she done? Probably gone and gotten herself fired.

His lips twisted as he chewed the inside of his cheek. It must be costing him to admit that she was right.

"No, Gray will get the story. It is his by rights."

"He asked you to give it to him, didn't he?"

"You aren't to work on it anymore."

She sagged. How foolish of her to believe, even for a moment, that her boss might think she was good enough to handle this. "What have I done wrong?"

"Nothing. Your work has improved a great deal in the past several weeks. You've done an exceptional job of making the case a sensational read. But it's time for you to hand it over to someone more experienced. The news has grown too big for you."

She stifled the laugh that swelled in her throat. "Because I'm small, that's why I'm losing this opportunity to prove to you how good I am? Or is it because I'm a woman?"

"Female reporters should confine themselves to writing about subjects they are familiar with. Mr. Tammen and Mr. Bonfils agree."

"So you men in charge feel I should be stuck with society happenings, you mean."

"Precisely. I'm glad you see it from our perspective."

She rose from her chair and leaned on Mr. Ward's tidy desk. "No, I don't see it from your perspective." This is what had happened throughout her life. Because she was a female, men believed she wasn't capable of more than bearing children, cooking, and keeping house.

"I've worked hard for you, sir. I have done everything you've asked of me. I've taken criticism and grown and learned from it. And I've done a good job on this story. You admitted it yourself. This isn't fair. This is a story primarily about women. Who better to write it than a woman?"

He scraped his chair back and met her eye to eye across the desk. "You're the one who wrote the editorial about the police department."

Polly gulped.

"You went behind my back to gain recognition for yourself."

She squirmed.

"You're gutsy. A trait I admire."

Was he genuinely complimenting her this time?

"A trait I admire in a man. In a woman, it is most decidedly unbecoming. But I will give you a chance. You and Harry will both write articles about the Shadow. I'll publish whoever's is best. And if you ever go behind my back again, it will mean the end of your career."

"Yes, sir."

"Those are my conditions. Do you agree to them?"

Of course. This was more than a story now. She had to stay on it.

Especially when she had an idea about catching the man responsible for these crimes.

Chapter 13

Monday, December 17, 1900

A. T. Lewis and Son Department Store in downtown Denver bustled with Christmas activity. Men crowded the jewelry counter, purchasing gifts for their sweethearts, while women pored over cologne and cufflinks. Amelia grabbed Polly by the elbow. "This is so much fun. Thank you for agreeing to come shopping with me. I still need presents for, well, everyone, and I couldn't think of a better person to help me."

For her part, Polly couldn't keep from staring at the scene in front of her. Never in her life had she been in such a beautiful store, filled to overflowing with everything a person could ever want or dare to dream to have. She could hardly catch her breath. Though Amelia clung to her, in reality it was Polly who needed the support.

"What do you think I should get Edwin?" Amelia surged forward in the crowd.

"I have no idea." Polly had difficulty forming a coherent thought. If she had to write an article about this place, she would never be able to find the words.

"You two have been spending a great deal of time together." Amelia stopped. Did she wink at Polly?

Ah, so that's why Amelia had chosen her for a shopping partner. Because surely she had plenty of friends from church and her social circles who were much more fashionable than Polly. Amelia wanted to find out what was going on between her and Edwin.

Was there anything? There couldn't be on Polly's part. She had to concentrate on her career. There was no time for other distractions.

"We've been working on the case. He's been giving me information so I can continue to write articles about it. Not that he's giving away anything the police wouldn't want the public to know, just details that might help solve these crimes. And he listens to me." Which endeared him to her.

No other man had ever taken her seriously. Had listened to her ideas and not called them stupid. Had talked to her and not through her or around her. She clasped that feeling close, savoring it for whatever time she could hold it.

"My brother is a good man."

"I think you had a great deal to do with how he treats women. You and your mother both."

"Yes, my mother is quite progressive. She believes that women should be treated as equally intelligent, capable, and worthy as men. I guess that Edwin shares our thoughts. Anyway, back to the Christmas gift. Whatever the reason, you've been with him for many, many hours these past few months. You must know what he needs."

"What he needs is rest. He's been working far too hard. When none of those men Detective Armstrong brought in ended up being the culprit, he pretty much had to start the investigation from the beginning."

"Well, I can't very well wrap that up and put a bow on it, can I? How about pair of gold cufflinks?"

What an extravagant item. Far beyond anything Polly would ever be able to afford. "I'm sure any gentleman would like that." They stopped in the men's department, and Amelia placed the order. Once that was done, they flitted around the store, picking out the rest of her gifts.

"Don't you have any presents to purchase?"

There was no way Polly could afford anything in this store. "I don't have anyone to buy for. I already bought a small doll for Sophie and a few trinkets for the other women at the boardinghouse. My brother doesn't live around here. My father is in St. Louis, and we don't have much to say to each other." Except for the newspaper clippings that Polly sent him. Ones he never acknowledged. But she wouldn't stop. She would keep on until she proved herself to him. To everyone.

"Oh, I'm so sorry to hear this. How awful for you. What are you planning to do for Christmas Eve?"

"Mrs. Mannheim is making a special dinner, though there won't be many there. Most of the women are heading home for the holidays. But we'll have our own fun. Perhaps I can persuade one of the other girls to play checkers or Parcheesi with me."

"You must come to our home then. You haven't seen a Christmas until you've seen a Price Christmas. The fire, the trees, the carols around the piano. It's magic."

"I wouldn't want to impose."

"No imposition at all. You'd be more than welcome. My mother adores you, and so does Edwin."

Polly's cheeks must match those of jolly St. Nicholas. "I don't know."

"I won't take no for an answer. So that's settled. Now, let's—" Amelia stopped as still as the mountains. She sucked in a breath and leaned against Polly.

"What is it? What's wrong?"

"Do you see that man by the cravats?" Amelia's voice was so quiet, Polly had to strain to hear it.

"Which one?" The place was crowded. There were many men at that counter and a few women too.

"The one with the tattered crushed hat on his head."

He was slight of build, but that's all Polly could tell about him from the back. "What about him?"

"I think that's the man who assaulted me."

Now it was Polly's turn to suck in her breath. "How can you tell? He isn't facing us."

"He's the right size and shape. I don't know. There's just something familiar about him. A feeling that I can't shake."

"You're positive?"

"No. But what if he's the Shadow?"

"Then we have to do something." Polly's mouth went dry at the idea of trying to apprehend him. But if he was the Shadow, they couldn't sit by and allow him to walk out of the store and assault other women.

Amelia stared at Polly, her eyebrows raised. "What? What are two women supposed to do? We can't arrest him."

Polly wiped her sweaty hands on her skirt. Her stomach flipped a few times. "We can follow him. At least find out where he lives."

"My hat." Amelia gestured to the dark purple creation sprouting ostrich feathers on her head. "It's the same one I was wearing that night. What if he recognizes it? He might try to attack me again."

"We'll stay far enough back and out of sight. We can't just let him go. Are you coming with me?"

Amelia nodded.

After a few minutes, the man moved away from the counter and headed toward the door, his back to them. Amelia and Polly slipped behind him, several people between them and the possible assailant. The possible Silver Shadow.

They wove through the crowd, around groups of shoppers. The man stepped outside to the sidewalk, and Amelia and Polly, clasping hands, purchases still with the concierge, followed a few seconds later.

He stood with his hands in his pockets, as if he didn't have a care in the world.

Then he glanced over his shoulder, just for a second. Not long enough for Polly to get a good look at him. He wasn't tall enough for her to see his entire face.

But she saw well enough to notice a scar above his right eye when he took off his hat long enough to scratch his head.

Something for her to tell the police.

In a flash, he took off.

He must have spied Amelia's hat.

"We can't lose him." With Polly pulling Amelia along, they took off at a sprint down the street.

Holiday shoppers crowded the thoroughfare. A light snow fell, coating the walks, turning them slippery.

It didn't help that the suspect was short. Polly couldn't keep her sights on him through the throng. Every now and again, she caught a glimpse of his dark, caped ulster coat. With one hand, Polly grasped her skirts. With the other, she dragged Amelia behind her.

"I can't keep going." Amelia gasped. "This hurts my head."

Polly released her grasp on her friend and sprinted forward. Every beat of her heart was a scream. *Get him. Get him. Get him.*

She drew closer to the man, never taking her focus from his charcoal-gray hat.

But he was fast. Very fast. Darted around people. Not hindered by skirts.

Polly breathed hard. "Please, let me pass." Though the crowd let him through, they didn't part for her.

"No, no. He's getting away." Her lungs cried for oxygen. She gulped air. Held her side to ease the pain of the stitch in it.

Try as she might, she couldn't catch the man.

A minute later, he disappeared, absorbed into the crowd.

She'd had him in her sights.

How could she have lost him?

Monday, December 24, 1900

Edwin couldn't help but stare at Polly as she sat across the parlor from him. The deep green gown she wore accented her tiny waist. The glow from the cheery, crackling fire set off the red highlights in her hair. Laughter floated from where she and Amelia sat with their heads together.

When she gazed up for a moment, his breath hitched. She smiled at him, and he did his best to shoot her a relaxed grin.

Even though she set every nerve tingling whenever she was around.

Mother swept into the room and clapped her hands together. "Edwin, are you ready to light the candles on the tree? And then we can open gifts." A childlike quality filled her voice. She loved this holiday as much as he did.

Yet when Edwin glanced at Polly, some of the glow had left her eyes.

"Come on, girls, quit your chatting and join us over here." Mother was the director of their family.

Polly and Amelia left their corner, Amelia claiming the wing chair that flanked the davenport. With Mother on the far end of the couch, that left Polly with the space beside Edwin.

He cast a glance at Amelia. He'd bet a year's wages she had orchestrated the seating arrangement. He knew her far too well.

Not that he minded. Not in the least.

Pine boughs covered almost every surface in the room, mingling their sweet fragrance with that of warm gingerbread. Each of them held a cut-glass cup of Christmas-red cranberry punch.

"Come on, Edwin." Mother sat forward on the edge of the davenport. "You know what time it is."

He nodded, a smile curling the corners of his mouth. As he lit the candles on the tree, he cast a glance at Polly every so often. Her eyes grew larger and larger by the minute. When he finished, she clasped her hands together. "I've never seen anything quite so lovely in my entire life."

Hadn't her family had a tree at home? Then again, she'd told him about her estrangement from her father. Perhaps they hadn't had the money for one. Perhaps they didn't celebrate the holiday with the fanfare that the Prices did. Few people could match them.

"And now it's time for gift opening." Mother's cheeks were pink, and her eyes were as bright as the candles.

Once more, Polly wilted at the mention of gifts. She had brought some with her when she'd arrived, so what might the problem be? He leaned over to whisper to her. "Is something wrong?"

She shook her head.

"You can tell me."

"My gifts aren't as grand as yours."

"You didn't even have to bring anything. Your presence is gift enough."

She turned to him. "That's what Amelia said."

"You should listen to her. Whatever you got, I'm sure we'll love." And he would.

A wild rap on the door interrupted the celebration. A few moments later, Nancy led O'Fallon into the parlor.

Edwin jumped to his feet, almost upsetting the glass of punch on the table at his elbow. "What is it?" He didn't dare take a breath, though he knew what O'Fallon would say.

"There's been another attack."

The ladies gasped.

What kind of monster was this, who beat women on Christmas Eve?

"She was walking home by herself from a church service. The next thing she remembers is waking up in her own bedchamber. It's a good thing her husband went searching for her. She might have frozen to death otherwise."

"Where was this?" As ever, Polly was at Edwin's side.

"Over on Corona Street between Ninth and Tenth Avenues. I don't know which church she was coming from."

Polly grabbed hold of the back of the sofa. "When will the women of this town be safe again?" She turned her gaze toward Edwin. Toward his heart in particular.

Her question was a good one and very valid.

O'Fallon played with the brim of the brown hat he held in his hands. "Such a shame about this woman. Her injuries are rather severe. We're doing all we can to apprehend this man. You know that, Miss Blythe."

"How could her husband have allowed her to walk home alone?" A tremor passed through Polly.

Edwin shrugged. "He probably figured it was safe enough on Christmas Eve."

"We have to do more to spread the word that women shouldn't be on their own in public, especially in the evenings."

Amelia touched her elbow. "Some women will refuse to listen. Look at me. I knew better. Goodness gracious, my brother is a detective and had warned me on multiple occasions, yet I got stubborn and set out on my own."

"Like I might have been tempted to do myself." Polly gave a wry little laugh. For a moment, she studied the floor, the tips of her shoes just peeping from underneath her skirt. "I might have prevented this."

"How?" Edwin and Amelia asked the question in unison.

"If I'd caught him the other day, he'd be behind bars right now."

Edwin shook his head. "That might not have even been our culprit."

Mother came to Polly and pulled her into a tender embrace. "We can't change the past. Everything that happens is part of God's will.

His plan. We don't understand it, but that's the way it is. You were able to give Edwin a new detail about the Shadow, if it was him. Combined with this attack, perhaps there will finally be an arrest. You don't know how God is going to use it."

Polly squeezed Mother. "Thank you for everything." She then turned her attention to Amelia. "You have become a good, dear friend of mine. I appreciate what you've done for me today."

She came to Edwin's side. "Please, take me to the woman's residence with you. I'm afraid this holiday has just turned into a workday." With this information, she would get a jump on Harry and have a fighting chance of getting an article in the paper.

"Of course."

"Thank you." Her eyes shimmered in the flickering candlelight. "Let me gather my things."

Once she had left the room, Edwin turned to O'Fallon. "What can you tell me about the case? How is the lady?"

"She was conscious when they brought her to the house, though she wasn't able to give much of a description of the man. The story is the same as all the others. Walking alone after dark. A man creeps from between houses or an alley and hits her over the head."

"Thank goodness she's going to recover."

"That's just it, sir. The doctors don't know if she will live or not."

Chapter 14

Wednesday, January 2, 1901

Tears blurred Polly's vision so much that she had a difficult time seeing the words she was typing.

Mrs. Young, the woman attacked on Christmas Eve, was gone. Dead. Just like Edwin's friend Rachel. She had suffered for more than a week before she passed away. When Polly got the news this morning, it was almost too much to bear. Two lives snuffed out without cause or provocation.

And other than Edwin, no one on the police force was lifting a finger to stop these crimes. The roundup of every man in the city matching the description of the culprit was a farce. It had yielded no results. The monster who was clubbing women over the head was still out there. Still free to terrorize them.

And somehow, some way, Harry had managed to beat her to the punch. His was the story that made the front page on Christmas morning.

Another editorial built in her until she couldn't stand it any longer. What the citizens of Denver and their police needed was a prod to wake them up and stop this man before another innocent woman lost her life.

But it hurt to have to write this. Two people were dead, numbers of others injured. Sophie suffered terribly, not in her right mind, all because Polly had decided to put her leisure ahead of her friend's request that they spend the evening together.

If she hadn't done that, Sophie wouldn't be in the state she was in.

Thankfully, Edwin had agreed to help with Sophie's expenses so she could remain in the familiar boardinghouse setting until they could arrange for someone she trusted to see her home.

With her embroidered-edged handkerchief, Polly wiped the tears wetting her cheeks. She glanced about the newsroom. Had anyone seen her crying? That would never do. If she had any hope of making it in this business, she had to be strong and tough.

At least on the outside.

Thankfully, the morning was young. Many of the men she shared the space with hadn't arrived for work yet. The two lone reporters who were here sat with their heads bent over their typewriters, likely too busy with deadlines to pay her much attention.

Then she glanced to her left. There was Harry, leering at her. He had noticed her tears.

"Aw, Miss Blythe, did you get a paper cut?"

She furrowed her brow.

"Did your kitty die?"

She swallowed around the knot in her throat. "I am not four years old, and I don't appreciate being spoken to in such a manner."

He changed his tone to a sultry beckoning. "I didn't mean to hurt your feelings. Of course you're a grown woman. Everyone knows that."

If it wouldn't have brought more jibes from Harry, she would have fanned the heat from her face. Instead, straightening her shoulders, she got down to work. Her fingers flew over the keys. For the most part, the editorial flowed, and she made very few mistakes.

To my fellow Denver citizens,

As you may know from recent articles in this same paper, the string of muggings by the Silver Shadow have continued, even over the just-past holiday season. The women of this fair city continue to live in fear and trembling. A walk to church or to the store might mean death.

And what have the police and the mayor of our hometown done to curb this fiend? Brought in a parade of men somewhat resembling the description several women gave of the Shadow. The surviving victims were not able to match any of them to the true culprit.

What a colossal waste of time and resources. Instead, the police should be combing the streets, interviewing witnesses and more-likely suspects, conducting searches, all in a true effort to catch this menace.

While there is one detective on the force who has a vested interest in the case and has been working long, hard hours to solve it, the chief of detectives, Captain Hamilton Armstrong, has been ineffectual at best, bumbling at worst.

That is why, good citizens of Denver, it is time for us to take matters into our own hands. Let us rise up, united in this cause. Protect your mothers. Protect your wives. Protect your daughters. Do not allow another woman to shed her blood or lose her life. Your inaction will sign their death sentences.

Most sincerely,
Miss Polly Blythe

As she pulled the sheet of paper from the typewriter's barrel, she fought back another wave of tears. There was no way she was going to allow Harry any further opportunity to mock her.

Sophie had been a good friend to her. She hadn't been such a good one to Sophie. This—she poked her finger at the paper—this was for Sophie and Rachel and Mrs. Young and Amelia all the others like them. So there would be no more Mrs. Youngs or Rachels.

Since Mr. Ward's dressing down several weeks ago, she'd been toeing the line. Since he had warned her not to go behind his back again, she needed to get his approval for this editorial.

As she stood, she patted the pocket of her skirt where Pa's latest letter rested. She didn't even have to look at it to know what it said. The words had seared themselves into her brain.

Polly,

I've had about all I can take from you with those ridiculous articles and editorials you've been sending me. You know how I feel about you being in Denver and working for that paper. That's not the proper place for a young woman. What is happening in that city isn't any of my concern. And these attacks on women are precisely why you should be married and running a home instead of out in the world alone.

If you will continue to defy me and live such a scandalous lifestyle, I have no wish to hear about it. The only letter I will accept from you is one stating that you are on your way home with a repentant heart and a willingness to act the way a proper young woman should.

Pa

What was it with all these tears threatening to flow today? She stiffened her spine. Pa could demand that she not send the articles, so she wouldn't. But one day he would be proud of her. He would have no other choice than to be proud of her.

Once admitted to Mr. Ward's office, she handed him the paper. "I wanted you to see that I'm acting in good faith by bringing you this editorial. My belief in this story is strong. Another"—her voice cracked, and she cleared it—"another victim has passed away. It was my obligation to write this letter. I pray that you will allow it to be published so that no more women suffer the same fate."

Mr. Ward sighed but took the paper she offered him. While he read it, all Polly could hear was the whooshing of her blood in her ears. Though not prone to it, she might even faint.

After a small eternity, her boss gazed from the page to Polly. "You're calling for a posse?"

"I don't know what I'm calling for. I certainly don't want violence. But I do want the men and women of this city to do whatever they can to stop this man from stealing another innocent life. This cannot continue. The circus Captain Armstrong created at the police station didn't help."

Mr. Ward nodded. "I'm with you on that. What a travesty to have a parade of men brought in just because of their looks. No probable cause at all."

"The *Post* has never been shy about calling out the city and the police for their handling of certain matters. Now is not the time to start."

Mr. Ward nodded. The wrangling between the politicians and

the newspaper was almost legendary. He had no choice but to agree with her.

"Not to mention, sir, that I've had a look at the photographs of criminals, the rogues' gallery, that Mr. Howe compiled. Hundreds upon hundreds of them on panels at the station. Though I got a look at the Shadow, I wasn't able to identify him either."

"I'm growing concerned about my own wife. Might she be next?"

Polly couldn't have hoped for a better response to her editorial. "That's exactly how many men are feeling. They want this culprit stopped and stopped now, before someone they know and love falls victim to him. So you're going to allow my editorial's publication?"

"You must amend it to contain some kind of phrase about not condoning violence. That whatever measures are taken must be peaceful and lawful. Once you have made that correction, you may bring it to the red room."

The red room. What they called the editorial office. "Thank you, sir, thank you." Polly just about floated out of Mr. Ward's office. If the citizens of Denver acted on her words, surely then Pa would be proud of her.

Monday, January 7, 1901

Every pew in Edwin's church was crammed with men. The air buzzed. There were businessmen in their suits and bowler hats, laborers in their dungarees with dirt under their fingernails, even a few gray-haired men who would probably rather be by the fire than out on such a cold night. Men filled every available space in the pews.

Granted, the church wasn't large, but the turnout was much bigger than he had expected. Edwin stood at the front, next to the simple pulpit, staring into the sea of men, Polly by his side.

"Look at this."

When he turned his attention to her, her eyes shone. Something that had been sorely missing since Mrs. Young's attack.

"People really do care. They want this man caught as much as you and I do. We're going to get him. I'm sure of it." Her voice held a hint of the fierce determination that flowed through her veins.

He almost reached out to draw her closer to himself. Almost. But not here. Not now. "I owe this to you. It was your editorial that put the idea in my head in the first place. And it was your reporting that caused this amazing response tonight."

"From the first day I met you, I knew you were the man to get this case solved."

"Oh, you did, did you?"

The color heightened in her cheeks. Not at all unattractive. But he couldn't spend the entire evening gazing at her. Other matters were more important. With a squeeze of her shoulder, he turned to the crowd. "All right, men, if I could have your attention, please."

The din of conversation continued, the men paying him little heed.

He drew in a deep breath and gave it all he had. "Gentlemen."

Not much quieting of the group.

An eardrum-popping whistle sounded beside him. Polly. He couldn't help but chuckle. Not many women could whistle like that. Or would even dare try. And it worked. The men settled down.

"Didn't know you had it in you, Miss Blythe."

She laughed. "I have a brother. Need I say more?"

He couldn't stop the silly grin that spread across his face.

"I believe the floor is yours."

"Of course." He raised his voice to be heard in the back. "Thank you all for coming this evening. As a member of the Denver Police Department, I want to assure you that we have been working as hard as we can to solve this string of strange muggings.

"But there is only so much the police can do. At some point we must turn to the residents to assist us. I know you are all concerned about your wives, sweethearts, and daughters. You have already been doing all you can to protect the women you love.

"We will not be able to rest easy until this menace is apprehended and brought to justice. We will need fortitude, commitment, and resolve. Who is with me in this fight?"

A great cheer rose from those gathered.

"Who will help me secure the safety of this city?"

Another rousing cheer.

"Who will bring this man to justice?"

Another hearty hurrah rang from the sanctuary's rafters.

"But how are we going to do it, Detective?" This from a middle-aged man with a high starched collar and a red cravat around his neck.

"We will organize into groups to patrol different sections of the city, particularly in the Capitol Hill area where most of the incidents have occurred. That is why Miss Blythe, the writer of so many articles on these crimes and the author of the editorial that spurred this idea, is with me. She will be the one taking your names and putting you into groups. She will give you your schedules, mostly during the early evening hours."

"And what do we do when we find him?" An unshaven man with a large, white Stetson on his head hollered from the back.

"There is to be no violence. Is that understood? The man is to be apprehended and brought to the police department. At that point, the officers will take over. You are not to shoot at him unless he shoots at you. Because he has used no weapon other than a metal pipe of some kind, we don't believe he is carrying a firearm."

"It would serve him right if he took one between the eyes." This from Rachel's father. His daughter's death had changed the normally gentle man into a raging bull.

The men were getting out of hand. Vigilantes often did, turning into wild men with no other mission than to cause chaos. They would have to be careful and dismiss those who couldn't follow the rules. The chief wouldn't be happy if Edwin's idea led to more incarcerations.

Polly tugged on Edwin's sleeve. "May I?"

He gave a single nod. "Of course." Perhaps, with her woman's touch, she could calm the crowd.

"Sirs, please look at this through the eyes of the women you love. Would they want you to hang for killing him? That would make you no better than he is. No. They would want you to use restraint. To hold your tempers in check and allow the judicial system to do its duty.

"Your job here is to make the streets safe for those you love to go about their business without fear. What this man is doing is unconscionable. Capture him, certainly. Make sure he faces a judge, of course. But don't become what he is."

A murmur ran through the crowd, but there were no more objections to the call for peace. Edwin mouthed *thank you* to Polly before turning back to the gathering. "If there are no further questions, we can begin getting organized."

Polly stepped to the table in the narthex, and men lined up for her to divide them into groups. Edwin sat beside her, filling up the schedule they had sketched out the evening before.

Some of the men requested to serve together. She honored those requests. Though quite some time passed before they had all the men assigned to patrols, they did manage to complete the job. At last the church emptied until only Edwin, Polly, and the janitor were left.

She waved the roster in front of Edwin's nose. "Can you believe what a response we had? All of these men are so willing to serve, it's amazing. I'm sure we're going to catch him. I just know it in my bones."

"Don't go getting your hopes up. I don't want you to be disappointed if this doesn't turn up a suspect. You're enthusiastic, and that's great, but there are times when we can't crack a case."

Though this case was more important than any he had ever worked on. For Rachel, for Amelia, for Sophie, for all the others, they had to solve it. They just had to.

She leaned against his shoulder. "Don't worry. With this many people on the job, there's no way we won't nab him. There's too much at stake to fail."

Chapter 15

A dark unsettledness descended over Denver as the crowd of men assembled in front of Edwin's church on this January night. The wind howled, a high-pitched wail, rattling the windows, sending skiffs of snow across the road and through the gathered assembly. Edwin pulled his coat tighter around himself and wrapped his scarf an extra turn around his neck.

Men stood shoulder to shoulder on the walk in front of the church and spilled onto the street. Curses came from those who couldn't drive their wagons or carriages down the road.

Every man who had signed up for this shift had turned up. A very good sign that the people of Denver were ready to be rid of the Silver Shadow once and for all. Polly would be pleased about that. They would catch him. They had to. Tonight was their night.

With the *Post* now kicking in another $100 for the reward, bringing it to $500, many of these men, no doubt, were here for the cash. But no matter. He didn't care what their motivation was if it brought the Shadow to justice.

Most of the men had dressed in dark clothing, making it difficult to pick them out in the winter's gloom. A few had pitchforks. No doubt, despite his warning at the church last week, several had guns. He prayed they wouldn't have to use them. A couple were even dressed like women, their not-quite-long-enough skirts brushing the tops of their work boots.

Edwin approached one of the men wearing a long, dark skirt, a pale blue coat that strained at the seams, and a blue bonnet. Far away, he might be convincing. Up close, not at all. Especially not with his blond beard.

"What's with the clothes, Thomas?" Edwin had to stifle a chuckle.

"To draw out the man. We've told our women to stay home, to stay safe. But without women on the street, we can't flush the man from the shadows."

"And you think he's going to believe you're actually a woman?"

"In the dark from the back, that's what I'm hoping. But don't worry. I brought protection." Thomas patted his hip. No doubt underneath that coat was a firearm.

"Just be careful. Remember, that's the last resort."

"Got it."

"Good luck." Edwin gave a hearty laugh and slapped Thomas on the back.

A flash of red underneath a gaslight caught Edwin's attention. A woman's coat. Small, dainty. That meant there was a woman inside that coat. Out alone. Though the men of the city were working to cleanse the streets of scum, the women had a responsibility to be careful and not be walking unaccompanied in the evening.

Wait a minute. He knew that coat. The way the woman carried herself with an air of sweet dignity and grace yet fierce determination.

Polly.

He groaned and clutched his head. What on earth was she doing here? She should be safe at the boardinghouse playing a game with her friends or at the office, writing an article.

Perhaps that's why she was here. That had to be the reason. Another story she wouldn't allow to slip through her fingers.

He moved away from the crowd to meet her before she reached him. "You're the last person I expected to see here tonight."

She tipped her head. "The last person? Really, Edwin, do you not know me better than that?"

Was she teasing or was she serious? He shrugged. "Maybe you should have been the first person I expected to see."

"That sounds more like me." Her brown eyes sparkled in the dim light.

"You still haven't answered my question."

"I don't believe you've asked one."

"Oh." Perhaps she was flirting. Or was she merely bantering? "What are you doing here?"

"I've come to volunteer my services."

"What services?"

"Patrolling the streets, luring the villain from his hiding place. If you don't have a woman, the man won't come out. He won't attack."

The same thing Thomas had said. The only difference was that Thomas was a man. An armed man. Polly was defenseless. "Out of the question."

"Why?"

The slight whine in her voice made it sound like she really was at a loss for why he would deny her. "Because I'm not going to put you at risk."

"Men will be all around me. I couldn't be safer at home in front of the fire."

"That may not be enough to deter him. He's targeted you specifically. What if he does strike? Will you fight back? If he injures you, how will you chase him down?"

"Well. . ."

"This is not the place for you. Look, we have men dressed in skirts to attempt to draw him out. We're forming this posse to keep you women safe, not to put you in harm's way. Your being here is defeating the purpose."

She crossed her arms in front of her and harrumphed. "'You women'? We aren't helpless, you know."

"I know, I know." He stepped backward. "But his target has been women. We, I, need to know you're safe. Please, let me walk you home, and then let me do my job."

"But I want to be here in case you catch him. Imagine the story I would get out of that. Once I write it, there's no way Harry or Mr. Ward or the *Post's* owners would ever look down on me again. I'd be a bona fide reporter. I'd have to be taken seriously."

"You would risk your life to be taken seriously? To prove that women are as capable as men?"

"I don't believe I'm risking my life."

"Don't be naive. You are. Please, I'm begging you, let me show you to the boardinghouse."

"And I'm begging you to allow me to stay."

"What are the chances that we're actually going to catch him tonight? It's not like he strikes every evening at six. This may take a while. We might have to wait him out, play a game of cat and mouse. He's proven he's smart. We have to outsmart him."

"And you don't think I am capable of outsmarting him?"

Why was everything he said tonight wrong? "Of course you are. And your help so far has been very valuable. I appreciate it. But this isn't a good way for you to be of assistance. Someone would have to keep an eye on you."

"Exactly." She crowed like a peacock. "If I'm walking around and someone is nearby—not within sight, but just close—then we can nab him before he has a chance to do anything to me. It's brilliant, really. Do you think a bunch of men dressed as women are going to make him leave the shadows?"

"Though I hate to admit it, Thomas isn't a very good woman. Not convincing at all."

"Not at six foot three. Come on, you have to let me help. Please?"

It was a wonder her father was so harsh with her. The way she gazed at him, hope filling her eyes, a small pout puckering her lips, was pretty much his undoing. How could you say no to that? Her plan did make sense. "Fine."

"What did you say?" She leaned closer.

"Fine. I said fine. Are you happy now?"

"Ecstatic." She gave a little squeal. "Thank you. You don't know what this means."

"But you have to follow the rules."

"And those are?"

"You must always be with a man. Have one who can see you, though we'll make sure you appear to be alone. You are not to go out without someone watching you. I repeat, not on your own. And if it's getting too dangerous and I feel it's best you aren't here, you have to go home. No begging or pleading or whining. Understood?"

"Perfectly. You won't have to worry about me."

Like he wouldn't worry about her. Something was growing in his heart, something he didn't want to name or label. But it meant he would always worry about her.

Blood pumped through Polly's veins as she meandered up and down the darkened streets of Capitol Hill. Sleet fell, stinging her cheeks, dampening what little light came from the streetlamps. She clutched her packages to herself, trying for all the world to appear like nothing more than a woman on her way home from the department store.

Even though she was anything but. It wasn't the cold that stole her breath. It was the prickling at the base of neck, like she was being watched, that gave her difficulty in drawing in air.

Of course she was being ridiculous. She was being followed, for her own safety, as Edwin had insisted.

At one point, she gazed over her shoulder. There he was, about twenty steps or so behind her. He had insisted that he be the one to guard her. He had his dark brown coat buttoned to the neck and his collar turned up over his ears. But she wasn't fooled. He watched her like a mother hen watches her chicks.

If the Silver Shadow did put in an appearance tonight, Edwin would be on him in a matter of seconds. She would be safe. At the thought, she sighed. Safe. To have a man such as him care for her. He respected her and what she did.

He was rare.

The evening wore on. From the way her feet ached and from the numbness in her fingers, she no doubt had traversed several miles, all up and down this same stretch of road. She had passed the Joslin Dry Goods building, the Kittredge Building, and the Masonic Temple several times. Pretty soon she would be able to sketch this area from memory.

Every now and again, they passed other men from the posse patrolling the street. She held back from laughing at the ones dressed like women, their skirts showing their ankles. The plumed hats they wore, though large on women, were too small for their big heads. They were ridiculous. What made them think the Shadow would try to assault them?

The streets quieted as people returned home for supper. A gnawing in Polly's stomach reminded her that she hadn't taken the time to eat between leaving the office and arriving at the church. By the time she returned to the boardinghouse, Mrs. Mannheim would have closed the kitchen.

Her mealtimes were firm. If you missed dinner, you were out of luck.

Like Polly was tonight.

But catching the Shadow would more than make up for it.

The sleet came down harder. Her cheeks stung from the cold. Several times she had to use her handkerchief to wipe her nose. Ice crusted her eyelashes.

This was crazy. The Shadow wasn't going to be out on a night like this. He was smart enough to stay home in front of a roaring fire. Oh, what bliss it would be to warm up next to the stove, a cup of coffee in her hands, a steaming bowl of soup in front of her.

Perhaps Edwin was ready to call off the search for tonight. She'd walked several blocks without seeing anyone else from the patrol. They must have all decided to go home.

As she turned to wait for Edwin and tell him she was finished for the night, she caught movement in an alley between a drugstore and a dress shop.

She drew in a breath. Couldn't release it. Though darkness and the storm cloaked the figure, he was slight of build. A crushed hat sat on his head. He pressed against the brick building of Schultz Drug Company.

If he wasn't the Shadow, why was he hiding in the alley? It had to be him. Just had to be.

Polly dropped one of her packages and bent to retrieve it, the sign she and Edwin had agreed upon if she needed him. Not two or three seconds past before he was at her side. "Let me get that for you, ma'am." He handed her the bag. "What did you see?" He whispered the question.

"He's down the alley between the drugstore and dress shop." A little louder, she said, "Thank you, sir. I appreciate it."

"You're positive?" His voice was low again.

"No. I didn't get a good look at him. And it's too dark for me to see if he has a scar. But if it's not him, why is he plastered against the side of a building in an alley?"

"You stay here." He darted off in the direction she had indicated.

Honestly, he must be out of his mind to think she was going to stay put and miss out witnessing the capture of the Silver Shadow. She crept after him, staying a good distance behind him. Just close enough to see what was happening.

As soon as Edwin approached the alley, the man raced down it. Edwin followed, as did Polly, discarding her no-longer-needed packages. But her toes were numb from cold, and the bite of the wind left it tough to breathe.

The three of them emerged onto Seventeenth Street. The man wove in and out of the people on the walk, barreling over an older woman, a book in one hand, her reticule in another. Edwin continued the chase.

Polly couldn't leave the woman lying on the sidewalk. She stopped and bent to help the woman sit up. "Are you hurt?"

"What's going on?"

Polly assisted the woman to her feet. "Are you injured?"

"Just my pride."

"I'm glad. If you'll excuse me. . ." Polly sprinted away, clutching her skirts with her frozen fingers.

Just ahead of her, Edwin tackled the man to the ground. At last Polly caught up with them. "You got him. Edwin, you got him." She almost danced a jig in the middle of the walk.

Edwin grunted, struggling to hold the suspect to the ground. The wiry fellow wrestled hard, but Edwin managed to pin his arms behind his back and subdue him.

The man raised his head. "What is this all about?"

"You are under arrest for a number of crimes. I'll enumerate them once we get you to the station." Edwin handcuffed the man, lifted him to his feet, and marched him ahead of himself and Polly. They made a brief stop at a callbox to alert the station.

She squeezed his upper arm. "I can't believe you truly apprehended him. Our plan worked to perfection. Now the city can put this nightmare behind us. Rachel can rest in peace. Sophie will have justice. And wait until I write this story."

"Don't get overly enthusiastic just yet."

Thankfully, they weren't too far from the station and arrived there in short order. What a blessed relief to step into the warm building. Edwin pushed the man into a chair. "What were you doing hiding in that alley?"

Polly took this chance to study the man in front of her. Yes, he was small in stature and in girth. Yes, he had a mustache. But was he the Shadow?

Edwin glanced at her, one eyebrow raised in question. She shrugged. This man didn't have a scar above his right eye. But she so wished he did.

"It will go better for you if you confess right now. Perhaps the judge will grant you leniency."

"Confess to what?" The man shrugged. "I didn't do anything other than seek some protection from the storm."

Just then the door to the interrogation room swung open and Amelia entered. "Ralph phoned me as soon as he received the call from the callbox." She peeled off her black leather gloves and brushed the snow from her deep maroon coat. "I came as fast as I could."

Edwin turned his attention to his sister. "I'm glad you're here. We apprehended this man lurking in an alley tonight. Do you recognize him?"

Amelia furrowed her brow and narrowed her eyes, tipping her head one way and then the other. "I'm sorry, Edwin. I just don't know. Everything after the attack is a blur. If I got a view of the Shadow's face, I can't remember it."

"So this man isn't the Shadow?"

"I can't answer that one way or the other."

He turned to Polly. "What about you?"

"I can't be sure either."

Chapter 16

H is hands shook so much, he could hardly make himself a cup of coffee. They had gotten smart to him. The cops. The people of Denver. Polly Blythe.

Especially her. The one who wasn't home with a husband and children.

He steamed more than the boiling water in his pot. They had to go and ruin everything, didn't they? Just when he'd been making progress. Just when he was driving women off the streets, keeping them at home where they belonged, they had to ruin that.

The posse would be patrolling the streets in the evenings from now on. Perhaps there were other areas besides Capitol Hill where he could hit. Then again, he couldn't take the chance. He had no idea where they may or may not be.

While it was good that the men of the city were protecting their women like they should, it wasn't good, because he couldn't continue his work. He wasn't finished yet. Wouldn't be finished until he had shown them the light. Had shown them the good and moral and godly way to behave.

He wandered into his bedroom and glanced at the picture on the little table beside his bed. The picture of her. The one who had stolen his heart then trounced all over it. Smashed it until it was dust.

He drew in a few ragged breaths.

This used to be a place of happiness and love. She had brought her feminine touches here. Pretty paper on the walls. A multicolored quilt on the bed. A bunch of flowers in the center of the kitchen table.

Now the quilt was gone, and the flowers had long since withered and died.

All because of her.

Even though he had worked hard and bettered himself, she still left. Left him for someone with even more money. He ground his teeth.

From the photograph, she smiled at him. Or was that a sneer? Did she know even then how she would betray him? Was she already betraying him when she sat for that portrait?

Heat rose in his chest. Curses be on her for what she did. He grabbed the photograph and threw it against the wall, smashing the glass in the frame, shards of it raining on the table and floor. He dashed into the kitchen, and from the small countertop, he grabbed a knife, raced back to the bedroom, and slashed the photograph until he had shredded it.

Until there was nothing left of it.

Like there was nothing left of his love for her.

She wouldn't stare at him with those hypnotic eyes any longer. Would never stir the feelings he'd buried the day he found out what she'd done.

With all of his might, he hurled the knife. The blade stuck into the plaster. He allowed a primal scream to rip from him. "Why? Why? Why? I gave and gave and gave. You took and took and took. Then turned around and left me with nothing." He shook his fist at heaven. "May God"—he stared at the floor—"or the devil deal with you and send the condemnation on you that you deserve."

He paced the house from one corner to the other to the other to the other. Over and over again like a caged tiger at the circus. What was he going to do? With armed men running the streets at night, he couldn't continue his crusade. And some of them were dressed as women. How ridiculous was that?

The men of Denver had lost their minds, emasculating themselves in such a manner. It went against everything God's law taught. Absolutely everything. The world had gone mad and turned upside down. It was up to him to stop this craziness before it got out of control. Before God rained His holy judgment on the earth.

He'd done it before in a flood. He would do it again. He had promised. This time, however, it would be fire and brimstone like at Sodom and Gomorrah.

He stopped in the kitchen and sat at the table, his coffee now cold in the cup. Ruined, spoiled, like everything in this world.

He had to think of a way he could do his part to keep the women of this city on the straight and narrow even though their insane menfolk prowled the evening streets. But how? That was the question. How would he go about it?

Was there a way to accomplish his mission?

Monday, January 14, 1901

Edwin sat in a chair in Armstrong's office, fiddling with a pen he'd picked up from his superior's desk. What did the man want? Edwin glanced over his shoulder. In a few moments, he would have his answer, because here came Armstrong, marching across the station like he owned it.

One day, sooner or later, he might.

He entered and shut the door behind him then took his place behind his desk. Edwin dropped the pen on the floor, bent to retrieve it, and returned it to where he had found it.

For several long moments, Armstrong gazed, narrow-eyed, at Edwin. Then he steepled his fingers and cleared his throat. "Well, Price, what do you have to say for yourself?"

"Pardon me?"

"It has come to my attention that you are leading a bunch of rabble-rousers who are patrolling the streets at night. A posse. An armed posse at that."

What he could say in response?

"Denver is no longer the Wild West, you know. This is a place of law and order now. That is how we operate. We don't send out civilians to do our jobs."

"Yet we could use the help on the case." He didn't dare voice what a disaster their roundup a couple of months ago was.

"You, of all people, should be a good example. As a detective, you are held to a higher standard. Then you go and pull a stunt like this. Are you after your family's money?"

"No sir, not at all. That's not why I'm part of the patrols. You have to understand all this man has taken from me. Because of him, our family lost a dear friend. My sister was attacked. She could have been killed." He bit his tongue to keep from mentioning that Polly, in a way, had lost a friend as well. "If I'm the one who captures the assailant, I'll donate the money to charity."

"Because you don't need it. You see this job as some kind of game. A way to pass the time." Armstrong leaned forward and curled the corner of one lip. "Don't you?"

"Not at all. This is serious business. I'm committed to keeping the streets of Denver safe for all of its residents, no matter their social status. I understand this isn't child's play. I've seen up close what this man is capable of. Why he must be apprehended and brought to justice as soon as possible."

Armstrong leaned back in his chair and lit a cigar, not bothering to offer one to Edwin. Just as well. He hated the sickly sweet smell of them. Every time Armstrong brought a match to one, Edwin's stomach churned.

"That won't be necessary." A smug smile crossed Armstrong's face. "We have a credible suspect in custody."

"How many this time?"

"You can cut the sarcasm. One. A single suspect. This time we've got him. No thanks to you and your posse."

"They aren't my posse." Well, maybe in a way they were. He had led them. Polly had organized them. "What evidence do we have against him?"

"He matches the description we have."

"And. . ."

"That's enough."

Not really. The description wasn't that specific. But arguing with Armstrong wouldn't get Edwin anywhere. And maybe, just maybe, they did have their man. "Please, sir, let me question him. Or at least be in the room when you do. And we should let Amelia and Miss Blythe know. They could come in and identify him from a lineup."

"Already done. You think I'm incompetent, but that's not the case. I'm pretty smart, all on my own. I wouldn't have made chief of detectives if I wasn't. And I didn't need your help to do it."

"Yes, sir. No insult intended. I want to make sure this is really the man and that we can take him off the streets once and for all."

"That's my goal as well."

"Then there should be no problem with me being in on the interrogation."

Armstrong sighed and puffed on his cigar, blowing blue smoke into the already hazy air of the office. "Fine. I'll be in the room. Once I make police chief, I'll have to appoint a new chief of detectives. We'll see how you do."

"Thank you, sir. You won't be sorry."

The Silver Shadow might be sitting in one of the interrogation rooms right now, getting ready to be sweated.

And Edwin was more than happy to do the sweating.

It was impossible not to get his hopes up.

O'Fallon met him on his way back to his desk. "You sure look happy about something. Thought when Armstrong called you in, you might be in some hot water."

"Just a little. But they have a suspect in custody in the Silver Shadow case. Armstrong is going to let me question him. Amelia and Polly have been summoned to try to pick him out of a lineup. Let me know when they get here."

"Aye, aye." O'Fallon saluted and gave a saucy wink.

Once Edwin had picked up the suspect's file, he hustled to the interrogation room. According to the intake notes, the man's name was Joseph Shaklee. Though he searched and hunted through the papers, he was hard-pressed to discover any evidence against the man. Armstrong had found an ulster coat in his possession, but that was hardly unique. Shaklee possessed a gun, but from what Edwin remembered of the reports from the victims' doctors and the coroner, the butt of a gun wouldn't leave the gashes the women had suffered.

Edwin sighed and stepped into the room. For a minute or two, he stood in the doorway, arms crossed, examining the purported Silver

Shadow. He was a slight man, very light skinned, with a dark, droopy mustache. He did have a scar above his right eye. As far as that went, he matched the description from the victims.

It was all Edwin could do to keep his lunch in his stomach. If this was the man who had killed Rachel and hurt Amelia, he deserved whatever fate the courts meted out to him.

Calm and composed, he nodded. "Mr. Shaklee?"

"Yeah, that's me. I don't understand what this is about. Why am I here?"

Armstrong entered the room and stood in the far corner, his gaze shifting from Edwin to Shaklee and back again. Almost like Edwin was the one being interrogated.

But he would do his job. If this man was guilty, he would get a confession from him.

Edwin plopped the file on the table, pulled out a chair, and settled into it, all the time staring into the man's blue eyes. "Why don't you tell me?"

" 'Cause I got nothin' to tell. The men who arrested me said I'd find out soon enough the charges against me. But I can't answer you unless I know what the questions are."

The man was intelligent. So was the Silver Shadow. He had to be to avoid detection this long. "Why don't you tell me about the night of August 24 of last year? Where were you that night?"

"You expect me to recall a night from six months ago?"

"Let me refresh your memory. That was the night you assaulted three women. All along Sixteenth Avenue. And one of them, Rachel Quincy, was killed. Do you recall that?"

Shaklee scratched the top of his head. "Now that you mention it, I do remember some mumblings at work about it. Something about these muggings getting out of control. Don't recall much more than that."

"Funny how your memory came back all of a sudden."

"Well, you can say whatever you want, 'cause I wasn't the one who did it."

"Do you have an alibi for that night?"

"A what?"

Edwin huffed out a breath. "An alibi. Can you tell me where you were?"

"Like I said, it was so long ago, I wouldn't remember. What day of the week was it?"

The weight of Armstrong's stare on Edwin pulled down his shoulders. He was getting nowhere with this suspect and looking incompetent in the process. The time had come for a different tactic. "What about this last Christmas Eve? It wasn't that long ago, was it? Surely you can remember where you were then."

"Yeah, Christmas Eve wasn't too long ago. That's an easier one to remember. I went to church with my family, and my wife cooked us a nice dinner afterward."

"What time was the service?"

"Late afternoon. I don't recall. My wife just tells me where to be and when to be there, and I listen to her." He chuckled. Edwin and Armstrong remained straight-faced.

"At any time that day were you out without your family?"

"Might have run out for a last-minute gift or something my wife needed for baking. I don't remember."

"We'll have to have a little talk with her then. Unless you'd like to spare her the humiliation?"

"How do I do that?"

"By confessing."

"But I don't have anything to confess. I swear it on my dear departed mother's grave."

Just then the door swung open. Amelia and Polly stood on the threshold, clasping hands.

Edwin stood and motioned them in. "Amelia, take a gander at this man. Study him well. Is he the one who attacked you?"

Both women stood wide-eyed and open-mouthed.

Chapter 17

As the two women stood in the interrogation room's doorway, Polly grabbed Amelia by the elbow to ensure that both of them would remain upright. Dust motes floated on the weak winter sunshine that streamed through the window high in the far wall. A man sat behind a long desk. Edwin stood to one side.

The entire office reeked of smoke and strong coffee. From somewhere behind her, a telephone rang. Then another one. A chilly draft crept up her skirts, and she shivered.

As she stared at the suspect who squirmed in his wooden chair, Polly's breath hitched. Beside her, Amelia gasped.

Edwin nodded. "I know this might be a shock and quite traumatic. But take a good look at him. Don't rush to any conclusions. We want you to be absolutely sure of your answer. Is this the man who attacked you, Amelia?"

Beside her, Amelia trembled. Polly swallowed hard.

As if she'd dropped down a well, all noise around her dimmed. The light narrowed until it spotlighted the suspect.

The man on the chair across the table bore a striking resemblance to the descriptions Polly had heard from the victims. He was small, hardly taller than she was, just like the man from the department store. His complexion was so fair he must work in a cave or something. Perhaps he was a silver prospector in a mine. And he did have a scar.

At first sight, Polly might say this was the culprit, the man they had been searching for since August. Five long months. By declaring him to be the man she saw in the alley, she could bring this case to a close. What a story she would have to write.

The temptation lingered for a moment in her heart.

But it wouldn't be true.

She honestly had no idea.

She turned to Amelia, who had faced her. Unspoken words passed between them in a raise of Amelia's eyebrows and a slight shake of Polly's head.

"I—" The word squeaked from Amelia's throat, and then she straightened. "I don't know why you continue to call me in. I didn't see his face. I'm not ever going to be able to identify him, even if you find the true culprit." Her voice broke.

Edwin's shoulders sagged. "Are you sure about that?"

"Positive. I'm sorry. I truly am. With all my heart, I wish I could tell you if this is the man who attacked me. I just can't."

Edwin focused on Polly. "What about you?"

"I'm swimming in the same stream as Amelia. I want this to be over so the streets are safe. But I couldn't tell you if this was the man or not. I came mostly to support Amelia. I've only ever seen the Shadow's back."

From the corner, Detective Armstrong, whom Polly hadn't seen right away, glared at them. "Take another look." His words were sharp. "Be absolutely sure. Because I'm positive this is our suspect. This is the man who attacked you, Miss Price. Sometimes women don't remember things correctly. Or they become easily confused. The fright of that night may be clouding your memory. Do you really want to free him to menace the streets again?"

Amelia bit the inside of her cheek. "Sir, I wouldn't be serving justice if I helped to put an innocent man behind bars." She glanced at Polly, who nodded. "I refuse to do such a thing. I want the case to be solved, but not at the expense of an innocent man's life. That would be wrong."

"Well said." Polly released her hold on Amelia. "We both wish we could help you, but we can't. Neither of us has ever seen his face." She stared at Edwin, the pulse in her wrist fluttering at the gaze he gave her. A sad sort of half smile that said he was disappointed but proud of them. A man who believed her word. Who believed in her.

Red bloomed in Detective Armstrong's face. "You're wrong. Both of you are confused. Muddled in the brain. How could you not have seen his face or remembered him at all? This is our culprit. I'm done here." His voice rose in pitch. "I'm going to ask the bailiff to take him to a cell. We'll get a confession."

The man rose to his feet so fast, he tipped his chair backward. It clattered to the floor. "You'll never get a confession from me, because I'm innocent."

"Sit down this instant, Mr. Shaklee." Detective Armstrong's voice boomed in the small room.

Mr. Shaklee picked up his chair and sat. Amelia and Polly each took a step backward, out of the room. Edwin followed them and shut the door behind him. "I'm sorry you had to go through that. Armstrong is so determined to solve this case to make himself look good that he's willing to assume the guilt of an innocent man."

Polly relaxed her shoulders. "So you won't be calling me or your sister in anymore?"

"Of course not." He hugged Amelia. "It takes some fortitude to stand up to Armstrong."

"How could I lie?" Amelia's voice was quiet but firm. "That would be so very wrong. It would go against everything we've been taught."

"You're right." Edwin loosened his collar. "As much as I wanted to believe this was our suspect, there isn't any evidence against him."

Amelia excused herself to use the restroom. Polly sighed. If only she didn't have to tell Edwin what she had to tell him. "Sounds like you've already had a pretty bad day, and I'm about to make it worse."

"Do I really have to hear it?"

"I'm afraid so. I've been trying to put together schedules for the nightly patrols. At first I had more than my share of volunteers. But it's getting harder and harder to fill the slots. There have been no new attacks since we started the program."

"That's kind of the point of it." Edwin adjusted his spectacles. Detective Armstrong exited the interrogation room, his face the color of Ma's summer tomatoes, and gave Edwin and Polly each a long, hard glare.

Polly turned from the man. He was out for political gain and nothing more. All he was interested in was a name for himself and a promotion. Justice was low on his priority list.

Once Detective Armstrong was down the hall and his office door slammed shut, she focused on Edwin again. "Yes, that's the point of it, but the men are growing restless. What they want to do is the same thing as your boss—find a culprit and string him up by his toes. They don't understand, or don't want to understand, that what we're doing is working."

"So where do we go from here?"

She touched his arm, his muscles taut beneath her fingers. Being so near him, she caught the scent of soap and leather. So manly. So pleasant it sent a burst of warmth through her. "I don't know if you'll like my idea."

"Why wouldn't I?"

"Because I think it's time for another editorial."

Wednesday, January 16, 1901

"Price. In my office. Now." Armstrong's voice was a barely controlled simmer, his cheeks redder than any cherry. Nothing but a miracle kept him from having a stroke.

When Edwin glanced at O'Fallon's desk, O'Fallon just shrugged his slender shoulders. Edwin didn't have any idea, either, what Armstrong could want. And getting called into the office was growing more and more tiresome by the day.

With leaden feet, Edwin shuffled toward Armstrong's lair, the tingling stares of many of his fellow officers and detectives on him. Like he was part of a parade or something. Worse yet, an exhibit at a freak show.

Since the debacle with Mr. Shaklee, Armstrong had been none too pleased with Edwin. Especially when Armstrong was forced to admit he had no evidence and had had to let Shaklee go. So when Edwin arrived at Armstrong's office, he slunk into the room and slouched in one of the chairs in front of Armstrong's desk.

"Well, Mr. High-and-Mighty, so glad you could make it."

Armstrong took a drag of his stogie and then downed a mouthful of coffee.

What bee had gotten under Armstrong's bonnet?

"You didn't close the door behind you."

Edwin rose to do so.

"Sit." Armstrong roared the command. "It's better if the entire precinct hears this. Your little sweetheart has written herself another editorial."

Edwin stifled his groan. What Polly had to say about the chief of detectives and his work so far would not be flattering. And she had written it with his blessing. "She's not my sweetheart." Although the thought wasn't unpleasant. He'd enjoyed spending time with Polly, getting to know her. She was spunky and fun and beautiful and—

"Price, are you paying attention to me?"

Whoops. Not the right time to be daydreaming about Polly. "Of course."

"Have you seen this piece of garbage the *Denver Post* produced?"

"No, sir, I haven't." He hadn't taken the time for breakfast this morning. The sweet saltiness of bacon almost beckoned him, but when he met Amelia in the hall, her eyes red-rimmed from another sleepless night because of headaches that plagued her, he lost his appetite. The only thing he hungered after right now was justice.

"Let me enlighten you, then." Armstrong cleared his throat. "Be sure to listen up, out there in the office. I want you to hear this too. 'Men of Denver, this situation calls for action, not complacency. You acted, and for a while, the muggings and killings of innocent women stopped. We praise God for that. But to sit back now and believe that your job is complete might well condemn another woman to death.'"

Edwin nodded. That sounded like Polly. And she was correct. Now wasn't the time to stop their patrols or to ease up on their efforts to capture this man.

" 'How can you fail your mothers, your wives, your daughters in this manner? Do you care nothing for them? You say you love them. Then show them that love by continuing the fight for safe streets. Let us continue in our search for the culprit. Let us see that he comes under the full weight of the law.'"

Armstrong waved the paper in Edwin's face. "She has quite the way with words, don't you think?"

All Edwin could do was swallow and nod. She did. She truly did.

" 'And what about our esteemed police department under the direction of Police Chief Farley and Chief of Detectives Armstrong? Let's turn our attention to them for a moment. How can we approve of this mass roundup of men, dragged from the streets and from their homes for no other reason than that they resemble the Shadow and cannot remember where they were on the nights of the attacks? How can we approve of men being locked up with no evidence pointing to them?

" 'This is an abomination of justice. A railroad job if ever there was one. Captain Hamilton Armstrong is gunning for the chief's job and will do whatever he has to in order to get a conviction. Anything to make himself look good in the eyes of the mayor. Even to the point of bullying witnesses into fingering the wrong man as the assailant.' "

Armstrong dropped the paper and pounded on his desk. "Does that little chit even know what she's saying? How could she throw such accusations around? Her first editorial was bad enough, saying we were trying to fix an election. This is worse. A hundred times worse. To accuse me of such things is unconscionable. I will not stand for it. Do you hear me? Rein her in, or I will be forced to sue her and the paper for slander. I think I will anyway. And your job might well be eliminated. Is that clear?" A vein in Armstrong's neck bulged.

Edwin rose and closed the door, clenching and unclenching his hands, forcing himself to keep inhaling deep breaths. "I was in that interrogation room with Joseph Shaklee. I saw how you tried to plant a seed of doubt in Amelia's mind. She said she couldn't identify the attacker, but you pressed her."

"That's good police business."

"Is it? Is dragging half the men of Denver, anyone with a scar and a dark mustache, into the station and holding them for as long as possible good police procedure? Not the way I was trained. In America, you are innocent until proven guilty. We've had no evidence against any of those men."

Now Armstrong's neck flamed as red as his cheeks. "And we will continue conducting those sweeps because they work. One of these days, one of these days very soon, we will get our man. Mark my words. And you will not get an ounce of credit for it, no matter what your role in the arrest is."

"That's fine with me. I'm not interested in fame or glory for myself."

"Of course not. You have your family's money."

Edwin's breathing quickened. "This has nothing to do with that. All I'm after is justice for the women who have suffered at this man's hands, and security for the women of Denver. Peace for them, knowing this menace is locked up and will never harm another one of them again."

With that, he turned on his heel and marched from the room, slamming the door behind him.

Armstrong was a twit.

But Edwin did need to speak to Polly. She was going to get him and herself in a whole lot of trouble if she didn't watch what she wrote.

Chapter 18

Miss Blythe."

While Polly crossed and uncrossed her ankles underneath her camel-colored skirt, Mr. Ward circled his entire office. She clasped her hands together to keep from fiddling with the darker brown sash around her waist.

"I told you that you could write another editorial about this so-called Silver Shadow, didn't I?"

"Yes sir, you did." In fact, he had acquiesced without too much of a struggle.

"And you wrote said editorial, did you not?"

"I did. And this time I did it with your full knowledge and consent." That should count for something.

"That may be the case, but I did not give you permission to smear the entire Denver police department and paint them with a black brush."

"I did no such thing, sir. All I did was tell the truth I have seen with my own eyes and verified with numerous sources."

"Is that so?"

"It is." She slid to the edge of the hard wooden chair. "The department is only following orders that come from Captain Armstrong. He's the one who ordered a sweep of the city and all those innocent men brought in. I was one of the witnesses he attempted to intimidate by pushing me to say that the man in front of me was the Shadow. But I didn't recognize him. I couldn't lie."

"You may be above lying, but you apparently are not above slander."

She rose to her feet as he continued his circuits of the room, a dark scowl crossing his face like a summer storm cloud. "I don't understand where this is coming from. There has never been any love lost between the police and the paper. The *Post* has never shied away from letting their feelings about the department be known. Not to mention that I did not slander a soul."

"Captain Armstrong believes you have."

"That's because he doesn't want the truth about his motives to become public knowledge. Not when he's gunning for the chief's job."

"Do you want to know what he thought of your little editorial?"

Polly thumped into her chair. No, she didn't really want to know. But Mr. Ward was going to tell her anyway. "What?"

"He thought it was a piece of trash. Worse than that, you made him angry. Angry enough that he is suing the paper for slander. And you will likely soon be slapped with a similar lawsuit."

What? A lawsuit? She'd never stepped out of line before, either in her personal or professional life. She had never been to court. If she lost, she certainly wouldn't be able to pay whatever settlement Captain Armstrong was awarded. This would be her ruin. She would have no other choice but to return home and admit to her father she was a failure.

She clasped her hands together to keep them from shaking.

"That's right, Miss Blythe. You have brought this problem on the paper and on your own head by your foolish, thoughtless, careless words. Remember that the pen is mightier than the sword. And you have cut Captain Armstrong deeply."

"This is nothing new for the *Post*. In the past, many editorials have been written about various government entities that have inflamed sentiment. To be blunt, the paper isn't known for making friends in high places. Rather the opposite."

"Inflame sentiment? Yes. Cause an uproar? Of course. But you have taken this a step too far. You don't know when to stop. How to walk that fine line between riling up people and making them madder than a nest of hornets."

"But what if all I said was true?"

"Who are the courts going to believe? The chief detective of the

Denver police force or a woman who only writes about society events?"

"Society events?" The words squeaked between her vocal cords.

"Yes, Miss Blythe. You have proven my point. Your gender should stick to writing what they know best—hearth and home. Anything else, you get yourselves into trouble."

"But, but—"

He cut her off with a wave of his hand. "That's all. You're finished for the day. Leave now—before I say something I truly regret. And if you're wise, you'll lay low and stay out of my line of sight for the next few weeks. If you can't behave, you will be fired. Is that clear?"

Polly bowed her head. "Yes, sir. But I need to wait for Detective Price to come and see me home." Heat rose underneath her collar.

"When I say now, I mean it."

"But the Shadow, sir. I shouldn't be on the streets alone."

He didn't answer, so she struggled to her feet and shuffled from the room.

When she returned to her desk, Harry grinned at her like the Cheshire Cat. "Well, well, well. That was fun."

What? Had the entire newsroom heard Mr. Ward's tirade? Polly groaned and glanced around. Thankfully, Harry was the only one left in the place.

"Nice going. Like he said, you only proved his point."

She lifted her head higher. "And what point is that?"

"That women should stay home and mind their place in the world. Why we put up with you in the workplace like this is beyond me. If you know what's good for you, go home. And stay there." Harry grabbed a stack of papers from his desk. "If you'll excuse me, I have a front-page article to turn in."

For a moment after he left, she stared at the half-written article in her typewriter. Did she turn it in or tear it into little pieces for the trash bin?

Though tears burned her eyes, a tiny smile escaped. She ripped the paper from the barrel, tore it in half, then in half again and again and again. Some of the tiny pieces fluttered to her feet like snowflakes.

She needed to get out of here.

Without bothering to pick up the scattered bits of paper, she grabbed her coat and reticule and headed for the door.

She stepped onto Sixteenth Avenue to a blanket of darkness. The streetlamps hardly cut through the deep evening. How had it gotten so late?

She turned behind her to the brick building with a glass storefront. Few lights were still on. Most of the staff had already gone for the night. No wonder the newsroom was almost empty. She hadn't really given it a second thought.

Where was Edwin? She shouldn't return to the boardinghouse without an escort. The Silver Shadow was still out there. She'd had too many encounters with him already. She gazed at the floor that held the newsroom. The other reporters must have either gone home or were out on assignment.

For the past few weeks, Edwin had walked her home in the evenings and was as prompt as the morning's sunrise. Had he gotten called away? She could hardly waltz back into the office and request Mr. Ward to walk her to the boardinghouse. No doubt, he would suffer a fit of apoplexy if she did. That would only exacerbate the situation. He'd told her to stay out of his sight. She would listen to him.

That left her with few options. What should she do?

"Watching for someone?"

Polly jumped at the voice behind her, then clutched her chest. "Valerie, you startled me."

"Oh, I'm so sorry." The switchboard operator's face softened. "I didn't mean to."

"I know. My thoughts were elsewhere."

"Perhaps on a certain handsome young man?"

She could play coy, but there was no doubt who Valerie was talking about. "He was supposed to walk me home."

"He stopped by earlier, but you were in a meeting with Mr. Ward. He had to leave but thought it would be okay if we went home together. Your place is only a few doors down from mine."

While she would miss the chats that she and Edwin had when he saw her to the boardinghouse, at least she had a solution to her problem.

The two women set out in the direction of their residences. As she moved along, Polly scanned the area around her, mindful of any men on the walk.

There weren't many. Tonight was quiet. Perhaps the cold temperatures kept most inside. She and Valerie spoke about fashion and what was going on at the office as they strolled. In no time, they arrived at Valerie's boardinghouse.

"I'll watch until you make it home."

"Thanks." The two parted ways, and Polly glanced around before setting off down the street.

She picked up her pace, her heart keeping tempo with her feet. She was almost there. Just another couple of houses or so to go. In her haste to leave the office, she hadn't pinned her hat the best she could, and now it was slipping.

She reached up to right it.

And pain shot through her wrist.

Edwin paced in the parlor of Polly's boardinghouse. When he'd asked the switchboard operator to walk home with Polly, it looked like he wouldn't be able to finish his work until much later. What a bonus that he'd been able to get off. Mrs. Mannheim informed him Polly hadn't arrived yet, but she should be here any minute.

Just as he was about to wear a hole in the carpet, a piercing cry came from outside the house. A woman's scream. A shrill, high-pitched screech of pain. He took off at a sprint, racing outside and toward the shriek. As he did so, he caught a glimpse of a shadowy figure running away.

Another assault.

"No!" His stomach jumped into his throat, cutting off his breathing as he hurried toward the victim.

By the time he reached the crowd that had gathered around the woman, the man was nowhere to be found. Though everything inside of him fought to chase the suspect, he instead went to check on the victim. "Excuse me. Let me through. I'm a police officer." The crowd parted.

There sat Polly on the ground, clutching her wrist. He stumbled backward.

"Are you all right, sir?"

The bystander's voice came from deep in a tunnel. No, he couldn't allow the fact that he knew the victim to disrupt the job he needed to do. A clamp tightening around his middle, he knelt beside Polly on the cold, hard ground. "What happened?"

"Oh, Edwin, is that really you? I—I can hardly believe it myself."

"I was waiting for you at the boardinghouse and heard a scream. I thought I saw the Shadow, but you don't appear to have a head injury." At least he hadn't spied any blood. Then again, it was quite dark, and the crowd limited what little light there was.

"He could have killed me."

His blood chilled. "Who?"

"The Shadow. It was him, I'm sure of it. He said in his letter he would get me."

"Where on your head were you hit?"

"He didn't hit me on the head."

"Are you sure? You're not making any sense. Up to this point, that's been his pattern."

"He tried to hit me on the head." She shifted positions, wincing.

The rest of his questioning could wait. He came to his feet and scooped her up.

"Oh, this is unnecessary. He didn't do anything to my legs."

He bent closer to her, catching a whiff of her sandalwood perfume. "Will you allow a gentleman to be gallant once in a while?"

That brought a soft note of laughter. "Then be gentle with me. I'm not used to this."

"I know. And it's a shame." Had those words really crossed his lips? How could he have spouted something like that? She must think him crazy. Or perhaps she would read more into it than he intended. How much did he intend?

If he was to get anywhere, he had to gather his wits again. Before he carried her to the boardinghouse, he addressed the crowd. "Did anyone see what happened? Anyone get a glimpse of the man who did this?"

The crowd stood silent. Miss Sanders, the woman who was supposed to have walked home with Polly, came forward. "I didn't take my eyes off her. It all happened so fast. He darted from between two houses, hit her, and was gone."

That was the consensus of those gathered. Though she didn't weigh much, his arms ached under Polly's weight. "If you remember anything, please contact the Denver police." He shouldn't have left two women out by themselves, but the Shadow had only ever struck women who were by themselves. And he'd thought that the distance of a couple of houses wouldn't make a difference. She wouldn't be alone that long.

How wrong he'd been.

The walk to Polly's home was short, and they arrived a few minutes later. Mrs. Mannheim met them at the door. "Oh my, oh my. Whatever happened?"

"Send for the doctor. Miss Blythe's wrist may be broken."

"It's not, I assure you," she objected.

He swept inside and deposited Polly on the davenport. "May I have a look?"

She gave him a glare that questioned his qualifications as a physician, but in the end, she nodded. Black and blue marks marred her fair skin, and her wrist had swollen to twice its size. As soon as he touched it, she winced.

"In my opinion, it's broken." He nodded to Mrs. Mannheim. "Please, send several of the girls out to summon the doctor. And make sure they stay together at all times." He didn't need another assault on his hands tonight. They had to go in a group.

He gazed at Polly, her eyes filming over with tears. He cupped her cheek. "I know you're scared, but it's going to be okay. We'll find who did this, and we'll find him soon. This can't go on forever." He prayed they would bring him into custody before another woman died.

"This has been the worst day of my life." The silvery tears spilled their banks and slid down her cheeks. Before this, she had been so strong. That facade crumbled before him. He sat on the davenport beside her and pulled her into a side hug.

"We're doing all we can to find this man. I'm thankful you weren't hit on the head. How did you manage that?"

"My hat. My silly hat was falling off, and I reached to straighten it just as he struck me."

"That was God's providence."

"I suppose. But my wrist really hurts. How am I going to type if it's broken? Mr. Ward is sore enough at me. He. . ." She turned to face him, so close her breath tickled his neck. "He took me off the Silver Shadow story. Not even a chance to compete against Harry. He put me back on the society pages. The city is suing the paper over my editorial."

Mrs. Mannheim bustled into the room. "Mary and Laura are going for the doctor. Let me get you some ice from the icebox. From the look of it, I think Mr. Price is correct in his diagnosis."

This sent a fresh stream of tears pouring from Polly's eyes. He pulled her close enough so that she leaned against his shoulder. "Do you know what Mother always says?"

A sniffle was all the answer he received.

"Things will look better in the morning."

She lifted her gaze to meet his. "In the morning, my wrist will still be broken. Mr. Ward still won't allow me to write about the Silver Shadow. And Armstrong will still be suing the newspaper. And me. I have no other choice. I'm going to have to go home to my father and tell him what a failure I am."

Chapter 19

Though no moon shone through his window and the house lay still and quiet, Edwin couldn't sleep. He tossed and turned until the quilts tangled around his legs. Another attack on yet someone else he cared about.

Cared about. He jolted upright. Why hadn't he thought of this before? How thickheaded could he be? He scrubbed his face. The idea held merit. Held a great deal of merit.

What if the Silver Shadow was singling out people who were important to him?

His shoulders sagged. No, that couldn't be it. While three women he knew had been attacked, he hadn't known the rest of them. But maybe it was a ploy on the Shadow's part to throw him off the scent. Oh, he didn't even know anymore.

Then again, Polly had received that threatening letter. It was likely the Shadow had targeted her.

He threw off the blankets, wrapped himself in a thick robe, and padded downstairs. Nancy often left a slice of cake in the icebox for him if he got in late or had an emergency call.

This qualified as an emergency.

But as he neared the kitchen, a light shone from underneath the door. Someone else was up. No time for him to enjoy a snack and try to get some thinking done. And idle conversation wasn't high on his list of things he wanted to do right now.

Still, he entered and discovered Amelia sitting at the table, forking a bit of the best chocolate cake ever into her mouth.

"Hey, that was mine."

She shot him an I-know-it grin. "You aren't the only one Nancy likes to spoil."

He sat beside her. "What has you up so late tonight?"

"Who says I'm not up early?"

She could be a little brat when she put her mind to it. He sighed.

She pushed back her plate. "Fine. I couldn't sleep either. I haven't slept well since the attack, and now with what happened to Polly tonight, I'm not sure I'll ever sleep well again."

"I understand. Until this culprit is behind bars, no one will rest easy."

Amelia peered at him, her eyes wide in her haggard face. "I'm sure this is hard on you, not being able to catch this man. You carry such a load because of what happened that night to Father. None of us blame you. You know that, don't you?"

That night. Father. No, he couldn't think about that now. Couldn't dwell on it and allow it to make him a two-time failure. Maybe more. He had to focus on the case right in front of him. "Do you think it's possible the Shadow is targeting women I know in particular?"

"You knew all of the victims?"

"No."

"Then I think that theory collapses like a chair under the weight of a fat man."

"Very poetic for the middle of the night."

Amelia cracked a small smile.

"Whether he is or not, I have to consider all possibilities. And I have to do something toward capturing him. Sitting behind my desk all day interviewing the string of men that Armstrong parades through the station isn't helping anything."

Amelia pushed the cake toward Edwin. "I can see by the way you're scrunching your forehead that you're formulating a plan."

He took a bite of the moist cake. Boy, no one baked like Nancy. "You know me too well."

"I learned how to read you so I wouldn't be surprised when there was a snake in my bed."

"You're right." He went to the icebox and poured himself a glass of milk. "Want one?"

Amelia shook her head. "No. What I want is to know what this plan of yours is."

"Since the posse disbanded, I'm going to take over patrolling the area where the Shadow has struck the most."

Amelia bit her lip. "By yourself?"

"What other choice do I have? Polly's editorial got her into a vat of hot oil, but she was right. Armstrong's only out for himself. He'll do whatever he has to in order to make himself look good."

"So you're going through with it?" Amelia grasped him by the hand. "Yes, I am."

"Be careful, big brother. I couldn't stand it if anything happened to you. This family has lost too much already."

Friday, January 18, 1901

Another society event to cover. Polly sighed as she left the boarding-house for a gathering in the posh Capitol Hill area of the city. Some women might consider such an assignment exciting. Getting to attend the best parties in Denver, meet all the right people, perhaps even make a good match for herself.

But not Polly. She didn't fit in, not the child of poor working parents. She hadn't had a mother to teach her how to behave properly or how to dress like a lady. She'd learned about etiquette in school, but it was the girls at the boardinghouse who had taught her which clothes were the most fashionable and how to wear her hair.

Action. Excitement. Thrills. That's what got Polly's mouth salivating and her heart pumping. Her stories should contribute something good to the world. Teach people something or help them in some way.

Thankfully, Mr. Ward had agreed to pay for a hired carriage for her so she wouldn't have to walk the streets after dark. Her wrist, now set in a splint, ached like the dickens. A warm cup of tea and a soft bed called to her. But not tonight.

Crowds were thin right now, even though it was quitting time at most businesses. Wait. Just ahead, she spied a familiar ginger-haired man in a long brown coat. It had to be Edwin. No one else carried himself quite so straight and tall as he did.

For a moment, he disappeared. When he turned, she spotted him again. But it wasn't another street he turned down. No, it was an alley. What was he doing back there?

He was up to something. They said reporters could sniff out a story. Whoever they were was right.

Hang the party. This was more important. At the very least, it had to be more exciting. She tapped on the roof to get the carriage driver to stop. Once he reined the horses to a halt, he jumped down and opened the door for her. "Are you sure you're wanting to get out, miss? It's terribly dangerous for women on the streets these days. I was to deliver you safe and sound."

The pain in her wrist pulled her back. She might be putting herself in harm's way. For what? A story? Recognition? No. To help make the streets safe so she would be the last woman the Silver Shadow would hurt. Whatever happened, it would be worth it. "It's fine. I won't be alone." Because she was going to find out what Edwin was up to. "Don't worry. I won't get you in trouble with Mr. Ward for this."

The driver tipped his hat, climbed back into the seat, and headed down the street.

When Polly approached the alley Edwin had disappeared down, she slipped in after him. Long evening shadows hid him until her eyes adjusted to the dim light. He stood against the opposite building, peering around the corner, so intent on whatever he was watching that he hadn't seen her arrive.

"Edwin."

He jumped and clutched his chest then spun around, his hand on the gun at his hip. "Polly? What on earth are you doing here?"

"I could ask you the same question."

"But you won't."

"I will. What are you doing here?"

"Polly, please go home. Now. Before it gets any darker. You shouldn't be here."

"You're on the lookout for the Silver Shadow, aren't you?"

"Yes, I am. That's why I don't want you here. You're only putting yourself and me in danger. If I do spot him, who knows what he'll do? Run? Shoot? No, I can't take that chance. Look at what he's already done to you."

A place deep inside her warmed. He cared about her. Other than her brother, no man had ever shown her such concern. Not Mr. Ward. Certainly not Pa. But this was her big shot. Maybe the city would relent and drop their lawsuit. "I'm staying."

He rubbed his bloodshot eyes, black leather gloves covering his hands. "I was afraid you were going to say that."

She settled in across the alley from him so she could watch the other side of the road. "Besides, you need me."

"Father used to warn me that women were always right." Edwin said it with resignation in his voice.

Polly chuckled. "He was a wise man."

"How's your wrist?"

She held up the broken appendage. "Throbbing. It's hard to type with one hand too. Took me forever to write up the christening announcement for the Hill's new baby."

"I can imagine. Sorry it's so painful for you."

"The wrist or having to write a christening announcement?"

"Both. You'll get your break. You're too good of a reporter not to."

"If I have a job after all is said and done." What would she do if she lost everything? "Maybe I should speak to the chief about this lawsuit. Is he a reasonable man?"

"Hard-nosed and by the book, but it couldn't hurt. You do have a way of bringing people around to your way of thinking."

"Thank you. That's the nicest thing anyone has ever said to me."

Edwin chuckled. "You're welcome."

They returned to their respective watches. Several women scurried along the road, no doubt anxious to be home before the Silver Shadow slunk out of hiding. They carried bags or pushed prams, the babies tucked in with piles of blankets.

Men wrapped in heavy overcoats and carrying briefcases sauntered down the street. A few couples were out and about, some of them with dogs on leashes. It was far too cold for a leisurely stroll.

Several times Polly opened the top buttons of her heavy wool coat and checked the gold watch pinned to her shirtwaist. Had the minute hand even moved?

Because she was coming from work, she hadn't dressed for standing in the cold for hours. Her thin leather boots weren't doing the job. Her toes were frozen. Her nose and cheeks stung. And the frigid temperatures exacerbated the pain in her wrist.

Edwin took a step or two toward the street. Polly dashed across the alley and peered over his shoulder. "Do you see something?"

"What about that man?" He pointed to one in a gray ulster coat with a crush hat on his head.

She leaned over farther. He was the right build. The coat and hat were similar to what the perpetrator had worn. "No, I don't think so. He's too tall. Too well dressed."

Edwin slid back into the shadows. "I'm beginning to doubt we'll ever catch him. I thought this was a good idea, but now I'm not so sure."

"It's something, and that's more than I can say for some at the department."

He turned his attention to her, his stare hard but not unfeeling. "But is it enough? Is it the right course of action? You do have to admit that Captain Armstrong has brought in an impressive list of suspects."

"I would hardly call them suspects. Just a bunch of men he swept from flophouses and saloons. And you haven't looked into Harry yet, have you?"

He blew out a breath. "No. I don't know. Maybe we should. It's no crazier than skulking about in an alley hoping the Shadow walks by. Would he stroll down the street, as if he didn't have a care in the world?"

"He must go out other than just to knock women over the head. He has to get groceries and other supplies, if nothing else, and maybe even go to work."

"So I'm not out of my mind for doing this?"

"I don't think so. You're doing what you have to in order to keep the streets safe for all the city's women. It's a good thing."

"Thanks for the encouragement. I needed that."

Polly returned to her post. Was Edwin right? Would the Shadow stroll down the same street where he had committed most of his crimes, mixing in with regular people going about their business? It could be that he lived miles from here. Maybe not even in Denver but in one of the outlying mining towns.

She continued to scan the crowds, which were a little heavier now. The women who were out, for the most part, were escorted by men. Either that, or they walked in groups. Good. They weren't giving the Shadow an opportunity to strike again.

She hugged herself to ward off the increasing cold. The buildings blocked the wind but did nothing to raise the temperature. Dressed as she was in a thin shirtwaist and wool skirt, she wouldn't be able to remain here much longer.

Wait a minute. Was that. . .? Could it be? Was it possible, or was she making herself try to believe it so this nightmare would end? He had his back to her, but he was the right height and wore the exact coat and hat that the Shadow had. He glanced over his shoulder, and she spotted his droopy black mustache. Wouldn't the Shadow have shaved it off by now?

The goose bumps that broke out now had nothing to do with the cold.

This could be their man. Then again, so many had been so wrong before.

"Edwin." She whispered as loud as she dared. He didn't acknowledge her. "Edwin."

This time he turned. "What?"

"That might be him."

"Really?"

"Maybe. Come here." Her legs trembled.

He did so, this time peering over her shoulder. "Which one?"

She pointed him out.

"Listen to me." Though quiet, his voice was firm. "I'm going to approach him. You stay here. No following me. If this is him, he might recognize you. He's threatened you and gotten to you once already. This is important. I won't have you jeopardizing your life for a news story. Do you understand?"

"Of course. Just hurry. He's getting away."

Chapter 20

Edwin had him. There he was, right in front of him, possibly the Silver Shadow, the man who had wreaked so much havoc on their city. And he was strolling down the street as if he didn't have a care in the world.

As a detective, Edwin didn't wear a uniform, so he wouldn't spook the man as he approached him. He could go up to him, maybe bump into him, and arrest him then and there.

No one had to get hurt. It would be easy.

And then Rachel and Amelia and all the other victims would have their justice.

The only problem was that an arrest was seldom as easy as it first appeared. He swallowed hard.

With one last narrow-eyed warning glance over his shoulder at Polly, Edwin moved from the shadows and merged into the flow of people going about their business on this bitter January evening. Everyone scurried, eager to get out of the cold. Eager to be in front of their fires once again.

Though every muscle in his body ached to break into a sprint and tackle the suspect on the sidewalk, he restrained himself. If he came at the Shadow too fast, he might start a chase. Or he might have a fight on his hands. And if the Shadow was armed with the pipe he used to slug women, Edwin might be in trouble. The suspect could attack him before he had a chance to draw his weapon.

Inhaling a deep breath of bracing air, Edwin zigzagged his way through the crowd, his pace rapid, his pulse pounding in rhythm.

Though the Shadow's crush hat bobbed up and down, never did Edwin allow the man out of his sight. If he did, he might not pick him up again.

The Shadow threaded his way through those out and about, always keeping just far enough in front of Edwin that he couldn't nab him.

Almost like he had a sixth sense informing him there was a cop behind him.

Edwin fisted his hands. Though he bumped into a woman loaded down with bags of groceries and into a businessman whose briefcase burst open, spilling papers into the street, Edwin didn't break off his pursuit. He just apologized and kept going.

In the cold, his lungs burned, but he kept up his pace.

Up ahead, there was a lull in the crowd. A break where there weren't any people. Now in front of the Shadow was a woman. Alone.

He pressed himself, going as fast as he could. He had to reach the Shadow.

Before he struck again.

Edwin brushed by a woman with two children in tow. "Excuse me."

"Watch where you're going. You could have knocked down one of my kids."

"Apologies." That was the only word he had time for.

The incident slowed him more. The Shadow was farther ahead now than when Edwin had started yet still within striking distance. He willed his legs to move faster.

The menace came ever closer to the woman. Edwin had to hurry. Couldn't let this happen again. Couldn't fail to protect those he was responsible for.

"Come on, Edwin, he's almost up to her. We can't let him get away."

Polly. Where had she come from?

He never removed his gaze from the Shadow, now almost within reach of the woman. In a slow jog, Edwin drew closer to them. Other than the woman and the Shadow, the road in front of him was deserted. Light spilled from storefront windows. In the distance, a dog barked. Another one, throatier, answered.

Without warning, the Shadow turned the corner, away from the woman, to a residential area where Edwin knew men sat and read the paper while their wives cooked dinner. Edwin followed. When he got around the corner, however, the Shadow was nowhere to be found.

Picking up his pace, Edwin peered between buildings. He peeked into an alley. Nothing but litter and refuse. Thank goodness the snow and cold kept down the stench.

Polly was no longer following him. What if the Shadow had turned to follow her? He had to find him. Them.

He tried several more alleys, all with the same result. The darkness deepened, and he had a difficult time making anything out in the gloom. For all he knew, the Shadow might have ducked behind some bushes. He might have slipped into one of the homes on this street. He might have doubled back.

One thing was for certain.

The elusive culprit—if it had been him—had vanished, like a shadow when clouds obscure the sky.

Polly. His heart tripped over itself. What if the Shadow had caught up to her?

He had to locate her.

Before she met the same sinister fate as Rachel.

Polly couldn't keep up with Edwin. A well-trained police officer, he was stronger and faster than she was. She didn't want to hinder him in apprehending the Shadow or saving that poor, unsuspecting woman, but at the same time, she didn't want to miss out on the story. If she could present that to Mr. Ward, perhaps he would relent and allow her to return to reporting real stories.

While it was a long shot, it was the only option she had.

Perhaps she could take a different route and head off the Shadow. A tremor shot through her at the thought of running into him again. He could have killed her last night. At the very least, she should be recovering from a head wound.

She had suffered a broken wrist. How would she apprehend him with only one good hand?

She had to be crazy for doing this. Did a job mean this much? Then an image of her father flashed in front of her eyes, the scowl on his face the stamp of stern disapproval.

She could do it. She would do it. The first step was to find him. When the rest happened, she would worry about it then.

She rounded the block, then headed in the direction they had last seen the Shadow. As she crossed the side street, she glanced both ways. The only one around was Edwin. No sign of the woman in front of the Shadow.

At that thought, Polly blew out a breath.

When Edwin ducked into an alley, she scooted across the street and continued onward. She crossed and recrossed streets, always aware of her surroundings. No chance of the Shadow coming behind her again.

The Shadow had never struck two nights in a row. Usually there were weeks between attacks. Armed with this knowledge, she relaxed a little. But just a little. He could change his pattern. He could seek her out specifically. If she had seen him, likely he had seen her. Her breath hitched, and not just from scurrying about.

By this time, she had wandered so far, none of the streets held any familiarity. This area of town was shabbier. The painted names in the storefront windows were faded. A stoop here and there was crooked. Smaller houses sagged, crowded together.

Where was she? She swallowed hard. She was so numb now, the cold didn't even bite anymore. Though she rubbed her hands together and spun in a circle, she couldn't get her bearings.

By now Edwin must have caught the culprit. She had missed out on the biggest story of her life. The one that might finally win her some recognition in people's eyes.

What was she going to do? Her growling stomach reminded her that she had missed dinner. Mrs. Mannheim wouldn't approve of her being out so late wandering the streets.

She didn't want to be out so late wandering the streets.

Wait. Up ahead there. Sudden warmth displaced the chill in her body. A slight man in a gray ulster coat with a crush cap. It had to be the man she'd seen earlier. He must have gotten away from Edwin.

If she knew where Edwin was, she could lead the Shadow to him so he could make the arrest. But she had no idea where she was, much less Edwin. No, it was up to her.

Yes, yes, she could follow him home. Find out where he lived. Then Edwin could go to his residence and arrest him there. It was perfect. She wouldn't put herself in danger, but she would lead the police right to the suspect they had been searching for all these months.

Edwin couldn't object to such a plan.

For several blocks, she followed the Shadow, maintaining a good distance between him and herself. Too bad she didn't have shopping bags or a Bible to make it appear like she had a purpose for being out at this time of night. No matter. As long as she kept her footfalls soft, he would never know she was behind him.

He slowed, perhaps ready to turn into one of the houses. She didn't let her gaze leave him for even a moment. This was it.

Just then she hit a patch of ice, and her foot slid out from underneath her. For a heart-stopping split second, she floated before descending. She was falling. And there was nothing she could do about it.

With a thud and a crack, she hit the frozen road. Pain shot from her wrist through her arm. A scream broke from her lips. She couldn't breathe.

The Shadow turned. No, oh no, he was headed in her direction. Biting her lip, she braced herself with her good left hand and scrambled to her feet.

He approached. He couldn't see her up close. If he did, he might recognize her. And then there was no telling what he would do.

She jumped to her feet and, clutching her skirts with her good hand, she spun and ran in the opposite direction, not bothering to turn to find out if he followed. That would slow her too much. Tears leaked from her eyes. She couldn't give in to them. Somehow, some way, no matter how afraid she was and how much pain she was in, she couldn't allow him to catch her.

A stitch in her side slowed her. Up ahead, on a cross street, several people scurried in and out of her view. If only she could make it there, she would be safe. Perhaps she would be able to figure out where she was and get back to the boardinghouse.

Everything would be fine.

As she headed toward the busy street, she repeated those words to herself.

She was almost there. By now pain and cold had numbed her to everything else. So close. Maybe there was a restaurant where she could get a cup of coffee.

Just a block. She had to keep moving forward. Now a couple hundred feet.

Someone reached out and grabbed her. Her heart jumped into her throat.

A deep, muffled voice spoke in her ear. "Just where do you think you're going?"

Chapter 21

Reaching across her body, the man, the Shadow, tightened his grip on Polly's bicep, cutting off the circulation to her hand. A surge of adrenaline shot through her veins, and she bit his arm. He didn't release his grasp. No wonder. All she got was a mouthful of wool coat.

She had to get away. This man had killed before, without a second thought. Nothing was stopping him from killing again. She wriggled in his hold. At least she tried to squirm. Move at all. Impossible. So she kicked him. Hard. In the shins.

At last his release slackened, and she freed herself. Like a bullet from a gun, she sped away.

"Polly, wait."

She stopped in her tracks. The deep voice was familiar. Why hadn't she recognized it before? "Edwin?"

"Yes, it's me."

Taking her time, she spun around. There he stood, a little sparkle in his eyes, even in the dim light. "Oh goodness." Her cold cheeks heated. "I can't believe I. . . Please, please forgive me. I thought you were the Shadow."

He approached her. "You had me scared out of my wits thinking the Shadow had gotten to you. Mrs. Mannheim is furious with me for allowing you to wander the streets alone."

"You checked at the boardinghouse?"

"I did. You're going to have to volunteer to wash and dry the dishes for a month to make up for the fright you've given the poor woman."

"And what about how you scared me out of my skin by grabbing me?"

"I called to you several times. Didn't you hear me?"

She shook her head. "I must have been too intent on getting away from what I thought was the Shadow. But surely you must have caught him. Tell me you have him in custody."

The brightness left Edwin's face. "I'm afraid not. He got away. Again. If it was even him."

Polly sagged. All at once, the cold seeped through to her bones, and she couldn't stop shivering. Edwin drew her to himself again, this time his hold gentle but warm.

"Slippery as a tadpole, he is. I don't know what it's going to take for us to catch him. And by us, I mean the police department. You shouldn't be out chasing him."

"Why not? You need the help."

"You broke the cardinal rule of law enforcement. Always be aware of your surroundings. In this day and age, that goes for being on the street alone."

"I thought I could head him off or send him your way."

"Has anyone ever told you that you are the most hardheaded woman?"

"Plenty of people. But in order to be taken seriously, I have to be."

"I can see that you're frozen to the core. Let me walk you home. You need a hot cup of tea and a warm bath. Perhaps I can even smooth things over with Mrs. Mannheim for you."

"Thank you. I appreciate it. Though Mrs. Mannheim might not allow you in the door. No gentleman callers after nine. It must be long past that by now."

"I imagine it is."

The frigid air dampened their conversation as they made their way to where Polly lived. How good it was to be in familiar territory again. She had lived in Denver for three years and knew much of the city, but she had gotten so turned around. Edwin was correct. A bath and a warm drink would set everything to rights.

As soon as they entered the cozy, lamplit parlor of the boardinghouse, Mrs. Mannheim bustled in from the kitchen, waving an envelope in her hand. "It's about time you're home. I'm glad Mr. Price was able to locate you. You have to stop scaring an old woman like me."

"You aren't old." Polly kissed Mrs. Mannheim on her sunken cheek. "And I'm sorry to have given you such a fright. I got turned around in the dark, that's all. I'll be fine as soon as I warm through."

"Perhaps this will do it." Mrs. Mannheim handed Polly the envelope.

She stared at the familiar scrawl that spelled out the address. Her father.

Could this night get any worse?

"What's wrong?"

Edwin's voice at Polly's side startled her. Hadn't he left? "Nothing."

"Your cheeks turned from pink to white in the space of a second."

"Just a letter from my father."

Still Edwin remained standing beside her.

Oh, he was probably waiting for a little gratitude. "Thank you so much for seeing me home. And for finding me. I'm sorry I put you to so much trouble. At least I can report that we saw the Shadow tonight. Perhaps it will bring a few more leads. And we know what neighborhood he frequents."

"We might have seen him. We can't be sure. Just promise me you won't get yourself into any more trouble like that." His tone was somber and his gaze hard and unflinching.

"I promise. I think I'll go upstairs and read my letter now. Thank you again, Mr. Price." Mrs. Mannheim hadn't left the room and wouldn't think it was proper for Polly to address Edwin by his first name.

"Good night, then. Sleep well."

"Thank you for everything, Mr. Price." Mrs. Mannheim showed him to the door as Polly dashed upstairs.

Her heart pounded, and not from the race to the second floor. Pa hardly ever wrote. His only response to any of the articles she had sent him was to tell her not to send them anymore. Everything she knew about her father, she learned from Lyle.

With a band tightening around her chest, she ripped open the envelope and unfolded the paper inside.

Polly,

He couldn't even address her as dear.

> *A friend of mine from church has brought to my attention your latest editorial in the newspaper and has informed me that you have stirred up a pot of trouble by writing this piece. There is even news that the police department might sue you for slander. And then who would be stuck with the bill?*
>
> *When you put pen to paper, do you ever stop to think about the consequences of your actions? How it might affect not only you but the rest of your family?*
>
> *I have tolerated your reckless behavior for long enough. Working as a reporter in a big city, living alone in a house with nothing but women, isn't befitting any daughter of mine. Other parents with loose morals may allow it, but I have come to the end of my patience and have seen the error of my ways.*
>
> *Since you have not returned of your own accord (even the prodigal son did so), I will be sending Lyle to collect you and deliver you home as soon as he can get away.*

What did Pa think she was? Nothing more than a package to be picked up and dropped off at the appropriate address?

> *You may expect him within a few days of this letter, so be prepared to come home. Do not delay him. He has much work to do and cannot be held up.*

A few days? That meant Lyle could be here anytime.

But she was so close to nabbing the biggest story of her career. She couldn't leave now. As soon as she and Edwin captured the Shadow, Mr. Ward would be forced to recognize the good work she was doing.

No. She wouldn't leave. No matter what Pa said. What could Lyle do? Tie her up and drag her home?

He sat at the kitchen table and spooned soup into his mouth, his hand shaking so much that he spilled most of it down the front of his shirt.

Curses. He couldn't allow those tailing him to fluster him. That would never do. Remain calm. Don't panic. At least Detective Price didn't know where he lived.

The call tonight had been a little too close for comfort. He wasn't even planning an attack. Was just strolling home after a drink or two at the saloon. Nothing bad. Nothing most men hadn't done at least a few times in their lives. Maybe more.

But the game was now wearisome to him. Yes, some had changed their behavior. Some had not. There were still plenty of women, he noticed tonight, who were out and about without any escorts. Who knew what they were doing?

Like that one who was right ahead of him. If he hadn't attacked Polly Blythe the previous night, the one tonight would have been a prime target. Then again, Polly Blythe was the one that needed to be taken down a peg or two. He rubbed his hands together.

But why were the police chasing him? He was doing them a favor. He was doing all mankind a favor. He was saving marriages and preserving families by making sure that women were in their rightful places.

Not like that snoopy female reporter. If only the blow he had dealt her had knocked some sense into her. Made her see reason. Or perhaps it was her father that needed some sense knocked into him. No respectable man who had his daughter's best interests at heart would allow her to strut the streets the way she did and hold a job that belonged to a man.

Giving up on the soup, he pushed the bowl away and rubbed his aching shoulder. What was it going to take for the men of Denver to wake up and keep their women in their rightful place? For women to see that it was best if they were at home with their husbands and families? The outside world held nothing but danger for them. They needed their men to protect them.

Running out on the men who took care of them would be wrong.

Very wrong. They would be too scared to do it.

What should his next move be? Whatever it was, it had to be dramatic. These attacks, one or two a night several weeks apart, were not working. He had to change tactics. Really get himself and his cause noticed.

But what? What would do the trick? He tapped his chin for a minute or two.

Yes, yes, that was it. What a brilliant idea. Why hadn't he thought of it before? There was that one night, right at the beginning, when he had attacked three women. That had gotten attention. A lot of it. That was when the people finally took notice of what he was doing.

There had to be a night, just the perfect night, when he could wreak havoc on the city. Make them finally understand what he was trying to tell them. They would be forced to listen to him then.

He clapped his hands a couple of times and allowed a small smile to bloom on his face. That's how good this plan was.

It wouldn't bring her back. He clenched his fists and ground his teeth. That was the worst part of it all. She would never be his again. She and her baby belonged to another man. God would have to deal with them for the heinous acts they committed, how they broke His Word.

But if he could save one man, just one man, from the ridicule, the censure, the derision he had endured, then what he was about to do would be worth it.

God had given him the job to bring order to the world again. And that's just what he would do.

Chapter 22

Monday, January 21, 1901

What's got you down, Polly?" Harry leaned over her typewriter, his breath stinking of onions and cigars and perhaps even a little whiskey. Enough to churn the breakfast she'd eaten.

"What do you want, Harry? I'm busy."

"Busy writing the society column. Did you know that another woman was almost attacked on Arapahoe Street last night?"

She lurched back in her chair so hard it almost tipped over. She fought to keep her mouth from falling open. "How did you know that?"

"I have my ways."

If she could have shifted back any farther, she would have. She kept her words as light as possible. "What ways would those be?"

"You don't really need to know, do you? Especially now that you aren't writing the Silver Shadow stories. That's my job now, isn't it?"

"Yes, but it is curious how you know about an attack that didn't even happen. How did you come by such information?"

"Like I said, that's my business, not yours."

Did he know these things because he was connected to the case? Part of it? The perpetrator?

Ridiculous. If he was, he wouldn't be crowing over her like he was now. He'd not show his hand. One thing you had to give Harry credit for, he was smart.

"Now, you'd better get back to your little fluff story before Ward gets really sore with you and fires you. Then again, it would be nice to return the newsroom to the way it should be." Harry slunk off like the slime he was.

She studied him as he settled at his desk. He was just goading her, that was all. That was all it could possibly be.

Then again, he did have a small scar above his right eye. But did it match the scar she'd seen on the other man?

Even if it did, that didn't make him the Shadow. Right?

Right. The zoo at the police station a few months back was proof that there were many men who could fit this description. None of them had proven to be the Shadow. Besides, what would a respectable man like Harry—no matter what she thought of him, he hadn't ever been in trouble as far as she knew—be doing skulking about the city, whacking women over the head?

She rubbed the splint on her wrist. Then again, he did know her. Knew she was working with Edwin to try to solve the case. That was a well-known fact around the office. Especially after Mr. Ward gave her that dressing down about her editorial.

Now, not only did her wrist throb but so did her head. Harry was right about one thing. She couldn't get on Mr. Ward's bad side. She had to get this article written and to press fast or she would endure his wrath again.

And pecking it out on the typewriter was an all-day chore.

But peck away she did.

About halfway through the article, a shadow fell over her desk. She glanced up through her eyelashes. A tall, thin man with a full beard stood over her. She jumped up, knocking her knee on her desk. Forget the pain.

Lyle was here.

In a flash, she was around her desk and enveloped in his hug. "Good to see you, Pols."

She squeezed him back. "I'm glad you're here. Although I wish it were under different circumstances."

"So you got Pa's letter."

"I did." She stepped from his embrace. "He shouldn't have made you leave work to come here to fetch me."

"Let me guess. You have no intention of going anywhere."

"You know me too well."

He glanced at her wrist. "What happened to you?"

"Just a little, um, accident." She stared at the floor.

"Oh no you don't. I can tell when you're lying. And that's exactly what you're doing now."

"But if I tell you, you'll send me straight home to Pa." She stamped her foot like a five-year-old. "You can't let him know what happened. Promise me that?" Now she gazed into his eyes, ones that mirrored her own.

"When you look at me like that, you know I can't deny you anything."

"And when I kept Willy Williams from beating you up on the playground because you were smart, you said you would pay me back someday. That day has arrived."

"You remember something from fifteen years ago?"

"I sure do."

"Fine. I promise not to tattle on you."

She shared with him what had transpired with the Shadow. "But I'm fine. My wrist will heal good as new, that's what the doctor says. Right now it's slowing me down in my work, but not for long."

"Can you take a break? Let's go somewhere we can talk."

"Sure." She informed Mr. Ward she was going for lunch and allowed Lyle to escort her to a nearby restaurant. Of course she knew that every Monday Edwin came here at noon, so running into him would be a bonus.

They settled at a white-cloth-covered table, and once they had placed their orders, Lyle leaned on his elbows, his face mere inches from hers. "I have to tell you, I tend to agree with Pa."

"You can't. You've always been the one to stick up for me to him. Without your persuasive arguments, he would never have allowed me to take this job."

"You threatened to run away from home if he didn't relent. In a way, you did, when you left right after your argument. Pa never said in so many words that you could do this."

"But I'm doing well. I've even had a couple front-page articles."

"This is dangerous."

"Not anymore. I'm back to the society pages, so that should make you feel better. Please, I'm begging you, don't take me home. I want to stay. I'm happy here. Really, really happy. And I'm careful not to be out at night without an escort."

Lyle sighed and leaned back in his chair. "I don't know what Pa expects me to do. I can't tie you up and drag you onto the train by your hair."

For the first time since Pa's letter had arrived, a weight lifted from her chest. Almost like a criminal who was granted a stay of execution. She jumped out of her chair and hugged Lyle around the neck. "I can't thank you enough."

"I'm going to have to tell Pa that you refused to budge. You do know that might be enough to bring him here himself. Then you won't be able to say no."

Just like that, the weight landed square on her breastbone, crushing the air from her lungs.

Edwin studied the small man with a scar above his right eye as Armstrong led him through the police station to the interrogation room. His dirty, wrinkled clothes hung on him, and he mumbled to himself. Once he had deposited the man in there, Armstrong returned to the main office and stood at the front of the room. "May I have your attention, everyone?" Armstrong straightened and stuck out his chest. The din of conversation and clatter of typewriters ceased. "Thank you. This morning we have a new arrest in the Silver Shadow case."

Groans rose from the group, Edwin's among them. Not another one. By now Armstrong had paraded half of Denver's male population through here. Edwin wouldn't be surprised when it was his turn to be questioned.

"Now, now. I'm confident this time we have our man."

O'Fallon leaned over to Edwin. "He says that every time."

All Edwin could do was nod.

"I have called a press conference for this afternoon at four o'clock to announce the Shadow's capture. Tonight I want our city's women to walk the streets with confidence, knowing they are safe from this menace. He's a lunatic, which we always knew was true about the Shadow."

Every man Armstrong dragged in, he declared to be crazy. Insane.

Out of his mind. That might be true. But being off in the head didn't automatically make someone guilty.

"As you know, there was another attempted attack last night on an older woman walking home from a prayer meeting." Armstrong's voice echoed through the room. "The victim said the suspect was wearing a uniform of some sort. In the residence of the man I just brought in, we discovered a pair of dark blue trousers, a shirt and coat of similar color, and a billed hat the Shadow could have used to fool the victim into believing he was with the police department.

"Thank you for your attention. Price, O'Fallon, I'd like to see you in my office in five minutes."

"Wonder what he wants?" O'Fallon frowned.

Edwin shuffled a few papers on his desk. "Probably to crow about how he caught the Shadow and we weren't able to crack the case."

"But you don't believe this is the man?"

"Who's to say?" Maybe he was. Maybe he wasn't. He and Polly could have been chasing him last night. This woman who was almost attacked? There were other muggers roaming the streets. It might have been one of them. Especially with this description of a uniform. That was new. Nothing Amelia had mentioned. Nothing any of the victims had described. In fact, they had all mentioned a gray ulster coat.

A few minutes later, Edwin was in Armstrong's office, O'Fallon beside him, both shifting in their chairs under the captain's intense scrutiny. "Well, Price, what do you think about this arrest? Jack Maryuissen is our guy. I'm sure of it."

Edwin swallowed hard. "I hope you're right, sir."

"But you don't think I am."

Edwin picked a piece of lint from his brown pants.

"Spit it out. Be a man and say what's on your mind."

That broke the dam holding back the torrent of words in Edwin's mouth. "I don't know. What I do know is that you can't keep bringing in men without basis for charges. The media is raking us over the coals for this, and so is the public."

Armstrong gripped the arms of his chair so hard his knuckles turned white. "And that's your fault for bringing in that little reporter and feeding her all this confidential information."

"I object to that." Edwin came to his feet. "I haven't told her anything that isn't on the record. You're the one who makes these grandiose announcements to the department, only to have to retract them a few days later. You're making us appear inept."

Armstrong's face reddened until it was as bright as a campfire. "You are dismissed. Both of you. This case is closed. No more investigation."

Was he afraid they would discover that once again he had brought in the wrong man?

"And I warn you. Both of you." Armstrong swung his gaze between Edwin and O'Fallon. "Your conduct right now and over the past few months has not been becoming of officers of the law. Watch what you say to that reporter. Otherwise you'll find yourselves out of jobs. Am I clear?"

"Crystal, sir." O'Fallon stood and saluted.

As they left the office and made their way to their desks, Edwin adjusted his glasses and sighed. "I don't know what to make of this latest arrest."

"Armstrong must be really sure of it this time, because he's calling a press conference. If he's confident enough to do that, I'd say this case is closed."

"But what about the woman who made that narrow escape last night?" Had he and Polly wasted their time last night chasing the wrong guy? "What do you make of her reporting that the culprit was dressed in a police uniform?"

"He might have changed his tactics and worn different clothes to throw us off his trail." O'Fallon sank into the chair at his desk. "I have a good feeling about this. I think this time we have our man."

Edwin sifted through the pile of papers in front of him. "I hope you're right. But think back to October when he was sure it was George Turner. Or David Pace in November. Then there was Joseph Shaklee a week ago."

"But did you see this Jack Maryuissen? He's a lunatic. Slovenly, talks to himself. Certifiably insane."

"That doesn't make him guilty."

"What about the uniform they found in his place?"

"It might well be that he attempted to attack that woman last night. But that doesn't make him the Shadow."

"I guess time will tell. Let's see what happens with Maryuissen. Remember, Armstrong told us no more investigating. I plan to listen to him. I need this job if Susan and I are going to get married."

Edwin gulped. He had no intention of backing off the investigation. Even if it cost him his position.

Chapter 23

E dwin, you're finally here." It was all Polly could do not to jump out of her chair in the restaurant.

He gazed at Lyle, his green-eyed stare icy. Why? He'd never met her brother before. "You were waiting for me?"

"Yes. I wanted to introduce you to my brother, Lyle."

Edwin's face softened. Could it be that he'd been jealous, thinking Lyle was her beau? Her heart fluttered. A man had never thought that way about her before.

"It's nice to meet you, Lyle." The two men shook hands. Edwin tipped his head and stared at Polly, like he was asking her a question.

She took her napkin from her lap and placed it on the table. "We were getting ready to leave. I want to show Lyle where I live so he can report to Pa that I'm perfectly safe and doing well here. That's what the letter I received from Pa was about. He's sent Lyle to fetch me home, but my brother is on my side and will have none of it."

She and Lyle came to their feet.

"I'll walk with you. That will give me a chance to get to know you." Edwin nodded at her brother.

"But you'll miss your lunch."

"I'm sure I can find an old sandwich stuffed somewhere in my desk." When she sucked in a breath, he laughed. "Don't worry about me. I'm fine."

"If you're sure." They made their way out the door and down the street toward the boardinghouse.

Edwin's strides were long and hurried. "I didn't have much time for lunch anyway. Captain Armstrong has called a news conference at four o'clock."

She gave a little squeal. "Does that mean they nabbed him? Do they have the right man this time? Did our detective work pay off?"

"No. This man supposedly attempted to attack an older woman last night a good number of blocks from where we were. While Armstrong is convinced this is the man in last night's case and in the Silver Shadow's, I don't know if they are related." He relayed the woman's description of the uniform.

Her shoulders sagged, and she slowed her pace.

Lyle grasped Edwin by the upper arm, pulling him to a halt. "That means the man who injured my sister continues to roam free, ready to strike again?"

"It's possible. It's also possible he's behind bars." Edwin shook his head.

Polly stopped too. That wasn't what she needed him to say to her brother. He could still change his mind and force her to return to Pa. But she wouldn't go willingly.

Edwin folded his arms. "We're close to cracking this case though. I feel it in my bones. Sooner or later, he's going to make a mistake. We'll nab him then."

"Can you assure me my sister will be safe?" Lyle mimicked Edwin's stance and frowned.

Edwin dropped his arms to his sides. "Even if it weren't for the Silver Shadow, no woman should be without an escort in the evenings. That's just common sense when you live in a city, whether it be Denver or New York or Chicago. Polly is smart."

Lyle tsked. "You could have been killed."

Polly touched his arm. "But I wasn't."

When they resumed their walk, the men chatted about various topics, most of which Polly tuned out. Before long they arrived at her residence and climbed the steps to the front porch. "See, Lyle, it's a nice place. Not run down a bit. And it's in a good neighborhood." No need in telling him that she and Sophie had been attacked right outside the front door.

As Polly entered with the men, Mrs. Mannheim was coming down the stairs with a dust rag in her hand. She shook her head. "You know when visiting hours are, Miss Blythe. And aren't you supposed to be at work?"

"You remember Detective Price, I believe."

"Oh yes. He was here when both you and Sophie were attacked."

Lyle tugged on Polly's arm. "Someone else here was a victim?"

Mrs. Mannheim didn't even give Polly a chance to open her mouth. "Why, yes. Back in September. Terrible misfortune. The poor girl just hasn't been the same since. And may I ask who you are?"

"I'm Polly's brother. I've come from Colorado Springs to make sure she is safe and well. Reports of these attacks have reached our father in St. Louis, and he's concerned."

Polly almost choked when she heard those words. Pa would never be concerned about her. He was only concerned that she find a husband and become a proper woman, relegated to the kitchen for the rest of her life.

"Well, other than Sophie's attack, I can tell you I run a tight ship around here. Mealtimes are set in stone, and I expect the girls to be here. Gentlemen callers are only allowed for two hours each evening and three hours on Sunday afternoons. And then only with a chaperone in the room."

Lyle relaxed his shoulders. "That's good to hear."

"See, little brother, I told you that you have nothing to worry about on my account. Between Mr. Price and Mrs. Mannheim, I always have someone looking out for me."

A creak on the stairs brought Polly's attention to Sophie making her way down. Not now. Not when Lyle was comfortable with things. He had been about to write a glowing report to Pa, no doubt about it.

As Sophie descended, she began to sing "Amazing Grace" at the top of her lungs. Her blond, wavy hair hung loose about her shoulders, and she was dressed in a striped skirt and a checkered shirtwaist. Lyle stared, openmouthed.

She made it to the landing and curtsied. "Welcome, welcome, each of you. It is so good to see you." She turned to Mrs. Mannheim. "Where are Mama and Papa? You said they would be here soon. I miss them so and long to see them. They must meet my secret beau. Though

I suppose when they do, he won't be so secret anymore." She giggled.

Mrs. Mannheim leaned over to Lyle, half covering her mouth. "She hasn't been right in the head since the attack. You have to forgive her behavior. Most of the time, she doesn't know what she's saying. Her parents don't have money for the train fare to get her, and she can't travel alone. Mr. Price is paying for her room and board while we work to find someone to escort her home."

Lyle spun and faced Polly. "You didn't tell me about this. Look at her. That could be you."

Again, Mrs. Mannheim jumped into the conversation before Polly had a chance to answer. "My, but it could have been. Polly is so fortunate that at the time of the attack, she was reaching up to fix her hat and was hit on the wrist and not the head. If it was hard enough to break her arm, imagine what it would have done to her skull." She shuddered.

He sucked in his cheeks, then puffed them out. "How in good conscience can I leave you here? Pa is right. This is no place for you. I'm going to have to insist you come home."

"But Lyle—"

"Oh, you are a nice man." Sophie came the rest of the way down the stairs and sidled up to Lyle. She tugged on his coat. "Did you bring me some candy? Maybe a dress for my doll too?"

"I'm not going home with you." Polly used her most authoritative voice. "Bad things happen there too. St. Louis could have its own Silver Shadow. Perhaps even worse. You can't protect me forever."

Lyle glowered. "Pa would protect you. That's his job until such time as you find a husband. Then the responsibility transfers to him."

"You make me sound like such a burden. Like a dog that needs to be cared for all the time. I'm self-sufficient and proud of it. I'll be careful going out from now on, and neither you nor Pa nor any husband will have to worry about me."

The mail slot creaked open, and several letters plopped to the floor. Sophie ran to pick them up. "I love mail time. It's the best part of the day."

"It brings her such happiness." Mrs. Mannheim shook her head.

"Let's see." Sophie paged through the envelopes. "Polly, you have a letter. Looks like a boy writing to you." She handed it to Polly.

No, no, no. This was the worst possible timing. Bringing Lyle here had been a mistake.

Edwin nudged her, and she brought her attention to him. He raised his eyebrows in question.

She nodded.

It was from the Shadow.

Polly was shaking as she held the letter from the Shadow in her hand. Edwin led her to the davenport before she had a fainting spell. She glanced at him, a single tear shining on her long bottom lashes.

He turned to Mrs. Mannheim. "Please, get her a glass of water."

The woman stood stunned.

"Please."

At last she scurried off.

Lyle sat beside his sister. "What is it?"

She shook her head, her focus burning on the note.

"She received a letter before from the purported Silver Shadow. Anyway, in the last one, he threatened her."

Lyle grabbed her by her good wrist. "That's it. You're coming with me. Pa had every reason to be worried about you. This is no place for a woman."

Her brother's sharp words broke her out of the spell, her eyes brightening just as Mrs. Mannheim returned with the water. In the far corner of the room, Sophie sat in a wing chair pretending to pour tea.

"No. Don't you see? It's more important than ever that I stay here and see this story through to the end."

"You aren't even working on the story." Lyle was almost shouting.

Upsetting Polly wouldn't do anyone any good. "Let's all stay calm."

"You want me to stay calm when my sister has been attacked and is receiving threatening letters from some deviant out there?"

"He hasn't attacked women in that way."

"Not yet. You don't know what his next move might be."

Lyle had a point.

Polly stood, brushing away Mrs. Mannheim's offer of the water.

"Stop talking about me as if I'm not in the room. I'm a grown woman, and I can make my own decisions. I don't care what you or Pa have to say, Lyle. I'm not going anywhere. This is my big break, my chance to become a true journalist. To prove to Pa and to everyone that I'm worthy."

What a shame if Polly had to leave, had to give up on her dream. But perhaps it was for the best if she went somewhere else until they could catch this man who was threatening her. It was only a matter of time until he attacked her. "Maybe you should go visit your father. Or if you have a friend you'd like to see, this might be a good time."

"I thought you were on my side." A muscle jumped in her cheek. "You've been the one who has been supporting me through all this."

He touched her arm. "I have. And I do. I don't want you to leave. But if it's going to keep you alive, that might be the best idea."

"We don't even know what the letter says." She waved the envelope in the air, then opened it, withdrawing a plain white sheet of paper.

Edwin leaned over her shoulder. Just as before, the words in the note were pasted together with letters cut from the newspaper.

IF YOU KNOW WHAT'S GOOD FOR YOU, WATCH YOUR STEP. OR I WILL GET YOU NEXT TIME. YOU'LL BE SORRY.

She handed the page to him, trembling like a poplar in the wind.

Edwin rubbed the back of his neck. If only Polly would see sense and leave. The last thing Edwin wanted was her blood on his hands. He had enough already. He couldn't risk losing her like Rachel. No, that wasn't true. Polly meant more to him than Rachel. Even if he had to go through life without her, knowing she was safe and well was the most important thing.

Lyle shook his head. "This situation is too dangerous."

Finally, Edwin had an ally. "I agree. I think you should leave, Polly. You never know who it might be that's after you. It could be someone closer than you realize."

She stood, arms akimbo, her gaze flashing from him to Lyle and back again. "I don't care what either one of you says. I refuse to give up on my dream."

"A dream isn't worth your life." He itched to take her in his arms and beg her to leave. But the time wasn't right. And there were too many people in the room.

"What kind of life do you have if you don't have dreams? Would either of you leave? What about Mrs. Mannheim? I don't think she's going anywhere."

Mrs. Mannheim held up her hands and backed out of the room. "This doesn't involve me. I don't want to get in the middle of siblings. But consider what he's saying, Polly. Look at Sophie. Do you want to end up like her?"

Sophie had curled up in the chair and was twirling her hair and singing "Mary Had a Little Lamb."

Edwin looked into Polly's eyes. "Mrs. Mannheim is right. Look at what happened to Sophie. What happened to those women who were killed. This man is serious. He isn't playing a game. For whatever reason, he hates women. And he has a special hatred for you."

"No. I refuse."

Edwin glanced over her head at her brother, who gave a single nod. "Then I have no choice but to carry you to the train station. Kicking and screaming if need be."

Chapter 24

Fire rushed from Polly's belly to her face, exploding out her ears. How dare Edwin say such a thing? Drag her kicking and screaming to the train station indeed. It was one thing for Lyle to speak that way. He was her brother. It was quite another for someone like Edwin to treat her in such a manner.

"Let's step outside, Edwin." She didn't even try to control the tone of her voice. All the better if he understood how fuming mad she was.

He held the door for her. If he weren't such a gentleman, she might have been tempted to slam it in his face and lock it. Instead, she moved to the porch then turned to face him. "What is the meaning of this? I thought you were on my side. That you understood how important this is to me. I don't see you trying to send Amelia away."

"Amelia is under the watchful care of my mother and myself."

"And I have Mrs. Mannheim and you. Not to mention that I'm very self-sufficient. And smart."

"Oh, are you?" His words rang with sarcasm. "I suppose getting a broken wrist was smart."

"I followed your directive. You're the one who arranged my escort that night."

He turned away and tugged on his collar. "You're right. I failed again to protect someone close to me."

"I'm sorry." She went to him and stood beside him, looking out on the street. "I didn't say that to make you feel badly. I shouldn't have said it at all."

"After Rachel and Amelia. . ." He cleared his throat.

She touched his sleeve, her fingers tingling and not from the cold. No matter how hard she tried, she couldn't remain angry with him. "Don't. The night the Shadow attacked me was no one's fault. That a man is after me for some reason."

"Can you think of what that might be?"

"Probably because I'm exposing his crimes. There's a reason he hides in the shadows. The Bible says that evil men commit their acts in darkness because they don't love the light. He loves operating in the background, committing his dirty crimes and slinking away. And now that I'm back on society page duty, he has no reason to come after me."

"That, I'm not so sure of."

She had said too much. She had swayed him back to her side, but now the pendulum might be headed in the other direction. "You understand how important this is to me, don't you? Lyle was given everything I was denied. I love my brother, and I don't wish to take away what he has, but I'm tired of being pushed to the side. If I return to Pa, he'll have me cooking and cleaning and canning from sunup to way past sundown. That's not the life I want."

Edwin turned toward her, so close now his breath warmed her cooling cheek. "And what is it that you want?"

Her throat constricted. What was it she wanted? What every little girl wanted. Her father to love her. To be proud of her. Someone to take notice of her. Pa didn't do that. Never had and most likely never would. No matter what she did, she could never be worthy of his love.

The thought almost doubled her over in pain. She clutched her middle. His sending Lyle here for her was proof he would never truly love her. All he wanted to do was to control her. "Please, don't send me back. I beg you."

"Has he hurt you?"

She closed her eyes against the memories. The times she didn't make the meal right or the house wasn't clean enough. He had never struck Ma. But her death brought out the worst in him. Unable to find her voice, she nodded.

Now he enveloped her in an embrace, warm and comforting. Like a bowl of hot soup on a cold day. Like a crackling fire on the hearth of a welcoming home.

"I think I understand why you want to stay. Why you keep saying you have to prove yourself." He spoke into her hair, his breath sending shivers across her scalp. "But you don't have to prove yourself to anyone."

She backed out of his embrace, one she never should have welcomed in the first place. "If you say that, then you don't understand. Not truly. I want to be taken seriously."

"There is one person who does take you seriously."

For half a second, her heart forgot to beat. Did he? Maybe she had misjudged him. Perhaps he sympathized with her more than she realized.

"The Silver Shadow."

"He's the only one? He's the only person who takes me seriously?"

"I didn't say he was the only one. But for right now he's the most important one. Please, even if you can't go home, there has to be somewhere you can go. Somewhere safe."

"I won't be moved. And despite your threats to haul me to the train station, we both know that was a bluff."

"So you're leaving me no other choice?"

"I'm afraid so, Detective Price. Whether you like it or not, you're stuck with me. I promise to watch my surroundings and not go out after dark."

"And I'll do a better job of protecting you."

"That's not your job. It's God's."

"Everyone needs someone to watch out for them."

"So, is it a deal?" She moved to shake his hand.

And he accepted it. "Deal. But so help me, if you cause me any trouble, I will make good on that threat. I wasn't bluffing."

Was that a good thing or not?

Pa,

 You may think of me whatever way you want, but I will not be returning to St. Louis. Not now and not ever in the future. While it was good to see Lyle, it was wrong of you to take him from his work and send him to fetch me. Disown me if you like. I will make my own choices.

I used to love you so very much. You made the sun shine each day and the moon beam at night. All I've ever wanted was for you to be proud of me.

But that will never happen, will it? Something changed in you after Ma's death. I don't know if you even realized it. You broke. And you tried to break me too. Because of that, I cannot return home. Denver is my home now. People here care about me and want the best for me. They encourage me to succeed. They celebrate my successes and cheer me up when I fail. Never, though, has one of these people raised a hand to me or tried to control me.

Perhaps you were trying to mold me into Ma, but I never could measure up. No matter what I do, I never will. It's time for me to stop trying.

Polly

Once he returned to the office, Edwin dropped the latest note onto his desk, sat down, and stared at it while rubbing his temples. This man had his sights set on extinguishing Polly. If only he could have gotten her to agree to leave Denver. Go somewhere, anywhere. But once he heard what she was willing to tell him of her story, he couldn't urge her to return to her father.

Imagine a man treating one of his children in such a manner. Despicable. Deplorable. Disgraceful. How could a person treat any human like that, much less his own flesh and blood? It was beyond Edwin's comprehension.

She was right. He didn't understand. Not fully. God had blessed him with a loving family. No one had ever raised a hand to strike him. But he did know now why she was so determined to succeed, to make her own way in the world. That was why she had something to prove.

He blew out a breath.

"What's up, boss?" O'Fallon returned to his desk, breadcrumbs from his sandwich scattered across his dark vest.

"Come look at this." He held up the letter the Shadow had sent to Polly.

"Another one?"

"Afraid so. There has to be a clue in here somewhere. Something that will lead us to this guy. We need to bring him in soon. Today, if at all possible. Before someone else gets hurt or killed."

"Namely, Miss Blythe?" O'Fallon twitched his blond eyebrows.

"Anyone." But yes, Miss Blythe in particular.

"Let me take a look." O'Fallon studied the paper for several long minutes then shrugged. "I don't know." He handed the note to Edwin.

He adjusted his glasses and peered at it again, so long and hard, his headache intensified until it throbbed like an African drum. Wait. What was that? He held the note closer. "Do you see this?" He pointed to one of the letters.

O'Fallon leaned over. "I don't see anything."

"This one isn't cut from newsprint. The paper is too white. And the letter is much smaller. Not from a headline like the rest."

"So you think it's from a typewriter?"

"Not think. I know."

"So our suspect owns a typewriter."

"Or has access to one."

A few seconds passed until understanding dawned in O'Fallon's brightened face. "Like Harry Gray does."

"Exactly what I was thinking. Miss Blythe has mentioned him before. He fits the profile."

"Wouldn't she have known though? She works with the man every day."

The ache in his head didn't dull. He drew in a full breath and released it. "I don't know. She never has gotten a good look at the Shadow. I didn't either, the other night. But it might be worth it to bring Mr. Gray in for questioning. It's time we at least chatted with him. Goodness knows, we've done that with men who've had less of a motive or means."

"And I'll take the note to a typewriter dealer. Perhaps he'll know what kind of model was used to form that letter."

"I like your thinking." His partner had been green when he first started working with Edwin about a year ago, but he was coming around. "You'll make an excellent detective someday."

"Thanks, boss." O'Fallon grabbed his hat and coat and headed for the door.

Edwin informed Armstrong of their findings. It was almost time for the press conference to announce the nabbing of the Shadow, and Edwin failed in his attempt to convince the chief to hold off, at least until they had a chance to question Harry Gray. Frustrated, he donned his own coat and headed out.

The walk to the *Post* wasn't long. Not long enough for him to truly gather his thoughts and steel himself. His stomach clenched as he swung open the big door and proceeded inside. Once he had shown his credentials, the secretary directed him to the newsroom. The incessant clacking of typewriters did nothing to ease the banging inside his head.

Polly peered from her machine and widened her eyes. She rose, a smile on her pink lips, but he motioned her to sit. He'd prefer it if this were a social call. Then again, if this closed the case, it would be a good thing.

For both of them.

After he had straightened his shoulders, he approached Gray's desk, right beside Polly's. To think the Shadow might have been within feet of her each and every day. His stomach tightened again. It all made sense. How the Shadow knew Polly's every move. Knew where she lived.

The pieces were fitting. "Mr. Gray?"

He glanced up, then back at his work. "What do you want?"

"I'm Detective Price with the Denver police."

At this, Gray snapped to attention and grasped the edge of his rolltop desk. Edwin peered at Polly from the corner of his eye. Her mouth was wide.

Gray swallowed a few times.

"I need you to come to the station with me."

"This isn't a good time."

"You don't have any say in the matter. We need to ask you a few questions about the Silver Shadow case."

Gray pushed his chair away from his desk. "Listen, maybe I look a little bit like the man described in the paper, but I had nothing to do with any of those attacks. Tell them, Polly. Tell them I didn't do it."

Polly slid forward on her chair. "Detective, I don't think he's—"

"Let's go, Mr. Gray."

"I have to tell my boss I'm leaving. And not of my own accord."

Edwin nodded, and Gray retreated to the editor's office. Polly rose and smoothed her dark brown skirt. "Edwin, do you have any evidence against him?"

"Perhaps. We're looking into it. In the meantime, I want to question him. I can't discuss it with you, but O'Fallon is working to substantiate it." If only he could pick up Gray's typewriter, so tantalizingly close, and compare the types. But he'd need a search warrant for that. "All I can tell you is that the case is falling into place. The man who killed Rachel and those other women, who hurt you and Amelia and Sophie, may have been sitting across from you this entire time."

At his words, Polly slumped to the floor.

Chapter 25

"What in the world were you thinking by shocking her with such information?" Amelia leaned over Polly, who lay on the davenport in the parlor, but she spoke over her shoulder at Edwin.

He fiddled with his pocket watch's chain. "I thought she was strong enough to handle the news. Don't worry. I sent a message, and her brother should be here soon."

"I can't imagine learning that the person who's hurt friends of yours, one very badly, and tried to kill you, was within feet of you this entire time."

"We have no absolute proof that Gray is the man behind these crimes."

"Just the possibility is beyond imagining. Although Polly once told me that he bore a fair resemblance to the Shadow."

"Still, she wasn't sure. I need to question him. To go over his alibis. To see if the evidence goes in his favor or ours." He knelt beside Amelia in front of the couch where Polly rested. Mother had filled her with warm tea and covered her with a blanket, and exhausted by her ordeal, she'd fallen asleep.

"You care about her, don't you?"

"Of course. She's a human being. I hate seeing what people can do to others created in God's image."

"That's not what I meant, and you know it."

"I can't become personally involved in this case. Even though Armstrong is wrong about many things, he's right about this. I can't allow my judgment to be clouded by a relationship with Polly. Or anyone, for that matter. Already, you're involved."

"You want to solve this case for more than my sake or Rachel's."

"For all the women who have been victims."

"Stop lying to yourself."

He couldn't. To do so would be to risk his job. "Now that I know Polly will be well cared for, I have to get to the station. I don't want to delay in questioning Mr. Gray. Goodness knows, if I wait too long, Armstrong is going to call a news conference and spread the word that, yet again, we've nabbed the Shadow. But this time the Denver police will be the laughingstock of Colorado."

Before he came to his feet, Amelia kissed his cheek. "For all our sakes, I hope this truly is the man. It's time for this nightmare to be over."

"I couldn't have said it better."

All the way to the station, Amelia's words replayed themselves in his mind. Had his focus for this investigation changed? Was he doing this for Rachel and Amelia or more for Polly? He shook his head. It didn't matter. What was most important was that he was out there, doing the hard work, trying his best to catch the man responsible for hurting these women. Each one of them mattered.

O'Fallon met him outside the interrogation room. "About time you got here, boss. I was getting worried about you."

"Polly fainted when I told her about Gray. Once she regained consciousness, I called for someone to bring Gray in and took her to my house so my mother and sister could dote on her for a bit."

"That was nice of you."

Thankfully, O'Fallon didn't rib him too much. Not like some others in the station might have. "Are we ready to get on with this? What did you find out?"

"The salesman at the typewriter shop wasn't very helpful. He didn't know a thing about what kind of type each machine produced or which one the letter might have come from. We'll have to keep doing our detective work and see if we can discover anything from this."

"That's a disappointment. I had hoped to be able to settle this case with a single question. Perhaps once we confiscate Gray's typewriter, we'll get better answers." Edwin led the way into the room where Gray sat at a narrow table, stroking his chin.

"About time you showed up. I have an important job to do, in case you've forgotten."

Edwin seated himself across from Gray. "Oh, we haven't forgotten. Not at all. What kind of typewriter do you use at the office?"

"What sort of question is that?"

"Just one we would like an answer to." Edwin didn't remove his gaze from Gray. Didn't even blink.

"A Remington."

"Do you have a machine you keep at home?"

"I don't believe this has anything to do with the case."

O'Fallon circled the table to stand behind Gray. "You let us determine that. Just answer the question."

"Um, no. They are much too expensive."

Edwin glared at Gray, the single electric lightbulb illuminating the windowless space. "You don't sound too sure about that. We can always get a search warrant and find out for ourselves."

"Fine. Yes, I have a typewriter at home. An Oliver."

Edwin clenched his jaw until he pulled back the words that danced on the edge of his tongue. "I'm warning you not to lie. It'll go easier if you tell us the truth from the beginning. One way or another, we will find out. If you have it in you, be honest."

Gray gave Edwin a narrow-eyed stare of his own. "You're too close to this case. It would be best if you recused yourself."

This was the kind of arrogance the Shadow would display. The man would be full of himself.

"You aren't the one giving the orders here." Edwin gripped the seat of his chair as hard as he could. Bile rose in his throat at the thought of Polly having to work with this man every day. At the thought of him harming Amelia and Polly and Sophie. At the thought of this man killing Rachel.

If he was the Shadow, he had wreaked too much havoc. "Where were you on the evening on August 24 of last year?"

"I don't remember."

"How about the evening of September 24?"

"How do you expect me to recall that far back?"

O'Fallon leaned over Gray's shoulder. "You'd better start remembering. Otherwise we're going to assume you were in the vicinity of the crimes when they happened."

Edwin couldn't take anymore. No more of this man's evasiveness. No more of this man's arrogance. He stormed out of the room and slammed the door behind him, the sound reverberating in the suddenly silent precinct.

Polly stirred and opened her eyes. The davenport on which she slept was blue, not brown like the one in Mrs. Mannheim's house. The blanket over her was pink, not green.

She rubbed her eyes.

"How are you feeling now?" Amelia, holding a silver platter with cups and a plate of cookies, smiled at her.

And the entire day's ordeal rushed back at her, like a wave on the shore. That's right. She'd fainted at the office, and Edwin had brought her to his house. "Much more refreshed than I've been in a long time."

She sat up and smoothed her hair and skirt while Amelia sat by her side and poured the tea.

Lyle was there too, sitting in an armchair near them. "What happened? You aren't the fainting type."

"I don't know. I'm the one who suggested to Edwin that Harry might be involved. Perhaps a part of me didn't want to believe it."

"Imagine, working side by side every day with that man who has done such terrible things." Amelia shuddered.

Polly bit into a lemon cookie, but the treat turned to sand in her mouth. "Neither of you has met Harry Gray, but I've sat at my desk and stared at him every day for the past several months. Ever since I got my first glimpse of the Shadow."

"I hear doubt in your voice." Amelia dabbed the corners of her mouth with her napkin.

"That's because I have a great deal of doubt."

"You don't think he did it." Lyle sipped his tea.

"No. I'm pretty convinced he didn't. He's a mean coot who doesn't give two rat's hairs about women and is as slimy as algae on rocks, but he didn't commit these crimes."

"Then this Shadow is still out there with a vendetta against you."

Amelia set aside her teacup. "Why didn't you tell my brother that?"

"I tried. He wouldn't listen. I'm afraid he might be getting as bad as Captain Armstrong, trying to solve this case with whatever suspect he can find, no matter what. Just to free himself from guilt and be done with this entire business."

"Guilt?" Amelia sat back against the sofa. "What does he have to be guilty about?"

"Rachel. Me. You."

"He's always been the protective big brother. Annoyingly so."

At Amelia's words, Polly sent Lyle a pointed glance.

"Sometimes I just wished he would leave me alone. The one time he did, I was attacked. What happened was not because of him, though, not in any way."

"There's no reasoning with him. The only way he'll absolve himself is by solving this case."

"You're right." Amelia shuddered. "If he never does, it will probably haunt him for the rest of his life."

Polly turned to her brother. "Would you be a dear and go to the kitchen and ask Nancy for an ice pack for my wrist?"

"Sure." He rose and exited the room.

Though her arm did throb, that's not the reason she shooed him out. He couldn't hear what she was going to say to Amelia next. "We have to help him find out who is behind these crimes."

"We?"

"Yes, we. We were two of the victims." Polly placed her napkin on the coffee table. "We could have ended up like Sophie or Rachel. Only by God's grace are we healthy and whole. Let's stop being victims and put this man behind bars, where he deserves to be for the rest of his life. Are you with me?"

Amelia fiddled with the white linen napkin on her lap, her hands lily white. Would she be willing to leave her comfortable home and put her life on the line to save others? Goose bumps broke out on Polly's arms. What she was contemplating was risky and dangerous.

Was it worth doing?

Yes. If it saved even one life, kept even one woman from ending up like Sophie, then it was worth it.

Amelia turned her cup in her saucer, and her voice was barely audible. "We have to do it, don't we? We have to help Edwin. Captain Armstrong's efforts aren't that serious." She smiled. "And I know you enough to sense that you have a plan."

"Of course I do." But would it work? And if it did, would one of them end up hurt in the process?

Chapter 26

Sweat poured down his back as he sat in his kitchen, the *Post* spread out before him. Perhaps he had fed too much coal into the corner stove. Then again, a chill permeated deep into his bones.

The little bit of light that emanated from the stove cast macabre shadows on the far wall where fleur-de-lis wallpaper hung. Long abandoned cobwebs hung like limp flags in each of the room's four corners. There he kept them, not bothering to brush them away, stark reminders of all he had lost.

Without a woman to cheer the place, what use was there in keeping it clean and pretty? Each night he slept on the filthy mattress, nightmares disturbing his slumber, her laughter as she left him echoing in his dreams.

What a fool he'd been.

But no more. The police were growing impatient. That idiot of a chief of detectives had announced yet another suspect in the case. This one he described as cunning and wily and mentally deranged.

He chortled. If only they knew the truth. Cunning and wily, yes, that described him like wet described rain. Mentally deranged? Absolutely not. Far from it. In fact, he had never been more in possession of his faculties than he was now.

The trouble was that they would discover the man they had in custody wasn't the right man. Again, they would appear incompetent in the public's eyes. And the public would demand that the true Shadow be ferreted out.

He was running out of time.

Down the street, the church bells bonged the top of the hour. Yes, the time had come. Who knew how many more opportunities he would have to make his point? He had to act now. And make his biggest, boldest statement to date. Write it with strokes of blood.

Perhaps then the doltish men of Denver would receive the message he had been striving to send for over six months. Never in his life had he dealt with such imbecilic people. When would they understand what he was saying?

With a surge of energy running through his body, he grabbed the grease-stained map from the table and unfolded it. He had marked in pencil where he had taught each of those women a lesson. Where would be a good place for what he had in mind?

He studied the map for a good long while. It was those uppity rich ladies who grew discontented with their lot in life. Staying in the Capitol Hill area made the most sense. And since the police weren't the brightest stars in the sky, if he moved to a different area of the city, they may not make the connection.

A connection they had to make.

His gaze wandered to one area of Sixteenth Avenue. Yes, he had been before. Several of his previous actions had been there. But there were plenty of good alleys for him to hide in.

And if they didn't get the message he sent on his next night out?

What would he do if they never understood what he was saying?

That would be a disaster of epic proportions. He would have failed. As he had failed at most everything he tried. Love. Work. Holiness.

God, why won't you make them listen? I'm doing this for You. Use me as Your instrument to bring justice and vengeance on this stubborn, stiff-necked people. People who refuse to obey Your commands and Your order for the world and for life. I am Your sword. I am Your fire. I am Your flaming arrow. May I destroy what is evil and restore what is good.

Don't allow me to fail again. Open their eyes that they may see. Open their ears that they may hear. Open their hearts that they may obey.

With reverence, he touched the cover of his mother's Bible that sat beside the map on the table. What a good, gentle woman she had been. She knew her place. Every day she worked hard, kept the house, cooked the meals. She served his father and him. Never once did she complain. Never once did she lash out. Never once did she cry.

She was a shining example of what every woman should be. Docile, submissive, servant-minded. He was doing this for her. To honor her and the Christian women like her who knew their place and cheerfully did their godly duty.

She would be proud of him. Sad that he had married the wrong kind of woman, but happy that he was now putting that to rights. His father would be proud too. He'd admire that he'd brought up his son in the right way and taught him the proper order of the world. He'd be pleased that his son was righting the world's wrongs.

Now, for the plan. Somehow, in some way, it had to involve Polly Blythe. She'd grown way too big for her britches. Even after the first time he had gotten her, she hadn't learned her lesson.

She was about as dim-witted as the rest of the city's denizens. He had been studying her, figuring out where she went and when. And when she might be alone.

He would decipher a good place to do it. Somewhere she passed on a regular basis. He would lie in wait for her. Spring on her like a lion springs on its prey. She would feel the full force of God's wrath upon her for how she mocked Him and flaunted the Almighty's laws.

He would mete out the justice she well deserved.

This time she wouldn't get away with just a broken wrist.

This time she wouldn't get away at all.

Thursday, January 24, 1901

Polly and Amelia had been thick as thieves the past few days. Polly's brother had left a day after arriving, and she had been over almost every night after work, sometimes enjoying dinner with them, always there after dessert was served. While the casual observer might believe them to be playing games with each other or discussing the latest fashions, Edwin wasn't so easily fooled.

They were up to something.

Something no good.

He hadn't become a detective for nothing. He would discover what they whispered to each other every night.

Tonight Polly and Amelia had arrived home together in the carriage just in time for dinner. His family wasn't as mired in social convention as other upper-class families were, though they did eat in the formal dining room every evening and always changed from their work clothes before the meal commenced.

Polly arrived at dinner wearing a mint-green gown with sheer sleeves and a matching belt cinched at her small waist. As usual, she wore her hair up. Though her clothing didn't match the elegant cream-colored gown embroidered in black that Amelia had changed into, Polly outshone his sister. She was tough as leather on the inside and most feminine on the outside.

He shook his head. Muddled thinking dulled his senses and his instincts. He couldn't concentrate on the case at hand if Polly occupied every space of his mind.

They'd had to free Harry Gray, at least for the time being. The *Post's* typewriter didn't match the type on the note. That, and the fact they had no eyewitnesses who could identify him. Now they waited for a judge to grant them a search warrant so they could nab Gray's home typewriter. The Oliver.

If he hadn't already disposed of it.

Mother seated him at dinner beside Polly. She was a born matchmaker, convinced that if one of her children didn't marry soon, she would die without grandchildren. And that would be a travesty of great proportions.

In between bites of his mushroom bisque, he leaned toward Polly. "What have you been keeping yourself busy with these days?"

"Still writing the society column for Mr. Ward. Though I beg and beg, he refuses to put me back on the case."

"Yes, I know. Gray has been haunting the police station for a while now. I'd much rather have you there."

She widened her brown eyes. "Do you have information for me? What about Harry? I'm surprised he's hanging around the department if he's still a suspect."

"He's like a specter. It's difficult to get much work done with him around, because we can't say much about the case. We don't want to tip our hand to him if he's involved. Ward hasn't taken him off the story? Seems to me it would be the logical thing to do."

"Harry belongs to Mr. Ward's all-boys club. I would have been sacked. Harry gets the juiciest story."

"I'm sorry about that."

"No sorrier than I am that you have to put up with him. Are you still hunting down the typewriter clue?"

"We are. I don't know if it will yield anything or not, but we keep on it. Has your brother arrived home safely?"

"He has. I'm so glad I convinced him that I needed to stay. I don't believe he was too happy about it, but he'll tell Pa that I'm not going to be coming home."

He grasped her hand for the briefest of seconds. "I'm glad to hear that. At least there's no chance of your father repeating his behavior."

She nodded. "I'm thankful you understand. And if you have anything else that might be of interest to me, would you mind letting me know? If I could get the scoop on the Shadow, Mr. Ward would be forced to take me seriously. It could get me off the society beat."

"So you don't like reporting on people in our circle?" He sipped his water.

"I never said that. There are plenty of well-to-do families that are as kind and charitable as yours. But it's writing about engagements and balls and coming-outs that has me bored to tears. I want excitement. I want a story that's going to get me another front page."

"Once you got a taste of it, you wanted more."

She cut a bite from her lamb chop and chewed it for a moment. "It's not that I'm after fame and fortune. I want recognition of hard work. Acceptance as a capable, intelligent reporter. That's what I would like."

He turned his attention to his green beans almondine. From the other side of the table, Amelia addressed Polly. "Are you up for another game of Parcheesi tonight?"

Edwin didn't miss Amelia's slight nod.

Polly sat straighter. "Of course. You know how much I look forward to our games."

"May I join you?" He glanced between the ladies. The clinking of forks against the Japanese china filled the silence.

Amelia huffed. "Why ever would you want to play a game with a couple of girls? As I recall, you were always anxious to get away from me when we were growing up."

Mother chuckled. "I do remember that being the case. But both of you have matured into fine young people. I'm sure Edwin doesn't want to get rid of you anymore."

"Certainly not. I would like to enjoy the company of two lovely ladies this evening, if that's not too inconvenient for you."

Amelia glanced at the ceiling, then back to him. "I suppose you can."

After dinner, they adjourned to the parlor where a cheerful fire graced the hearth, bathing the comfortable room in a warm glow. Mother relaxed on the davenport, her knitting needles flying.

Amelia set up the board, and the game began. Neither woman spoke much. "How are things with your tutoring, little sister?" He rolled the dice across the board.

"Fine. I still love volunteering there. The children are working hard, and it's good to see them making progress in their studies. Knowing that giving them an education will help them be successful in life is very rewarding." Amelia motioned for him to finish his turn.

Her answer was stiff and rehearsed. "Fine." He moved his piece a few spaces. "You both can drop the pretense. I know you have something up your sleeves. You've been sitting here night after night, plotting some kind of scheme. I'd like to know what it is."

"Just a party." Amelia waved him away and took her turn.

"For my birthday?"

Polly nodded with too much vigor. "Please, don't make us go and spoil the surprise."

"The surprise is that my birthday isn't until October, so I don't think that's what you've been planning."

Polly yawned. "It's getting rather late, and I do have to be at work first thing in the morning. Word is that a big engagement announcement is coming from one of the city's finest families. If you don't mind, because the weather is so cold, I hate to bother your carriage driver, but that would be divine."

"Oh no." As Polly rose to her feet, Edwin grabbed her by her good wrist. "You aren't getting away that fast. In fact, neither of you are going anywhere until I get some answers."

And by the twisting in his gut, he would be getting answers he didn't like.

Chapter 27

I'm still waiting for the answer to my question." Edwin tapped his foot and crossed his arms.

And here Polly had hoped to make a quick getaway from the Price home. No such luck. Edwin was too good at his job. But he wouldn't like the plan she and Amelia had come up with. Would probably veto it outright. "Well, see—"

Amelia stepped between Edwin and Polly. "We're only trying to help."

He heaved a sigh. "I had a feeling it had something to do with the case. What have you two concocted?"

"Don't tell." Polly whispered the words in Amelia's ear.

"But I can't lie." Amelia faced her, her eyes large in her thin face. She must not be used to stress like this. It was clear she didn't enjoy the adrenaline rush as much as Polly did.

Edwin raised his eyebrows. "The truth. It will always find you out anyway."

Amelia barreled on. "We want to help you solve the case."

"And that's it?"

Amelia shuffled her feet.

"We have to do something." Polly's voice grew in intensity but not volume. "Every day I come home from work, and there is poor Sophie, sitting by herself in the corner of the parlor, playing with dolls or talking to imaginary friends. She was such a bright and vibrant woman. Nursing was her passion, her calling. And now she needs to be nursed. What a shame. What a waste of a life.

"And the man who did this to her continues to roam the streets. What are we supposed to do? Sit back and watch this menace do as he pleases and hurt more women? Do you want to see more young ladies end up in Sophie's situation? Or Rachel's?"

"Of course not." Edwin took his glasses off and rubbed his eyes wearily. "But you two can't go off by yourselves and try to lure him out. One or both of you could end up in Sophie's condition. Or Rachel's."

Polly straightened. "If it saves just one woman's life, then it's worth it, isn't it?" Though she said the words, her stomach recoiled at what she was implying.

"There's no need to be foolish or rash. The department is working on it. If we weren't able to draw out the suspect when we had the posse, what makes you think it's going to work now?"

Polly sighed. "Did you really believe that a bunch of men dressed as women were going to fool someone as wily as the Shadow? He could tell from a mile away they were men. I saw them myself. Women—at least most of them—don't have beards."

"I'm doing the best I can. I brought in Harry Gray. We're still investigating him. With patience, we will bring him to justice."

"But you had to let him go." Polly shook her head. "With each passing day, the chance of someone else getting hurt or killed rises. The clock is ticking. It's only a matter of time before he—whoever he is—strikes again. We have to apprehend him before it's too late."

Red slithered up Edwin's face, and he fisted and relaxed his hands. She had pushed him too far. "Don't you think I want to do that more than anything? I have a personal stake in this. Rachel. Amelia. You." He stared at her with such intensity, she had to break the gaze. "More than anyone in this city, I want the Shadow caught. I need irrefutable proof."

"Then let us help you."

"No. The answer is no. Absolutely not. It's too dangerous. Don't you see? I couldn't bear for anything to happen to either of you." But he stared at Polly as he spoke, and her breath caught in her throat. "Already both of you have been injured. Next time you won't be so lucky. I guarantee that. And Harry knows you. Knows your patterns. Knows what you look like. If it is him, you're an easy target."

"But it's not." Couldn't the man see reason?

"Why are you so convinced he's the wrong man?"

"He's slimy and has no love lost for me, but he wouldn't do this. His typewriter didn't match. Not to mention that he often works late at the paper. I'm sure there were times when the crimes were being committed that he was sitting at his desk."

"But you couldn't swear to it in a court of law."

Polly studied the tips of her shoes. "No." Then she stared him in the eye. "But neither could I swear in a court of law that he wasn't."

Amelia swiped at her eyes. "If you won't allow us to go out, then what can we do? We can't sit by and let this man ruin our lives, to keep us prisoners in our own homes."

"Pray. That's the best I can tell you." Edwin turned to Polly. "Are you ready to go? I'll see you home."

After she said her good nights to Edwin's mother and to Amelia, he ushered her into the relative warmth of the carriage. Darkness cocooned them. He reached for her hand, his fingers smooth and cool against hers. "Please, promise me you won't do anything foolish."

His husky words, so full of emotion, tore at her heart. "I don't want to be careless. I do value my life."

"That's good to know."

"At the same time, I hate being helpless. Can't you see? All my life, that's how I've felt. Helpless against my mother's death. Helpless against my father's anger. Helpless against my lot in life. Here is a way I can be useful, a way I can contribute to the community's well-being. I can protect other women."

"It's just that he's already hurt you. What's to stop him from doing it again? Especially since he has marked you. You're too bright and have too much of a future ahead of you to end up like Sophie. I couldn't stand it if that happened to you."

"But—"

"I'm begging you."

"Isn't there any way I can help?"

"Keep writing. I know you've been reassigned, but keep after Ward and see if he'll relent. And if I can get O'Fallon on board so that one of us will always be with you, perhaps, just perhaps, we can arrange one night for you to walk the street."

She couldn't help herself. She hugged him around the neck. "Thank you. Thank you."

"This is only a maybe."

She'd find a way to turn it into a yes.

Friday, January 25, 1901

Harry sat on the edge of his chair behind his desk and yanked the paper from his typewriter. Several choice words flew from his mouth.

If Polly didn't need both hands to type, she would cover her ears. "Mr. Gray, please remember there is a lady in the room."

"This is the precise reason there shouldn't be a lady in the room. Men aren't free to be who they were created to be when they have to watch out for women's sensibilities." He muttered another swear word.

"Mr. Gray."

He kicked his metal trash can, tipping it over and sending several wads of paper skittering across the floor. The newsroom door opened, and Harry sprang up. He was as jumpy as a baby bunny.

Polly stared at him. "What has gotten into you?"

"None of your business." He sat back down, inserted a fresh piece of paper into his machine, typed several words, and jerked it out again.

He was nervous, that was for sure. But what had left him as fidgety as a child at the end of a long sermon? Could it be he had a guilty conscience? Had she been mistaken?

She shivered at the thought of sitting across from the Shadow.

Harry rose from his seat and paced back and forth, murmuring under his breath. He was the right height and build. The scar. The pale face. All of it matched.

The door opened once more. If possible, Harry went whiter than ever. Edwin strode through the newsroom entrance.

She smiled at him, hoping to keep the pleasure she felt at seeing him from showing on her face. But Edwin kept his attention trained forward and didn't even glance her way. He swept past her and, without knocking, marched straight into Mr. Ward's office.

She glanced at Harry and raised her eyebrows. He shrugged.

Oh, but he did know what was going on. That's what had him in such a state.

The silence that fell over the newsroom was like the silence before a storm. No one stirred. Not a single key clacked on a typewriter. Stranger still, not a telephone rang.

You could have heard a mouse squeak.

If only she could hear what Edwin had to say to Mr. Ward.

Harry marched to the coatrack and nabbed his ulster coat from it so fast he tipped the tree over. Without stopping to pick it up, he dashed toward the door.

Making a getaway.

But not if Polly could help it.

She sprang to her feet and sprinted to catch up with him. Just before he reached the door, she grabbed him by the arm and pulled him back. "Where do you think you're going?"

"Release me. This is a free country. I don't have to tell you where I'm headed."

By now a crowd had surrounded them. "Making a break for it, Gray?" A tubby older man pushed his way through the curious reporters.

"This is not any of your concern, Ford. Nor is it any of Miss Blythe's here either."

She crossed her arms. "You've been waiting for this all day. You knew he was going to come here to. . .what? Arrest you?"

Harry peered down his nose at her. "You think you know it all, don't you, because you're sweet on that detective. Well, you don't. You can't identify me as the Shadow, can you?"

Polly stood there so long, Ma would have asked if the cat got her tongue.

"See, you can't. So I have nothing to fear from that detective."

How much did Harry know? If he'd been hanging around the police station, probably a great deal. Maybe more than Polly. Perhaps they had gotten those results on Harry's home typewriter. It could be that Edwin had evidence she didn't know about. Solid evidence that Harry was the Shadow.

"Gray."

Polly turned. Mr. Ward stood in his office doorway, his face flaming redder than any fire. Edwin wasn't in her line of vision.

"Get in here. Now."

The crowd around Harry parted so he could make his way to the editor's office. Once Harry disappeared inside, Mr. Ward stepped out. "Get back to work, all of you. No lollygagging. You all have stories to write." He slammed the office door shut.

The room erupted into a crazy din. With a thump, Polly sat in her hard, wooden chair. A chill like a lump of ice settled in her stomach. There could only be one explanation for everything.

Edwin was about to arrest Harry.

Polly pressed on her abdomen. Had she been wrong this entire time? Had her attacker and the attacker of all those other women—the murderer of two of them—been sitting right beside her?

A wave of dizziness overtook her, and she leaned on her desk to keep from slumping to the floor.

Edwin wouldn't be here if he didn't have solid evidence. Something undeniable. Something that was sure to get a conviction.

Though she pecked out a couple of sentences, she couldn't concentrate on her work. The clock hands must be stuck, because they hardly moved. She couldn't breathe.

Just when she was about to crawl out of her skin, Mr. Ward's office door swung open. Harry emerged first, his hands cuffed behind his back, Edwin pushing him forward.

"And don't you ever come back!" Mr. Ward. Polly had almost forgotten about him.

As Edwin pushed Harry out of the room, Harry turned back and pierced Polly with a glare so sharp, pain exploded in her chest. "This isn't over, I promise."

Polly shivered. If Harry was the Shadow, he was capable of anything.

Chapter 28

Monday, January 28, 1901

Men pressed shoulder to shoulder inside the too-warm, too-small police station. Three o'clock. Edwin didn't need to open his pocket watch to know what time it was. Shift change. Captain Armstrong's daily briefing.

The man droned on about various muggings, none of which fit the Shadow's pattern, several burglaries, and a violent dispute over a mule, leaving one man shot and another man on the loose.

"Finally, gentlemen, we have a suspect in custody in the case of the Silver Shadow."

This news from the captain perked Edwin's attention. Of course he'd been the arresting officer, but still, it was his case.

"I have worked hard to bring this man to justice. Through my hard work, I solved the case. You see how well my tactics worked. I brought in many possible suspects and questioned them. This is what led to Harry Gray's arrest yesterday."

Edwin's mouth fell open. When he glanced at O'Fallon, so had his. How could the captain take credit? Wasn't it Edwin and O'Fallon who had done the hard work?

But of course Armstrong would seek the glory. The man would do whatever he had to in order to get ahead.

"I will be calling a press conference this evening to make the announcement. The Denver Police Department can stand with their heads held high. This wasn't an easy case, but with persistence and perseverance, I managed to crack it. To think that it was a well-respected reporter. I can't imagine it. That should serve as a reminder to never overlook anyone."

Edwin had to hold himself to his seat to keep from leaving the meeting.

"Of course this menace made bail this morning, so we need to keep a close eye on him. I cannot allow him to perpetrate this crime on another woman before his trial takes place. I'll be requesting a speedy blow of justice to rain down on him. And I will not be mentioning his release in the press conference. That is to be kept within the department. No one else is to know. Is that clear, Price?"

Edwin nodded. How was this possible? Gray was free? Out there to strike more women? He had to be madder than the hatter in *Alice in Wonderland*. There was no telling what he would do. The captain said they needed to keep a keen eye on him.

That is just what Edwin intended to do. There was no way he was going to let the man out of his sight. Not for a single second. Even if that meant Edwin wouldn't sleep between now and the trial. That's one thing on which he agreed with the captain. The sooner this man was brought to justice, the better.

Armstrong concluded the meeting a few short minutes later. Edwin and O'Fallon turned toward each other, nodded, and made their way out the door.

The bracing cold air heightened all of Edwin's senses. "Can you believe that Armstrong denied us the credit for nabbing Gray? Without our work, the man would still be running the streets."

"Technically, he still is." O'Fallon gave a half shrug.

"And why would a judge issue him bail? He's guilty of two murders and the assault of numerous women. Men like him should never be allowed to roam the streets again."

"Unfortunately, Gray has some money. It'll get you everything." O'Fallon gulped. "Oops, I didn't mean you."

"No offense taken. And it's not that I want the recognition. I would just like to not have Armstrong strutting like a peacock and crowing about his achievements when he has none to crow about."

O'Fallon chuckled. "I understand. Now I guess we'd better locate Gray."

They turned down Champa Street. "I know he was fired from the paper, so we won't find him there. The best thing to do is take the streetcar to his house. That's where he's most likely to be. Unless he's hightailed it out of town."

"He's such a slimy fish, I wouldn't doubt it."

This was why working with O'Fallon was such a pleasure. The man could shed a good light on any situation and cheer Edwin up with a single line.

After a short ride, they came to the Capitol Hill neighborhood, the same one in which Edwin lived. Queen Anne homes sat on large lots beside Greek revival houses and homes that featured Romanesque touches. It was where the Browns and the Sheedys, two of Denver's most elite families, lived.

O'Fallon whistled. "Gray must sure be doing well in the newspaper business."

"Perhaps he comes from old money." Though Edwin didn't know of any Grays living in the area. "Perhaps he's related to someone here. At any rate, according to Polly, he's a crony of her boss."

"Well, that explains plenty."

They arrived at the address, a brick Georgian with a spacious yard. When not covered in snow, it must boast the greenest lawn on the block.

The maid who opened the door informed them that Harry Gray lived in the carriage house and that she had seen him leave earlier that day.

When they went to the back to investigate, what they discovered substantiated the woman's observation. The shades were drawn. Every single one of them. Edwin nudged his partner. "Look at that. He doesn't appear to be home."

"That's not good. What do we do from here?"

"Let's find out." Edwin strode up the walk and knocked on the door. No answer. No one, nothing inside stirred. No one peeked around the shades or through the curtains.

"I don't have a good feeling about this. My gut is telling me something is very wrong."

"He doesn't seem to have any intention of returning soon."

Polly. Edwin had caught what Gray had said to her yesterday as he led him out of the newsroom. Something to the effect of this not being over yet. Gray had been anything but kind to her. Could he mean her some harm? Especially if he was the Shadow and had only injured her. She was a witness.

So was Amelia. They were both in danger. Who should he go to first?

As if reading his mind, O'Fallon tugged on Edwin's arm. "The streetcar to the *Post* first. Then to your house."

Edwin headed in the direction of the nearest stop. "Hurry, O'Fallon. I have a feeling we don't have a moment to lose."

Beside Polly, Harry's rolltop desk sat empty. There wasn't a scrap of paper on it, not a pencil, not his pressman's hat, not his typewriter. Word had filtered into the office that Captain Armstrong had called a news conference for this afternoon.

That could only mean one thing. Before she and Amelia had a chance to put their plan in place to catch the Shadow red-handed, Edwin and his partner had come up with evidence to charge Harry. She shuddered, a reaction she'd been having quite a bit in the past twenty-four hours, ever since Edwin had arrested Harry right in front of all the reporters.

With Harry not available, she had managed to talk Mr. Ward into allowing her to write an article about the arrest, but he, deeming the angle she had taken about Edwin and O'Fallon's hard work on the case not sensational enough, had moved it all the way back to page twelve. Not even as good as her first article.

He wasn't about to give her a break. No matter what she did, it wasn't good enough. Just because of her gender. She wrote ten times better than half the men on this staff. What was it going to take?

Well, no time like the present to get back to work. Within a few minutes, she was involved in writing her latest article on the upcoming high society Valentine's Day wedding of a Miss Greer and a Mr. Howe. How scandalous it was that the attendants would wear red gowns and the bride carry red flowers. Shocking.

It wasn't really, but according to Mr. Ward, she had to make it sound that way. As soon as she had this finished, she was headed to the police department. Though she had begged and pleaded with Edwin last night, he had refused to give her more information on Harry's arrest.

She didn't want him to lose his job because he fed her information he shouldn't. Then again, she had to keep her job to avoid getting sent home to Pa.

With a flourish, she pushed the final period on her article and unrolled it from her typewriter. Edwin had informed her that the Remington Harry used at the office wasn't the one used to type the letter in the threatening note, so that must mean he had a different model at home that was the one.

That had to be how they had cracked the case.

Well, no time like the present to get this to Mr. Ward for his approval so she could get out of here and get to some real reporting.

Just as she stood, movement at the newsroom door caught her attention. When she recognized who entered the office, her heart caught in her throat.

Harry.

What in the world was he doing here?

His eyes, those piercing blue eyes, glazed over, like he didn't see any of them. Like he had tunnel vision.

He marched in the direction of Mr. Ward's office. Polly held her breath. Caught the glint of something shiny in Harry's hand, still half in his pants pocket.

Mr. Ward charged from his office. "I thought I told you never to come back."

"I'm not here to work." From his pocket, Harry pulled a revolver. "I'm here to give you all what's coming to you."

Mr. Ward held up his hands. "Back off. This would be the biggest mistake of your life. We're friends."

"You fired me." Harry's voice was at a near-shriek pitch. "Friends don't fire friends. You never defended me, never stood up for me." He leveled the pistol at Mr. Ward's heart. "This is what you deserve for the way you treated me."

"Come on, Gray. Be reasonable." Mr. Ward took a step back.

"The time for reason is over." Harry cocked the gun.

Heart thrumming, Polly rushed forward, in between Mr. Ward and Harry. "Stop." She held her hands up the way a traffic cop might. "You don't want to do this."

"That's where you're wrong, missy." Harry glared at her with those eyes as blue as a winter's sky.

"You're already in a heap of trouble. Don't add to it." She forced herself to stand up straight. Show him she wasn't afraid, even though she fought to keep her knees from trembling.

"Much of it is thanks to you." Harry never took his gaze from Mr. Ward. "You were the one who told the police the Shadow has a scar. You were the one who showed that detective the letters."

She sucked in a breath and worked to steady her shaking hands. "So it was you all along?"

"No, you numbskull. It wasn't me. You made it look like me. Led the police to even consider me a suspect. If not for you, I wouldn't be out of a job. I wouldn't be facing a judge who could sentence me to swing. If you had stayed home where you belonged, a good daughter, a good wife, a good mother, none of this would have happened to me." He spun and trained the pistol at her head.

Was this it? Was this the end of her life? There had to be more to it than this. The constant running after the next big story. Seeking validation from her father and every other man on the planet. The pursuit of fame and fortune.

In that heart-stopping moment, it dawned on her. What did it matter what Pa, what Mr. Ward, what Edwin thought of her? What was most important was what God thought about her.

And what was that?

She didn't know. Heaven help her, she didn't know. That thought sent her swaying. "Please, Harry, you can't do this. Think about it for a minute. I don't believe you're the Shadow. I truly don't. If I refuse to finger you in court, they can't convict you."

"Even though there's a pile of evidence against me."

"It's no good unless they have a written confession from you." She didn't know if that was true or not, but she had to bluff. Had to get him to put down the gun.

Mr. Ward moved beside her. "You wouldn't dare shoot a woman."

"What do I have to lose at this point?" Harry widened his eyes and fingered the gun's trigger.

"I never thought you'd stoop this low." Mr. Ward's voice wobbled.

"Harry. . ." Polly's throat swelled shut.

"You took everything from me. Absolutely everything. And now I'm going to take everything from you."

One shot rang out, echoing around the newsroom.

Mr. Ward fell.

Edwin appeared in the doorway, face red, panting.

Harry spun around.

Another shot.

Edwin crumpled.

Chapter 29

Pain split Edwin's arm, a searing, white-hot heat. The impact of the bullet knocked him from his feet.

Harry raced by him.

No, no, they couldn't allow him to get away. With a gun, he was more dangerous than ever. More lethal than he had been before.

Polly was at his side. "Edwin, are you all right? You've been shot. You're bleeding so much."

Though his arm throbbed, he clambered to his feet. "I have to catch him. Can't let him escape."

"You're in no shape to—"

Before she finished the sentence, Edwin was out the door and in pursuit of Gray. His breath came in ragged gasps as he fought off the pain. Blood dripped down his arm.

Just as Edwin caught sight of Gray, the man exited onto the street and blended into the crowd. "Stop him!"

None of the pedestrians heeded his call. Though it hurt more than the dickens, Edwin pushed by people, keeping Gray's crush hat always in view.

Gray cleared a group of men and broke into a full-out sprint. A moment later, so did Edwin. *Can't let him escape. Can't let him escape. Can't let him escape.* He focused on that mantra to keep himself moving forward and to hold the pain at bay.

Gray turned down a side street, then turned again onto Seventeenth Street. Here in the financial district, the sidewalk was even more crowded, the streetcar clanging down the middle of the road.

Now Edwin managed to make up some ground. "Police! Let me through. Stop that man!" Running and shouting at the same time took every ounce of effort and energy. He fought off a bout of vertigo.

Gray surged ahead then yelled over his shoulder, "Let me go, unless you want some of these people to die." He brandished his weapon.

As the crowd of businessmen scattered, Edwin reached for his gun. The world spun around him. Purple dots obscured his vision.

Gray leveled the weapon.

In a single motion, Edwin withdrew his revolver.

Raised it.

Squeezed off a shot.

Fell to his knees.

As if an apparition suddenly appeared, there was Polly at his side. What was she doing here? "Edwin, you're bleeding. Let me help you."

"Why are you here?"

"You're shot and bleeding. I had to follow and make sure you were okay."

She was so beautiful with the late-day light streaking her hair with red.

Was he dying? Had he already passed away? "What about Gray?"

"He's down. I don't know. There's a crowd of people around him."

No, he hadn't moved to eternity.

"Do you want me to find out how he's doing?"

"Yes, please." He squeaked out the words.

With a rustle of her skirts, she left his side. Very soon, she returned. "He's dead."

All Edwin could do was nod. Though the cold chilled his body, his soul was colder still.

Polly wrapped something around his arm. Maybe a handkerchief? Her ministrations did nothing to stop the throbbing. Once she finished with that, she helped him to his feet and hailed a passing carriage. "I'm going to take you home. Someone used the call box at the corner to summon the police to deal with Harry. You need medical attention."

Most of the way to his house, he could do nothing more than stare out the window at the passing scene. Wives scurrying home, their arms loaded with groceries to make dinner. Men hustling down the street to finish their business for the day. Children dawdling on their way home from school.

Her featherweight touch on his arm brought his attention back to her.

"Are you all right? Are you in much pain?"

"No." The word was short and curt. He softened his tone. "No. It doesn't hurt that much."

"But this has something to do with Harry, doesn't it?" She touched his good arm again. "You've been so supportive of me. Let me do that for you. Please?"

He sighed. How could he tell her? What would she think of him? For a moment, he stared into her brown eyes, so deep, so rich, so sincere. There was no sign of prying in her face or in her tone of voice. No sign of digging for dirt. She wanted to help him. It was as simple as that.

"How do I start?"

"From the beginning. Whatever it is, I can handle it. You didn't judge me. I promise not to judge you."

"You might change your mind."

"Never. Because no matter what happened in the past, I know who you are today."

"I thought what happened today would absolve me of my guilt. Of this weight that has been hanging around my neck since my father's death. But it hasn't." He scrubbed his face, wincing with the effort. "It hasn't."

"What happened with your father?"

"When I was eleven, one night I heard a noise from downstairs. The rest of the family was asleep, including Nancy." He stopped to catch his breath. "The house was quiet. So still. I was still awake because sometimes I liked to see how long I could stay up before I gave in to sleep."

"That's why you can handle all those late shifts."

"I suppose I was in training for it already back then."

"Go on."

She wasn't going to let him off the hook. He stilled his shaking hands. "I snuck down the stairs and tiptoed to the kitchen. There was a man leaving the butler's pantry with a big sack. I assumed he was stealing the silver."

She covered his hand, her own so warm and soft against his. So steadying to him. He relished the comfort it brought. "I was so intent on this man that I never heard my father come behind me. He charged into the kitchen, demanding the thief return the stolen goods.

"The intruder came after my father, stabbed him, and they fought." Edwin choked on the tears that clogged his throat.

"Oh Edwin, I'm so sorry. How horrible for you."

"All I could do was stand there and watch them fight. For a long time, they struggled. Father did everything he could. Punched. Kicked. But he was losing strength from loss of blood. And I stood there. I knew where my father kept his guns. I knew how to use them. I did nothing. Nothing to help Father. Nothing to stop that thief. That murderer. After what seemed half a lifetime, the thug stabbed my father again. The fatal blow."

"You were just a boy."

"I was old enough to help. At that moment, I vowed to become an officer, to find my father's killer. But I never did find him. When Rachel was attacked and then Amelia and then you, I thought that if I caught the Shadow, that would make me feel better. That I would have done someone some good. If I couldn't avenge my father's death, then I could avenge someone else's."

"But it hasn't made you feel better."

"No. It didn't bring back Rachel. And even if I could somehow, miraculously, catch my father's murderer, it won't bring him back either."

"Because you are trying to do something best left to God. He's the One who will avenge. He's the One who will bring about the final judgment for each of us. That's what you have to trust in. And you must know that you did a very good thing today, even though it may not feel like it right now. You stopped a man from killing others. Mr. Ward was up and yelling by the time I left the newsroom. He's going to be fine. You saved countless lives."

Edwin turned to stare out the window once more. Yes, he had

saved lives. Throughout his tenure on the force, God had used him to save numerous lives.

Perhaps what Father's murderer had meant for evil, God had turned into good.

Friday, February 22, 1901

The little light there was that filtered into the almost windowless police precinct was fading fast. Good thing the Shadow was dead. Buried. Never able to harm another Denver woman again.

That freed up Edwin to stay at his desk and work late. There was a glimmer of hope now that he'd be able to get through the caseload that had piled up on his desk while he'd pursued the Shadow.

Accolades for Edwin had poured in after Gray's death. Even Armstrong didn't attempt to take credit for that act of justice. He claimed he'd known all along that Gray was their man, but he did acknowledge that Edwin was the one who had brought his reign of terror to an end.

But his heroics had come too late for Sophie, Rachel, Polly, Amelia, and all the other victims.

Even though it was late and the flesh wound on his arm ached something fierce, he kept at his work. Armstrong was demanding answers in that bank robbery from a few weeks ago. The man didn't even give Edwin a chance to catch his breath.

A faint rustling came from in front of him, along with the scent of sandalwood. He didn't even have to look up to know who stood there. "Polly. To what do I owe the pleasure of this visit?"

She sat on the edge of the chair, all prim and proper. He glanced up to discover that she wore her pressman's hat. This was a professional visit, then.

"It's been a while since the shooting."

"I saw your headline on the front page."

Her face outshone the sun. "Even Mr. Ward said I did a good job. The world must be coming to an end."

A chuckle built in his chest, but he suppressed it. It was wrong to laugh when he'd killed a man. No matter how vile that man had been.

"I don't think you came here, though, to talk about that."

"No." She touched her hat. "A little time has gone by since Harry died. I was wondering if you were ready to give a statement about it. About the entire case, really, and how it feels to have it come to such a dramatic close."

He could hardly think about it, much less speak about it. "Not right now."

"You can't keep it bottled inside. You have to have someone to talk to."

"Please, Polly. I know you mean well. And I understand what a boost this would be to your career. But I don't want to. It's over and done with. All I can do is pray I'll never find myself in a situation like that again."

"I can tell by the bags under your eyes and the stubble on your chin that you're working yourself to death. Please, promise me you'll go home and get some rest."

"In a few hours."

"Now."

He glared at her, but her expression was soft. Full of kindness and compassion.

"Boss." O'Fallon, who had gone for some supper a while earlier, raced across the room.

Edwin's heart leaped, then sank. What could possibly have him in such a state?

"We are getting reports that a woman has been attacked at Sixteenth Avenue and Clarkson. She's hurt badly."

In a flash, Edwin was on his feet, grabbing his coat from the rack in the corner of the room. He spoke to O'Fallon over his shoulder. "Do we have a name?"

"Mary Short. She's been transported to the hospital. But you should know, it's a single blow to the head. Nothing stolen. No other, um, violation."

By this time Polly was at Edwin's side. "The Shadow."

"More likely a copycat." Edwin prayed it was.

"I'm coming with you."

"No." Because if it was the Shadow, if they had been wrong about

Gray, the streets were more dangerous than ever. "You stay here. I don't know what condition we'll find her in."

"You don't have time to argue with me."

That much was true. "Then let's go." At least with her near him, he didn't have to worry about her.

They hustled from the station and hurried to the hospital. Edwin sprinted toward the nurses' station. "Edwin Price, Denver Police. I'm looking for the woman just brought in who was attacked. Mary Short."

"We have a woman here who was attacked, but her name is Emma Carlson."

"What happened to Mary Short?"

"That I don't know, sir. But the doctor is treating Miss Carlson right now. If you'd like to wait, I'll let him know you're here so you can speak to her as soon as she's able."

If she was able to give him any details.

He made his way to the waiting room where Polly sat on a chair, jotting in her notebook. When he approached, she glanced up. "What did you find out?"

"Mary Short isn't here, but another woman is who was also attacked."

"Did Ralph get her name wrong?"

"I don't know. He's usually pretty good with such details. Though he's newer to the force, he's smart and has a lot on the ball. It's not like him to make such a mistake." It couldn't be that there were two attacks. It just couldn't be.

"It's possible that, in the confusion of the moment, someone gave him the wrong name."

"That's a little more likely." With each passing minute, it became clearer that Gray hadn't been their man. That someone else was the Shadow.

"Stand back, stand back."

Edwin spun. Several men carried someone in from the street. He bustled toward them. "Denver police. What do you have here?"

One of the men said breathlessly, "The Shadow got her."

Chapter 30

The eye-stinging odor of antiseptic sent a few tears down Polly's cheeks as the orderlies brought in yet another woman, the latest victim. A few voices carried, quiet yet intense. The metallic taste of blood hung in the air.

It just couldn't be. Not three victims in one night. Not again. This hadn't happened in six months.

She stared into the dazed face of the woman who had blood pouring from a wound on the back of her head. Polly rubbed her own aching wrist.

The woman grabbed for Polly. She leaned close.

"I have to tell you something."

"Conserve your strength. You'll need it to recover."

"No. Now. Before it's too late."

Goose bumps broke out all over Polly. Did death tug at the woman's soul? Was the Lord waiting for her on the other side of the Jordan? How did she know? "What?"

"He came at me. From an alley."

"That's why they call him the Shadow."

The woman shook her head, blood matting her curly black hair to her head. "I saw him."

"Just a minute." Polly motioned to Edwin, who conversed with the first nurse they'd encountered at the hospital.

He strode over.

"This woman saw the Shadow."

"I'm Detective Price. What can you tell me?"

"Not much time."

Lord, please don't take another victim home. Let her testimony be what breaks this case wide open.

"Don't worry. I know where I'm going."

Polly couldn't breathe.

"Small. Thin. Pale. Scar above his right eye."

Everything they already knew.

"Wore dark blue. Like a policeman." Her chocolate eyes misted over as her gaze bore into Polly's.

"Just like the last one."

"Don't discount the things that are right in front of you."

An orderly, dressed all in white, blood staining his clothing, rushed over. "We have to get her to surgery."

Polly squeezed her hand one last time. "God be with you."

"Bless you. And curse him."

She watched until the door closed behind the woman, the din of the waiting room fading around her. The world spun, and she wobbled on her feet.

Someone caught her, strong arms kept her from falling to the floor. "Let's get you to a chair." Edwin's tenor voice as rich as King Midas.

Supporting her all the way, he led her to a seat in the far corner of the waiting room. For a while, she sat with her head down until the crazy tilt of the earth righted itself. "I'm so sorry. I don't know what came over me."

"This is too much for you. I'm going to take you home." He was on his knees in front of her, clasping her hands.

She sat up so fast, the whirling came over her like a tornado. "No. It just hit me. All these women. I could have been one of them. And that last one. She's talking as if she knows she's going to die." She transferred her grasp to Edwin. "Please tell me she isn't going to die."

"I can't know that. None of us knows."

"Three, Edwin, three of them tonight. This madness has to end. The women of this city have to be safe again. Whoever is doing this is out of his mind. Sick and deranged. And it's time to stop him."

"Don't you think I've been trying?" He furrowed his brows.

"No, no, I'm not blaming you. But you and Ralph are out there on your own. Captain Armstrong isn't giving you the support you need to work this case properly. So if he isn't willing to help, I am. He can slap me with as many lawsuits as he wants."

"Out of the question." Edwin spoke with such force that the other conversations in the room died down.

She kept her words soft and even. "You don't have a choice anymore."

"Ugh." He rose from his knees and spun in small circles in front of her.

At last her world steadied, and she came to her feet and took hold of him by both shoulders. "Look at me, Edwin."

He adjusted his glasses, his green eyes magnified behind them. "Don't make me do this, Polly. Please, don't ask this of me, because I can't ask it of you."

"You aren't asking. I'm offering. And I'm not giving you the chance to say no."

"You almost fainted a few moments ago. You're not strong enough for this kind of work."

"I'm hungry. I haven't eaten since lunch, and then not much." At least that's the story she was going to tell him. It might be the truth. She didn't have much in her stomach.

He shook his head, more vehement this time. "What if I lose you?"

"You won't. You'll be right beside me, protecting me. I trust you. You know this is the right thing to do. Together we can bring this man down. Stop this from becoming a recurring nightmare."

"Aren't you scared?"

"Yes, I am." Her painful wrist was a constant reminder of what could happen. "But we can't allow this man to go unchecked. Much longer, and women will be prisoners in their own homes. That's no way for a woman to live." She should know.

Edwin drew her close. Even though they were in public, she allowed him the liberty.

He whispered into her hair. "Thank you. What an amazing gift you are, an incredible woman. I promise to take care of you. I'm not going to let anything happen to you."

"I'm going to hold you to that." But it might be one promise he wouldn't be able to keep.

Friday, March 1, 1901

Still, still, still. After all this time, months on end, the people of Denver still didn't understand what he was doing. How he was saving them. Saving them from the tortured life he led.

Why couldn't they get it through their thick skulls? Why couldn't they see what was right in front of their faces? As long as women ran wild and free on the streets at all hours of the day and night, nothing would be right in the world. His mistake had been to allow his wife a degree of liberty. He'd believed he was being a good husband, a liberal man, responding to the times.

How wrong he had been. Women's suffrage, women's freedom, women's liberty were nothing more than a farce that brought ruin and destruction on both men and women.

Couldn't these husbands and fathers see this? Couldn't they understand that by allowing their wives and daughters such long leashes they were only choking themselves in the end?

The end. Yes, it was time this was over. He had sent his strongest message yet. The woman at the *Post* termed it Hell Night. Apropos, considering that was where she was headed.

Polly Blythe. Instead of learning her place, especially after he got her on the wrist, she continued to wax poetic about how he needed to be caught and taught a lesson so that women could continue their gallivanting.

When he'd missed her head, he should have given her another whack. Been done with her once and for all. She would be one less female standing between him and the salvation of the Denverites' souls.

He'd planned to get her the other night. She'd been his prime target. But he hadn't gotten his chance. She'd been with that detective.

He laid the morning edition of the paper in front of him, searching those ridiculous red headlines for the letters he needed. When he discovered one, he picked up his scissors, cut around it with a great deal of care, then pasted it onto a blank sheet of paper.

The work was painstaking but worth it. She needed one final warning.

Some time went by before he had the message spelled out. This time he'd managed to find all the letters he needed in the headlines. No need to type out a letter. That had been dangerous, giving the police a chance to track him down. Then again, there were many typewriters of his kind throughout the city.

It was the one thing his wife had left him. She had been a typist at a bank. Thankfully, this time he had what he needed from the headlines.

He folded the paper, making sure the edges were straight and sharp. Then he placed it in the envelope and sealed it. With a pencil, he wrote her name on it, careful to use block letters so no one could trace the handwriting to him. Though the extra effort took time, it would be worth it to protect his anonymity.

With that, his final plan was in place. He wouldn't kill her outright. He would strike and leave her to bleed to death. Somewhere they would never find her. So that she would suffer in agony the way he had.

If they didn't get the message this time, that was their problem. Jesus had shaken the dirt from his sandals and left cities condemned. Once he finished with Miss Blythe, he would do the same.

The paper had printed a description of him so that women could be on the lookout. He could change his appearance easily enough. He had already shaved his mustache months ago. Though facial hair was the true mark of a man, he had gotten rid of it.

They also printed that he wore an ulster coat and a crush hat. Well, the coat he couldn't do much about. He only had the one, and it was plenty cold out. Then again, he wasn't the only man in the city who owned such a coat. He pulled it on and did up the buttons.

He did, however, have another hat. He grabbed his bowler from the coatrack next to the door and jammed it onto his head. The winds were whipping up outside, howling around the corners of his house.

He glanced at himself in the hall mirror. There. A completely different look. No one would recognize him. Not even his coworkers at the mine.

When he went to work, that was. This job of putting women in their proper place was getting to be a full-time occupation.

As he shut his door behind him, a smile crept unbidden onto his face. Though this wasn't as enjoyable as a rousing sermon or a picnic with a beautiful woman, there was a level of satisfaction in going about the Lord's work.

Because lunchtime was approaching, the streets were extra busy today, heads bent against the gale. All the better for him, allowing him to blend in with the crowd. He didn't have the privilege of living in a posh section of the city, and he wasn't near downtown, so it was quite a walk. To take the streetcar would cost too much. He'd used what he had to keep body and soul together and the *Denver Post* arriving on time every day.

Once he finally arrived, he peered into the spotless front window of the *Post*. There a secretary sat typing away. Then she stood, several folders in her hand. These, she placed in a filing cabinet behind her. At last she shrugged into her coat and grabbed her reticule from her desk drawer.

She was going to get a bite to eat. He'd been watching. She did that every day at this time.

Soon she left the building, her skirts swirling around her ankles. Another working girl flaunting herself. She'd get the message too.

Before anyone else could go in or come down the stairs, he snuck through the door, placed the letter where Miss Blythe would be sure to find it, and hightailed it outside.

All the while, his heart sped faster than a train across the prairie. The rush of what he was about to do fueled him.

This was his last chance.

This time there would be no mistaking his message. He would send it loud and clear.

He would put an end to Miss Blythe.

Chapter 31

Polly, this came for you. It was sitting on my desk when I arrived after lunch. I have no idea how it got there." Gretchen handed Polly a plain envelope.

No, not plain. Her name was penciled on it in block-style letters.

She dropped the note as if it were made of burning coals, and it fluttered to the floor.

"Polly, are you okay?" Gretchen's voice resonated like it came from deep in a cave.

"It's from him."

"From who?"

"The Shadow."

"Oh my." Gretchen pulled Harry's chair over and sat beside Polly. "What does it say?"

"I don't know if I can read it."

Gretchen picked up the envelope and sliced it open with a hairpin. "Do you want me to read it aloud?"

It was all Polly could do to force herself to give a single nod.

"Oh dear."

"What is it?" Like a lightning bolt, a surge of energy burst through Polly, and she launched from her chair and grabbed the paper from Gretchen.

I WILL GET YOU.

That was it. Four small words. Four small, powerful words.

Icy fingers curled around her stomach. The Shadow was still out there.

"Thank you, Gretchen." Polly managed to eke out the words, though her voice was strained, even to her own ears.

"Let me get you a glass of water. You're as pale as Harry always was."

Definitely not a compliment. "Thank you." As soon as Gretchen left to retrieve the water, Polly picked up the phone and had the operator put her through to the police station. After a few transfers, she got through to Edwin.

"Edwin, it's Polly."

"Polly. How are you?" The telephone line crackled, probably because of the wind, and his voice was tinny. But there was no lilt to it, only a heaviness. She pinched the bridge of her nose.

"Has something happened, Edwin? What is it?"

"You're getting to know me too well."

She shuffled a few papers on her desk and waited for him to continue.

"Josephine Unternahrer, the woman from the hospital, never woke up after having surgery. Her husband is devastated."

She sucked in a lungful of air. "No. I was praying so hard she would survive. She was awake enough when they brought her in that I thought for sure she would make it. But she had this feeling, didn't she? Somehow, she knew she wouldn't survive."

"Her wounds were too severe. Surgery is risky as it is. The doctors just weren't able to save her."

"We've been saying this for months, but this has to stop. You have to put me out there as a decoy. He's still after me. He's targeting me, but he's also attacking other women. None of the others got notes though, at least that we know of."

"I'm not sure the notes you've gotten were from the Shadow. Gray may still have been the one who was sending those, trying to scare you away from the case so he could grab the headlines."

"They were from the Shadow."

"How can you be sure?"

"Because I got another one this afternoon."

She could almost feel his taut nerves through the phone line.

"What does it say?"

" 'I will get you.' "

"That's all?"

"Yes, that's it."

"Are you at the *Post*?"

"Yes."

"Don't go anywhere, no matter what. I'll be over there later. I have to go to court this afternoon to be deposed on another case. I want to see the note, to figure out any clue he may be giving us."

"It's time to act." Even as she spoke the words, her body trembled. "You know that, don't you?"

A long moment stretched between them. He still struggled with involving her. If only it hadn't come to this. If only they had been able to snare the Shadow long ago.

"This is the only way, Edwin."

"How am I supposed to allow someone I care about to put herself in harm's way?"

The chill of a few minutes ago was replaced by a warmth that spread from her chest to her fingertips and her toes. He cared about her. How could she not reciprocate those feelings? Other than Lyle, he was the only man in her life who had encouraged her and respected her for who she was.

"I care about you too." She whispered the words into the receiver. "But we have to draw him out. Too many women have died. We can't allow there to be any more victims."

He heaved a heavy sigh. "I agree." The words had cost him. "Even now, Armstrong has another parade of men in here. All of them have air-tight alibis."

"So no luck with them."

"No. When did the note arrive?"

"Sometime around lunch."

"Just about the time the room was most crowded with Armstrong's suspects. I have to hurry to make it to court. Remember what I said. You stay put until I get there. It shouldn't be long, but you never know when lawyers are involved. I'll be there as soon as possible. We'll work out something then."

"I'll behave. I promise. Since Harry is, well. . . Anyway, Mr. Ward has given me a meatier story to write, so I'll be occupied for a while."

He blew out a breath. "That makes me feel better."

"Don't you trust me?"

"Not as far as I can toss an elephant."

She chuckled as they signed off.

The rest of the afternoon flew by on eagle's wings. Edwin had yet to put in an appearance. Where could he be? What could be taking him so long?

The hours ticked on, and the newsroom emptied. The quietness of the building only amplified the howling of the wind. The place creaked. Almost swayed.

At last an older man she knew only as Peter the janitor wheeled in his barrel of water, a rather limp mop in one hand. "Quite the windstorm we're having, isn't it?" He started his work at the far end of the room, close to the window overlooking Sixteenth Street.

"Almost like a chinook, except for the warm weather that comes with those winds."

"You're here late."

"I'm waiting for someone to walk me home."

"Good thinking."

If possible, the wind picked up more.

Then came a terrible crash.

Glass tinkling.

The lights went out.

Polly jumped, her heart knocking hard against her ribs.

In a few moments, her eyes adjusted to the dark. A gray figure lay on the floor. She rushed to his side, almost tripping over the piece of telephone pole that had broken through the window. "Peter, are you okay? What happened?"

"Glass stabbing me." He gasped, his words difficult to hear above the roar of the wind.

"Where?" Polly shouted.

"My chest. Get help."

"Okay. Hang on." She picked her way back to her desk, but the telephone wasn't working. She returned to his side. "I'm going to have to go out. I can't call anyone. Don't go anywhere. I'll find a phone and be back as soon as possible."

Bracing herself against the wind, she made her way to corner near the *Post's* offices where there was a call box. If only civilians could use it. She had to keep going. Find the doctor who had treated Sophie.

At first there were plenty of other people bustling to and fro, hurrying to get out of the wind. Not a throng, but a smattering here and there. It was a dangerous night to be out. Garbage and other debris flew through the air.

And then she was alone. Her breath hitched.

Where had everyone gone?

But the doctor's office was near. Only one more alley to cross until she made it there. When she approached it, she slowed and peered around the corner of the building. The evening had deepened, though, and there was nothing but darkness. The frigid wind blew across her arms and bit through her coat. She drew it around herself with one hand. With the other, she lifted her skirts and scurried across what might as well have been a gaping canyon.

With a whoosh, she released her breath. There. She had made it.

And then the world went black.

Cold. She was so cold. Polly shivered from head to toe, unable to stop the convulsions that seized her. Yet each one that wracked her body sent slivers of pain slicing through her.

She opened her eyes to complete darkness. It didn't matter if they were open or shut. Either way, no light found them. No light illuminated the place she was.

She tried to lie as still as possible. Little by little, she curled into a ball to conserve body heat. That helped. At least it stopped the shivering, though it did nothing against the piercing cold.

What had happened to her? Her head felt like it could explode. A violent pounding inside her skull. The back of her skull, in fact.

She grasped at memories as if they were torn pieces of paper floating on the air. The window shattering. Leaving the office. Hurrying for the doctor. Being alone.

So alone.

Was she still? "Hello?"

Though she tried to scream, the word came out as nothing more than a whisper.

"Hello?" That was a little better. A little stronger, though her head ached worse than ever, a thousand hammers pounding inside her brain.

She held her breath, waiting for an answer. Nothing. Only the wind howling above her.

"Hello?" Her cry echoed. That meant she was in an enclosed space. What enclosed space? Where? Near the doctor's office?

If she could get up, she might be able to find her way out of wherever she was and get there.

Little by little, she raised herself to her elbows. Bright lights flashed in her eyes, her world spun, and waves of nausea washed over her.

She groaned but clenched her jaw. Gingerly she caressed the back of her head and was met with something warm and sticky.

Blood.

The Shadow had done this to her. He must have been watching. Must have known she'd left the office alone. Must have been waiting for the opportune moment.

One she provided for him.

But she'd had to help Peter.

Peter. *Dear Lord, let him be alive.*

No use dwelling on that now. She had to get out of wherever she was. She had to find help before it was too late. Before she ended up like Rachel.

The Shadow could come back and finish the job. Maybe he knew he hadn't done away with her when he brought her here. Why not kill her? Maybe someone had seen him. Maybe he'd had to stash her somewhere and then he would come back later and do her in.

Or maybe he was torturing her.

Now. Now. She had to get out now.

Gritting her teeth, she pulled herself to her hands and knees. Dirt. She sifted some of it through her fingers. Wherever she was didn't have a floor. She crawled, small stones biting into her palms and knees, until she bumped into something hard. Searing pain raced through her head, down her neck and back, collapsing her to the ground.

Turning to the side, she vomited. What had she been doing? She had to think, but pondering anything sent shards of pain digging into her brain.

Yes, yes. She had to get away from the Shadow. Get out of here before he returned.

Her breaths shallow, she fought to a crawling position once more. What had she been doing? Finding a way out. She had bumped into something. That was it.

She reached out, touched the cold, hard object in front of her. A stone. She ran her hand all around. Stones on top of stones. Up and down and sideways.

For a while, she crawled, feeling the stone wall. No breaks in it. None that she could find. Then came a corner. It turned at a ninety-degree angle.

What was this? A basement?

She had to stop. Wait for the pain to subside. Wait for her mind to clear. What was she doing again?

Trying to get away from the Shadow. Was he behind her? Why was she crawling?

She struggled to kneel. Her brain spun, and her head pounded. Keep going. Keep going. So she did. Until she couldn't go anymore.

She lay in the dirt, staring upward into the darkness. *God, help me. I can't help myself. Edwin can't help me. Only You can. I've been trying so hard all this time to be independent, but apart from You, I can do nothing. I can't even get myself out of this mess. Lord, I need You. Oh, how I need You. Every hour I need You. Be near me now. Help me out of this situation. Even if You don't, I am ready to meet You face-to-face. You are my true Father, my helper, my protector. I'm so thankful You see me here, even when no one else can. Please, Lord, please.*

As she stared upward, a few pinpricks of light danced above her. Stars. Were those stars? Or was she seeing things?

"Hello? Hello? Help me! Help me!"

Chapter 32

Edwin ran the almost-empty blocks from the streetcar stop to the *Post's* offices. Though he'd promised Polly he would be there so they could try to lure the Shadow from the darkness, he'd had an emergency call come in at the last minute. A double homicide.

As his feet pounded the pavement, he prayed he would discover Polly still at the office, fuming at him for being late, but safe and sound. Or that she had found someone to walk her to the boardinghouse.

Ignoring the stitch in his side, he approached the paper, glass from various broken windows along the darkened street crunching underneath his feet. He glanced up at a gaping hole in the newsroom window.

He flew up the stairs. "Hello. Hello." His chest heaved, and he reminded himself to draw in a few deep breaths of the bracing February night air. "Polly? Are you here?"

A moan came from near the window. Or where the window had once been. "Polly?"

"It's Peter. Janitor."

"Peter, I'm Detective Price. What happened?"

"Window broke. I'm hurt. She went for help."

"How long ago?"

"Long time. Happened around six."

It was after eight. No. He wouldn't panic. The wind and the damage must be slowing her. That had to be it. "I'll make sure you get help." And he'd find Polly too. Something must have happened to her. He refused to allow his mind to imagine what that might be.

He tried the call box on the corner, but the phone wasn't working.

Fighting the worsening wind, he hurried as fast as possible to the station. No one there had heard about the broken window or received a call for help. He had someone telephone for a doctor.

As quickly as he could, he briefed the officers on the situation and sent them to search for Polly. He and O'Fallon struck out together.

His partner clapped him on the back. "You care for her."

"Yes. A great deal." He couldn't imagine not having her in his life. She'd become so dear to him. Very, very dear. Nothing he could examine right now. "The most important thing is finding her. And bringing her home safely."

Lord, don't let the Shadow have gotten to her. Please, Father, protect her. I cannot.

Just like the night of the robbery.

He sucked in a breath. He could never perfectly protect his family. That was God's job. His was to do his best and leave them in His hands. Leave them to His perfect will.

But Lord, please, help me find her.

How long Polly lay on that dirt floor staring at the stars, she couldn't say. It might have been five minutes. It might have been five hours. She was so cold, she didn't even notice it anymore. She'd stopped shivering long ago.

Every now and then, she called for help. Each cry took every bit of strength she had. Each was weaker than the one before. Each rest in between was longer.

And it was all useless. No one would hear her over the rush of the windstorm.

She lay still, conserving her energy so she could call for help again. Where was she? She might be in a lightly populated area. Maybe even in the country. Or at an abandoned mine.

If that was the case, they wouldn't find her for a long, long time. Long after her soul was with the Lord. If she had any chance at survival, she would still have to be in the city. And God would have to send someone to come and rescue her. Someone with incredible hearing.

But no one knew where she was.

She turned her head to allow her tears to trickle down her temples.

Not that she was afraid of death. No, she knew heaven would be wonderful. She cried because of all she would miss out on with Edwin. He cared. Maybe he even loved her.

She loved him, wanted to be with him all the time, for the rest of her life. To be loved and cared for was incredible. If her life did end tonight, at least she'd had the chance to experience those feelings. And she had been cherished. Not all men were like her father. There were those who respected her and, even when she was stubborn and headstrong, still gave her her independence.

Any moment now, the Shadow could return to finish the job he started. If she could manage to learn his identity before he ended her life, perhaps she could leave a clue to help Edwin solve the case. If it was within her power, she would be the last of the Shadow's victims.

"Help. Help. I'm down here. Please, help me." Those few words exhausted her.

She rested and prayed for deliverance.

None came.

Her weighted eyelids refused to stay open any longer. Warmth and peace beckoned to her. She embraced them. The throbbing in her head dulled.

Lyle would be sad. He would miss her. She wouldn't have made it as far as she did without his support. He fought for her when she couldn't fight for herself. He kept her believing.

"Goodbye, Lyle. You were the best big brother. I hope you know how much I love you.

"Goodbye, Sophie. You won't notice I'm gone. I still regret not being a better friend to you. I love you too.

"Goodbye, Amelia. Thank you for being my friend and for your many kindnesses to me.

"Goodbye, Edwin. I wish I'd had the chance to tell you how much I love you. I hope you know. You are the only man for me.

"Welcome me home, Lord."

Edwin and O'Fallon had traced the streets up and down for hours. The tip of Edwin's nose stung with the cold, and his toes and fingers had long ago gone numb. His cheeks were windburned. But if he was this cold, imagine how cold Polly would be if she was still out here. For her, he had to keep searching. He couldn't give up until he found her. No matter how terrible the conditions.

With each tick of his pocket watch, hope slipped away. Where could she be? When the Shadow attacked a woman, he always left her lying on the sidewalk or on the road. Every time Edwin came across a working call box, he checked in with the station to see if Polly had showed up.

She hadn't.

"Boss, I know you don't want me to say it—"

"Then don't. We aren't giving up. We aren't going home. Not until I know where she is."

They searched for a while longer. No luck. *God, where is she?*

With a tug on his coat, O'Fallon stopped him. "We're not going to find her tonight. It's cold and dark. Let's catch a few hours of sleep and start fresh in the morning. There are other officers looking for her. You'll be more good to her when you can think straight."

Edwin stopped and rubbed the crick in the back of his neck. Defeat did not come graciously to him. "Maybe you're right. Maybe it's time to head for home." But it was so cold. What if she was out in the elements? She would freeze before they found her.

O'Fallon slapped him on the back. "We'll find her. Don't give up hope."

But his tenuous grasp on hope had slipped. It was gone. He turned. As he did so, the moon spotlighted a building under construction. The basement had been dug and part of the floor put in. What if. . .?

"Let's search there." Edwin shouted to be heard above the wind. He tamped down the energy flowing into his veins.

"Can't hurt." O'Fallon followed him across the street and to the building.

"Light the lamp and hold it over here."

A ladder had been pulled out and set to the side. "Bring the light closer."

When O'Fallon did so, Edwin's knees went weak.

Chapter 33

A light shone above Polly. The light of heaven? Whatever it was, it was beautiful and warmed her from the outside in. Even if it was the Shadow come back for her, there was the light.

"Polly? Polly! Are you down there?"

That voice. So familiar. As warm and as welcome as the light.

She parted her lips to answer but was unable to form any words.

"O'Fallon, I'm pretty sure that's her down there. I'm coming for you, sweetheart. You just hang on."

Could it be? How was it possible? That was Edwin's voice, telling her he was coming for her. No, it wasn't him. Her mind was playing tricks on her.

There was an article in the paper once. It had made headlines at the time, about a miner who got lost in the mountains in winter. The cold confused him, made him see things and hear things that weren't there. Between the cold and the gash on her head, that had to be what was happening.

"Can you answer me, Polly? Please, talk to me."

Was it crazy to talk to a hallucination? Probably. But if this was the end, what harm was there in it? Gathering her strength, she forced her mouth to move. "Edwin, darling, is that you?"

Laughter, as clear as Christmas bells, rang out above her, singing even above the wind. How lovely it was. Music, joyful and melodic. "It's me, Polly. Thank God, I've found you. Are you hurt?"

Was she? Yes, yes. "I am. Please help."

"Hand me that ladder, O'Fallon." Shuffling from above. "I'm

lowering it. Soon I'll be right beside you. Don't worry. You're going to be fine. I promise, you're going to be okay."

A moment later, the end of a ladder landed on the hard ground beside her. Not more than a few seconds after that, Edwin descended and was at her side.

He touched her cheek, smoothing back her hair. What bliss. He wasn't a figment of her imagination. He was real. "You're here."

"Of course I am. Hold on a minute." He turned his attention to the light. "O'Fallon, run to the nearest call box. Get us a carriage to take Miss Blythe to my house. Hurry." He focused on her again. "I had to find you. I wasn't going to give up until I did."

"The Shadow."

"That's what I was afraid of. Did you see him?"

"I don't know. I can't remember much. You're here."

He chuckled again. Oh, that he would laugh like that forever. "We have to get you out of here and get you medical attention. Can you stand?"

Could she? Why hadn't she tried that before? "I don't know."

"Okay, let's do this. I'll carry you, but you're going to have to hold on to my neck with all your might."

"I'm not strong."

"You're stronger than you think. Are you ready?"

She closed her eyes. "Yes."

When he scooped her in his arms, her stomach churned, and beams of pain slammed against the back of her head. She bit her lip so she wouldn't cry out.

"Hang on. I've got you. We're going up now."

Yes, Edwin was here. She had to hold him around the neck. So she did. Upward, upward, closer to the light.

Then a sudden gust of cold air hit her. "Am I out?"

"Yes, yes, you're free." As gentle as a mare with her newborn foal, he laid her down, spread his coat on the ground, and shifted her to it. On her side, so the pain in the back of her head wasn't as intense.

"Oh, Miss Blythe. You don't know how happy we are to see you." Edwin's partner was there, that stubborn golden curl blowing in front of his eye.

"I'm happy to see you."

Edwin waved him away. "Hail the carriage when you see it." O'Fallon raced to do his bidding. He rubbed her arms with some vigor, a measure of warmth returning to them. "How long were you down there?"

Down where? She fought for the answer. Oh yes, in that place in the ground. "I don't know. Why are you here?"

Nothing made sense. He cradled her in his lap and held her close. "Please, Lord, please, don't take her from me."

The light faded.

"Polly, Polly, stay with me." He couldn't have found her just to lose her. But she had just gone limp. In the dim light, he managed to make out the rise and fall of her chest. *Lord, please. Send that carriage. Fast.*

He had hardly finished the prayer when one approached, swaying in the wind. O'Fallon stood in the middle of the street, flagging it down for all he was worth. As soon as the driver reined the horses to a halt, Edwin swept Polly into his arms and sped toward the conveyance.

In no time at all, he had her settled, and the horses were clip-clopping down the street. He left O'Fallon with a backup to watch the house under construction in case the Shadow returned there with the idea of finishing Polly off. It was curious that he had thrown her in a basement like that. He hadn't done that with any of his other victims.

Dr. Klein met them as soon as they pulled up to the house. He helped carry Polly inside and to the guest room at the top of the stairs. Then the doctor closed the door and denied Edwin entrance.

Amelia rushed to his side. "Thank the Lord you found her. We've been frantic since your call. Then we didn't hear anything from you and—"

Mother joined them. "We've been praying and praying. Where was she?"

Edwin related everything he knew. "What if she doesn't recover?"

Mother rubbed his arm. "God's will is perfect. He cares for us like a hen cares for her chicks. Whatever happens, He's working for our good."

Oh, how soon he forgot what he had just learned. It was up to God to take care of Polly. Yes, there were things he could do, but in the end, she was in the Lord's hands, not his. The same with Father. The same with Amelia. He inhaled, long and slow, then released his breath little by little. "You're right."

"You have to let it go." Mother's words were as soft as lamb's wool. "Your father wouldn't want you beating yourself up over what happened all those years ago. I'm at peace. He's at peace. You need to be too. Don't drive yourself so hard. Don't blame yourself so much."

He kissed her cheek. "Thank you. I will try. With God's help, I'll try."

That didn't stop him from pacing up and down the hall in front of the room where the doctor examined Polly. Nancy brought him a cup of tea, but he couldn't sit to drink it. Mother urged him to eat, but he couldn't stomach anything. Amelia was the most help. She paced with him.

Finally, the gray-haired doctor exited the room, clicking the door behind him. "She's sleeping."

"That's good, isn't it?" Edwin rocked back and forth on his toes.

"Yes, very good. I've cleaned and stitched the wound on the back of her head. She has a concussion. That explains her confusion. I also have hot water bottles and blankets piled on her to warm her. Hypothermia was setting in."

"What is the final prognosis?" Edwin couldn't bring himself to ask if she would die. The word refused to cross his lips.

"If there is no swelling or bleeding of the brain and we can ward away infection, she will be just fine."

"She'll regain full mental capacity?"

"Yes. Any confusion associated with a concussion is usually temporary. What happened to her friend, from what I heard, was due to more bleeding and a more severe brain injury than what I believe Miss Blythe to have sustained."

"Praise the Lord." Mother grabbed Edwin's hand. "Isn't that great news, Son? She's going to be okay."

He couldn't speak. The swelling of his throat prevented him from uttering a single word. *Thank You, Lord. Thank You for taking care of her and watching over her. You do a much better job than I do.*

At last he found his voice. "Can I go in and see her?"

Dr. Klein nodded. "I'll be back in the morning to check on her. If there is any change in her condition, let me know right away."

Mother went to see the doctor out while Edwin stole into the bedroom. Polly lay in the four-poster canopy bed with a swath of white bandage around her head. Just like Amelia. Just like Rachel. Otherwise, underneath the mountain of quilts on top of her, her face was unmarred and her countenance peaceful.

He pulled up a chair. "I could have lost you tonight. I'm so thankful the Lord spared your life and led me to you. I'll never know just how I managed to locate you. It was all Him. He's the One who watched over you. But if I ever get the chance, I want to love you and cherish you for the rest of my life."

She didn't stir at his proclamation. Not that he expected her to. Perhaps it was rushing matters too much. In the right time, in God's time, it would happen. For now, she was alive and safe. That was enough.

For three days Edwin kept vigil at Polly's bedside, sleeping very little, always alert and attuned to her every need. Finally, exhaustion took hold and he must have dozed in the chair, because the next thing he knew, Amelia was shaking him by the shoulder. "There's a telephone call for you from Captain Armstrong. He says it's important."

Edwin jumped from his chair and raced down the stairs to the front hall where the telephone sat on a small table. He picked up the receiver. "Armstrong. Do you have something? Please tell me it's good news."

"About the best news you could have."

"You've caught the Shadow."

"Yes, we have. A Mr. Frederick went to the doctor's office a couple of days ago and, while he was waiting, overheard a couple of men talking about the Shadow's description, especially the clue that he wore a blue uniform. Lo and behold, Frederick showed up at the station first thing this morning and said he knew a fellow who owned a uniform like that. A man named Al Cowan. Frederick even claims to have seen the attack on that Blythe woman but didn't stick around to help her. We checked it out, and sure enough, Cowan had a blue uniform and a metal pipe at his place. Brought him in an hour ago."

"Is there blood on it?" Cases always hinged on these little details. This one more than others.

"It's plenty stained. Been used for something, that's for sure."

"Has he confessed?"

"Maintains he's innocent as a babe, but we both know differently. This is the man."

"You're sure?"

"More sure than I am of my own name."

Edwin allowed himself to relax his shoulders. Perhaps Armstrong was right. Perhaps this was the man after all.

"You can rest easy, Price. This nightmare has come to an end. No more Shadow lurking about our city."

"I pray you're right, sir. I truly do."

"I am."

He'd been wrong so many times before.

"Trust me. Every now and again, I manage to do my job correctly."

"I never said you didn't, sir."

"You didn't have to. I wouldn't have called you at home if I wasn't positive."

Perhaps Armstrong was right. Perhaps the Silver Shadow was behind bars at last and the citizens of Denver were safe again.

He hung up and retraced his route up the stairs to Polly's room. He stood in the doorway studying her. Even with her hair bound in the bandage and dark circles under her eyes, she was the most beautiful creature he had ever beheld.

"What did the captain have to say?" Amelia had snuck up beside him.

"Polly was the Silver Shadow's final victim."

Chapter 34

Wednesday, March 27, 1901

Polly sat straight and stiff in the courtroom gallery at Al Cowan's trial. Because he was the detective on the case, Edwin wasn't able to be with her. She rubbed her still-aching head. Some days she didn't have headaches or confusion. Stressful days, like today, were horrible.

All day long, District Attorney Lindsley badgered Cowan. The lawyer paced in front of the witness box. "Where were you on the evening of March 1?"

"This is the third time you've asked me that question." Cowan stared steely-eyed at the DA.

"And I'll keep asking it until I get a satisfactory answer."

"It's not going to change. I was at home."

"Alone?"

"Yes. I live alone. No one saw me there, but no one saw me anywhere else either."

"You let the court determine that. Where did you get that metal pipe the detectives found in your possession?"

"I don't remember."

"But it is yours."

"I can't remember buying it." He scratched his head.

"How did it come to be in your possession then?"

"Might have borrowed it. Don't know."

"You don't know how you came to have a metal pipe?"

"No."

"What did you use it for?"

"Don't think I ever used it."

"So you either borrowed it or bought it but never used it?"

"Something like that."

"To be clear, you never used it?"

Cowan's face reddened. "I don't know."

"You don't know, or you're refusing to say?"

"I don't know." Cowan was shrieking.

The prosecutor leaned right into Cowan's face, nose to nose. "You bought it so you could attack these women, isn't that the case?"

"No."

"Be truthful now."

"I am!"

"You're under oath. Don't lie to the judge. It will go worse for you. You attacked those women. Killed four of them, didn't you?"

The slight man rose. "No! No! No! Absolutely not. I'm telling the truth."

Polly shifted in her seat. She and Amelia held hands. Amelia leaned over and spoke in a whisper. "It's pretty clear he's lying."

"The entire matter is making my head throb." Polly rubbed the back of her neck.

Mr. Lindsley held up the gun that had been found in Cowan's home. "You are the Shadow. You did this to these women."

"No!"

"Why? Do you hate women so much?"

Cowan's cheeks flamed. A muscle in his jaw twitched.

"You hate women, don't you? Don't you, Mr. Cowan? Your wife ran off with another man. Her baby wasn't even yours."

"Objection." The defender's voice carried throughout the crowded courtroom. "Badgering the witness."

"I'll allow it, but move along, Mr. Lindsley."

"Just answer the question, Mr. Cowan. You are the Silver Shadow, aren't you?"

"Leave me alone!" Cowan leapt up and grabbed the revolver out of the prosecutor's hand. He waved it in Mr. Lindsley's direction. "You're a dirty skunk, and I'm going to kill you."

Amelia screamed. Edwin rushed forward. Polly's head spun. What was he doing? He'd been shot once already. Wasn't that enough? Her heart pounded as hard as her head.

In a flash, Edwin, bad arm and all, grabbed the gun from Cowan and tossed it to the side. It skidded across the floor and thumped to a stop against the empty jury box.

Edwin pressed on Cowan's shoulders and forced him into his seat. "Don't go anywhere."

Polly concentrated on returning her breathing to its normal pattern. She glanced at Amelia, who clutched the chair's armrests, her fingers white.

With a bob of his head, a ginger lock falling in front of his eyes, Edwin motioned to the judge. "He's under control. We can continue."

"Thank you, Detective. Please, Mr. Lindsley, resume your questioning." The judge slid back from the edge of his large black chair.

"You and your wife are divorced, are you not?"

Cowan dropped his gaze to his lap. "We are."

"How long ago?"

"A few years."

"Has the divorce skewed your view of women?"

"Absolutely not."

"Did you particularly target Miss Blythe because she is a successful female reporter?"

Polly picked at a nonexistent piece of lint on her skirt.

"I didn't target anyone. I'm not the Shadow."

The slender attorney with prominent ears leaned over the defendant. "But you can't provide an alibi for any of the nights in question."

"I live alone."

"Mr. Cowan, I believe that you injured Miss Blythe. I also believe you killed Mary Short, didn't you? You lured her to a vacant lot and struck her with a metal pipe."

"I never did any such thing." Cowan's blue eyes blazed as bright as the summer sky.

"Oh, but you did."

Mr. Rees, Cowan's lawyer, stood and loosened his tight collar. "Your Honor, I believe this line of questioning has gone on long enough. My client has sat in jail for almost a month without charges being brought against him. He is suffering. When he was arrested, he weighed 155 pounds. Now he weighs less than 135."

Edwin, still standing behind Cowan's chair, let out a loud half chuckle.

Mr. Rees glared at him. "Oh, sneer if you will, but I would like to see your impervious soul go through what this man has had to."

Color rose in Edwin's cheeks. Poor Edwin. Mr. Rees's accusation was rather laughable.

The judge allowed the district attorney to continue, but Mr. Lindsley had only a couple more questions before Judge Rice dismissed the defendant.

The attorney general turned to the black-robed judge. "Cowan says he isn't the Silver Shadow and that he doesn't hate women. Yet he matches the description given by more than one victim. He has no alibi. And the weapon of choice was found in his house. It's a perfect match to the wounds on all of the women. Sir, in light of the fact that Mr. Cowan waived his right to a jury trial, and in light of the evidence presented and Mr. Cowan's own testimony, the State asks that you find him guilty."

Guilty. Polly relaxed her shoulders. Al Cowan was the Silver Shadow. She had never been surer of anything in her life.

Could this nightmare be almost over?

Al Cowan strode from the witness box, his gaze straight forward, his shoulders back. Edwin returned to his chair and rubbed his aching upper arm, now more painful because of having to hold Cowan down. He glanced at Polly and Amelia behind him. Both of them flashed him small smiles, but he focused his attention on Polly. She was healing but had some time to go before she was fully herself again.

How brave of her to be here. To sit through this testimony. The way she bit her lip let him know she wasn't feeling well. This tension couldn't be good for her headaches.

As soon as Cowan returned to his seat beside Mr. Rees, the judge picked up his gavel. "I'm calling for an hour recess. I'd like to see both attorneys in my chambers." With a strike of wood against wood, Judge Rice dismissed court.

As soon as he left the room, Edwin made his way to Polly's side. "How are you holding up?"

"I'm so glad you're here. And glad you're in one piece. When you went after the revolver, I almost had a heart attack. Isn't one gunshot wound enough?"

"Well, I just thought I'd make both arms even."

"That's not funny." She frowned.

"Don't worry about me. I'm tough as old leather."

Amelia leaned across Polly. "I agree with Polly. You're crazy."

"It's my job. And I'm fine. Lindsley's badgering got to Cowan. He only brandished that gun for show. He knew it wasn't loaded. Why don't we get some fresh air?"

It was one of those warm late winter days in the city, and while Amelia decided she wanted a stroll, Polly wasn't up to it, so she and Edwin settled on a bench in front of the courthouse.

"They're going to convict him, aren't they?"

"I think that's why the judge called for the recess. If my guess is correct, he's ready to rule."

"Then this nightmare is truly over."

"Yes, it is. And I'm going to make sure you get the best care you can while you recover. You're going to move into the house with my mother and Amelia and me, and I'm going to watch you like a hawk. You aren't well enough to return to the newspaper yet, and Mother will be more than happy to see to your every need."

His eyes softened. "Don't you see? Polly, I feel deeply for you. I can't imagine my life without you, and with God's help, I'm going to make sure that I always have you in it. Forever."

She scrunched her forehead.

He swallowed hard. "Don't worry. You don't have to say anything now. When you're feeling better. When you're up to thinking about it." Pushing her too hard might push her away. But he'd had to say something. If nothing else, he had learned that God never promised tomorrow. Even if she didn't reciprocate his love, she now knew how he felt for her.

How he would always feel for her.

"I love you too."

He startled and gazed at her, her eyes as green as the pines that covered the lower slopes of the mountains.

"That is what you're telling me, isn't it?"

He closed his gaping mouth. "Yes. Yes, it is. I love you, Polly. And one of these days, I'm going to do a proper job of proposing to you."

"You'd better." She laughed, a silver-bell kind of laugh.

Who cared that they were in public? Let them cause a scandal. She was the most beautiful woman in Denver. And she'd all but said she would marry him. As the sun slipped behind the Rockies, he slid closer, pulled her toward him, and kissed her.

For a moment, there was no Silver Shadow, no crazed witnesses, no overzealous chief of detectives. Only the sweet softness of her lips as she returned his kiss.

Bliss.

Pure heaven.

Sun after the rain.

A promise that better days were to come.

Chapter 35

Friday, August 23, 1901

Polly blew a stray hair that had loosened from her pins and fallen in front of her eyes. She didn't have a minute to take her hands from her typewriter to smooth it back. Already she was running late finishing this article on how the police had finally cracked the case of the bank robbery from last winter.

A conviction. Praise the Lord for that. Two fewer menaces wandering the streets of Denver.

Since Al Cowan's guilty verdict, a certain peace had fallen over the city. Little by little, women started going out alone again. Word was that Al Cowan was wasting away to nothing in his jail cell.

Perhaps he would find his own peace.

Six months later, Polly could now allow herself to relax. She could walk down the street without looking over her shoulder every few seconds. She could sleep without nightmares accosting her. She had no more headaches.

And Captain Armstrong never filed a lawsuit for that editorial she had written.

Mr. Ward lumbered past her desk. Though she didn't so much as glance up from her article, the whiff of cigars and the heaviness of his step gave him away. "Don't worry, sir. I'll have this article done in no time. Even if I have to stay late tonight."

He stopped in front of her desk, and this time she lifted her gaze from the page she was working on. "No doing. You are to leave promptly at five. Not a minute sooner and not a minute later."

She leaned away from him and stared with a bit more intensity.

What had become of the old curmudgeon? "Excuse me?" Surely she had heard wrong.

"Five o'clock. On the dot. Understood? Sam is under orders to make sure you obey."

She glanced at the sandy-haired junior crime reporter who had replaced Harry. Her counterpart nodded. "If you don't do what Mr. Ward is telling you, I lose my job."

Ah, there was the lovable Mr. Ward after all. "Well, if you two say so." Still, the entire matter was out of the norm.

She completed her article, and true to his word, Sam all but shoved her out the door at five. Once she arrived at the boardinghouse, events took an even stranger turn. Mary insisted on styling her hair, Bea chose her outfit, and Laura applied the tiniest bit of rouge and lip coloring.

"What is going on here?" Polly asked the question for the thousandth time. "There's nothing special about tonight. I'm only having dinner with Edwin."

Her three friends exchanged glances.

Oh no, something was up. "What is it? What aren't you telling me?"

"Us?" Bea pointed to herself. "Nothing. Nothing at all." Though she feigned innocence, she didn't do it very well.

Could it be? Could this possibly be the night she'd been anticipating for six long months? Since her attack, she'd seen Edwin almost every day. At first she'd lived with his family, and he'd been most attentive to her. Then, when she returned to the boardinghouse, she had dinner with them just about every evening. Either that, or he took her out. Sometimes, when one or the other of them had to work late, they would be at the *Post* or the police station for a picnic of sorts.

Altogether, these past months had been almost perfect.

If only Sophie were here and in her right mind. She would be squealing over Polly. But Sophie wasn't at the boardinghouse anymore. Her parents had finally been able to get her home. And even if Edwin was planning some kind of surprise, he never would have told Sophie. She'd been the worst at keeping secrets.

With a quick prayer for her friend, Polly relaxed and allowed the others to fuss over her.

At precisely six thirty, Edwin's carriage arrived. All of her housemates stood in the doorway, waving and cheering as they saw her off. A few of them dabbed their eyes. Goodness, you would think she was leaving them for good.

What a strange day it had been all around. At least she could put it behind herself and enjoy the evening with Edwin.

As she made her way to the street, Edwin stepped out of the carriage and bowed. "Good evening, milady."

"Not you too. Can't anyone act normal today?"

He straightened and pecked her on the cheek. "You look lovely tonight."

"That's much better."

He helped her alight before settling in next to her. Almost before the carriage rolled a block, he was fidgeting in his seat.

"What is it?"

"What is what?"

"Something's going on. Everyone has been on edge today, treating me specially. Am I dying?" she asked, though the answer was pretty obvious.

He chuckled.

"That's not very funny."

"You, my dear, are not dying. Very far from it, I pray."

She blew out a breath. "Then what?"

"You'll find out in short order."

Though she pressed him, he refused to say more, so she sat back and gazed out the window at the city. A soft dusk fell, blurring the sharp edges of the scene. Here and there, electric lights flickered on, giving the entire tableau a warm glow.

Though she drank in the evening, Edwin did not. He shifted in his seat, patted his pants pocket, and shifted again.

"How was work today?"

"Have I told you how lovely you look tonight?" They blurted the words at the same time, then fell into laughter.

A moment later, the carriage rolled to a stop in a park. A cheerful fire and several torches illuminated a table set with sparkling silverware and gleaming china. A man in a suit stood to the side.

She turned to Edwin. "What's going on?" Though now there was no doubt in her mind, she would play along with the surprise. Hopefully, he wouldn't keep her in suspense for very long.

"Dinner."

He assisted her to the ground, then held on to her as he led her to the table. Once they were seated, and after Edwin had given thanks, the waiter approached and lifted the silver domes from their plates. Roast lamb, fresh green beans, and baby red potatoes greeted her with their mouth-watering aromas.

"I don't know what the occasion is."

"Does there have to be one?" Even in the gathering darkness, she caught his wink. "Every night spent with you is a special occasion for me."

"Well said."

The meal was delicious, and Edwin was more charming than usual. Six months ago, such happiness seemed almost out of the realm of possibility. Now here she was, her heart about to burst.

Especially if he didn't get to it.

For a long while, she stared at the stars, a few just now winking in the sky overhead. When she turned her attention earthward, Edwin was no longer seated across from her. She turned to the side.

He was beside her, down on one knee.

She gasped. "Edwin."

"Just let me get through this. I love you, Polly Blythe, more than I ever imagined I could love a woman. Life with you is a daily adventure, one I want to experience for the rest of my days. I want to laugh with you, celebrate with you, and rejoice with you. As long as God gives me the strength, I will treat you as the special, vibrant, talented woman He made you to be. Will you marry me?"

She brushed his cheek to find it damp with tears. That sent a few of her own pooling in the corners of her eyes. "You are the most incredible man I have ever met. I know I can trust you today and every day from here forward. Yes, of course I'll marry you."

He stood and pulled her to her feet. Then he drew her so close that their hearts pounded against each other.

And he kissed her the way she prayed he would kiss her every day for the rest of their lives.

Author's Notes

This is the fourth book I've written as part of the True Colors crime series. I've enjoyed every minute of it. Each of the books is so very different, yet the depravity of humanity is much too real in all of them.

The Silver Shadow is the most fictionalized of the four. I first read about this series of crimes in Denver between 1900 and 1901 in a book called Famous Crimes the World Forgot by Jason Lucky Morrow. And it's true that the world has forgotten about these attacks perpetrated on the city's women in those years. The only record of them is the chapter in Morrow's book and a few old newspaper articles.

This gave me little to go on in crafting the book but much leeway in the writing of it. The *Denver Post* was a real newspaper at the time, owned by Harry Tammen and Frederick Bonfils, two flamboyant young men who ran their paper in much the same way. They were all about juicy stories and sensational headlines, even going so far as printing them in bold red ink so the city's residents wouldn't miss them. They often tangled with City Hall. They even staged small fairs and circuses at the paper.

The paper was first called the *Denver Evening Post*. "Evening" wasn't dropped until 1901. To keep things simple, I referred to it as the *Denver Post* from the beginning.

Mr. Ward was also a true character and was apparently much as I described him in the book. A woman was on staff at the *Post* in 1900, hired to give stories the feminine touch that would appeal to female readers, but he didn't care much for her. He was a hard-nosed man.

Police Chief Farley and Chief of Detectives Armstrong are also historical characters. Armstrong was gunning for Farley's job and landed it later in 1901. Once the story of the Capitol Hill Thug hit the papers and a reward was offered, Captain Armstrong went after his suspects with gusto, dragging in anyone who matched the description given by several women. He continued with this tactic until Al Cowan was arrested.

The posse organized in January 1901 was factual. Some of the men did indeed dress up as women in an attempt to lure out the Capitol Hill Thug. This lasted for about a month before the men lost interest in the cause. During this time, there wasn't a single incident in the entire city. Why didn't the thug strike elsewhere? No one has ever figured that out.

One of the victims was indeed left in the basement of a home under construction. Why the Capitol Hill Thug changed his MO is unknown, especially since his attacks on two other women that night followed the same pattern as the previous victims.

At the turn of the century, wealthy people didn't go to the hospital. They were seen as places only for the poor. You would be better treated at home. From my research, most of the women who were attacked were not transported to the hospital. Even those who were maids were brought to their employers' homes and cared for there. I did find some evidence that on Hell Night at least one of the women was treated at the hospital, though Josephine Unternahrer ultimately died.

The windstorm was real, but it occurred on March 2 and 3, 1901, and it was a warm chinook wind, bringing temperatures soaring into the seventies. I really wanted Polly to be cold in the basement, so I exercised some creative liberty.

Alfred Cowan was rounded up with a group of other men at the end of February, soon after Hell Night. He was an unemployed laborer who lived at a boardinghouse and on the fringes of society. A few days after Cowan was brought in, Albert Frederick overheard the details about the reward money at his doctor's office. He went straight to the police and fingered Cowan as the man he had seen attacking Mary Short just a few nights before. Cowan was held in solitary confinement, and Captain Armstrong insisted on questioning Cowan alone.

At the pretrial hearings in March and April 1901, Mr. Rees, Cowan's attorney, grilled Mr. Frederick with ferocity, badgering him, pointing out inconsistencies in his story, and producing witnesses who testified to Frederick's morphine addiction. At one point, Frederick was so unnerved that he grabbed Cowan's revolver, which was sitting on the bar near him, and waved it around the courtroom. He was disarmed and restrained, but soon after that, the prosecution dropped the charges against Mr. Cowan.

Cowan was immediately arrested on charges of lunacy, but he conducted himself so well at his insanity hearing that the judge was forced to release him. Two weeks later, he left Denver and was never heard from again.

Before he left the city, another woman was attacked. Police rushed to Cowan's home, only to find him asleep. He was definitely not the Capitol Hill Thug. A few more attacks happened that summer, and then, as mysteriously as they began, they stopped. Mr. Frederick was given train fare and traveled to New York City. I hope my readers will forgive me for exercising my literary license to make the streets safe for Polly by convicting Mr. Cowan, even though the real Capitol Hill Thug was never caught.

Victims:

Elva Jessup, twenty-eight, attacked August 24, 1900, survived. She was walking home from a synagogue service. She was married to Alvin Jessup in 1895. They divorced in 1911.

Georgia "Lillian" Bell Mellon, forty-five, attacked August 24, 1900, died eleven days after the attack. She was a divorced music teacher and was survived by two small children.

Emma Carlson, twenty-three, attacked September 24, 1900, survived. She was walking home from a church activity.

Annie McAtee, attacked October 5, 1900, survived. She was the sister of a wealthy Denver merchant who put up a $200 reward for the capture of the Capitol Hill Thug.

Mrs. Carrie S. Young, forty-six, attacked December 22, 1900, survived. She lived in Denver until her death in 1930.

Julia Dohr, forty-six, attacked January 6, 1901, survived. She was attacked while walking to a residence where she was employed as a housekeeper. She was shoved into a cellar. Sometime between 1901 and 1910, she moved to California and died there in 1924.

Marie Frazer, eighteen, attacked February 16, 1901, survived. She was struck while walking home from the hairdresser and managed to stumble to her home.

Mary Short, forty, attacked February 22, 1901, died one day later.

Emma Johnson, thirty, attacked February 22, 1901, survived. She was hit on the way home from the Swedish Methodist Church. She was employed by the renowned Denver physician Frank Waxham.

Josephine Unternahrer, twenty-eight, attacked February 22, 1901, taken to St. Joseph's Hospital, died a few days after surgery. Her husband remarried the following year.

Eliza Monroe, attacked April 19, 1901, is believed to have survived.

There likely were several other victims, although those cases cannot be confirmed.

Acknowledgments

Behind every book, there is a great team, and this one is no different. It wouldn't have come into being or be in the shape it's in without a good number of people.

Thank you to Barbour Publishing and their amazing staff. I so love working with all of you! Becky Germany, my deepest appreciation to you for believing that I could write these stories and do them justice. Ellen Tarver, my fabulous editor, thank you for cleaning up this manuscript. I know it was a hot mess when I sent it to you. You've gone over and beyond. I'd be lost without you. Shalyn Sattler, Abbey Warschauer, and the entire marketing team, thank you for doing your jobs so well and making mine so easy. And a round of applause to the cover designers for the entire True Colors Crime series. The covers are truly magnificent.

To my agent, Tamela Hancock Murray, thank you for believing in me every step of the way. Thanks for your encouragement and for your help. Most of all, thanks for being a listening ear and a friend.

Thank you to my family for putting up with me while I write. This book has especially consumed me. I appreciate your patience when dinner was late, the laundry wasn't folded, and the dishes weren't done. Your love and support through it all mean the world to me.

Thanks to my critique partners, Diana, Jen, and Jenny. Where would I be without you ladies? I shudder to think.

To my faithful prayer partner, Janet, thank you, sweet friend. To know that you care enough to pray with and for me is an amazing gift that I am so grateful for.

Thank you to all of you, my fabulous readers and ardent supporters. You make what I do every day possible. You have given me my dream job. For that, I will forever be grateful. I cannot thank you enough.

And to my Lord, who lit the spark inside of me and gave me my love for reading and my passion for writing. I can only pray that I use the talents You have bestowed on me to Your honor and glory. Soli Deo gloria.

Liz Tolsma is the author of several World War II novels, romantic suspense novels, prairie romance novellas, and an Amish romance. She is a popular speaker and an editor and resides next to a Wisconsin farm field with her husband and their youngest daughter. Her son is a US Marine, and her oldest daughter is a college student. Liz enjoys reading, walking, working in her large perennial garden, kayaking, and camping. Please visit her website at www.liztolsma.com and follow her on Facebook, Twitter (@LizTolsma), Instagram, YouTube, and Pinterest. She is also the host of the Christian Historical Fiction Talk podcast.

True Colors. True Crime.

The Scarlet Pen (July 2021)
by Jennifer Uhlarik

Enjoy a tale of true but forgotten history of a 19th century serial killer whose silver-tongued ways almost trap a young woman into a nightmarish marriage.

In 1876, Emma Draycott is charmed into a quick engagement with childhood friend Stephen Dee Richards after reconnecting with him at a church event in Mount Pleasant, Ohio. But within the week, Stephen leaves to "make his fame and fortune." The heartbroken Emma gives him a special pen to write to her, and he does with tales of grand adventures. Secret Service agent Clay Timmons arrives in Mount Pleasant to track purchases made with fake currency. Every trail leads back to Stephen—and therefore, Emma. Can he convince the naive woman she is engaged to a charlatan who is being linked a string of deaths in Nebraska?

Paperback / 978-1-64352-929-5 / $12.99